ALSO BY KIM SAVAGE

After the Woods

BEAUTIFUL

BROKEN

GIRLS

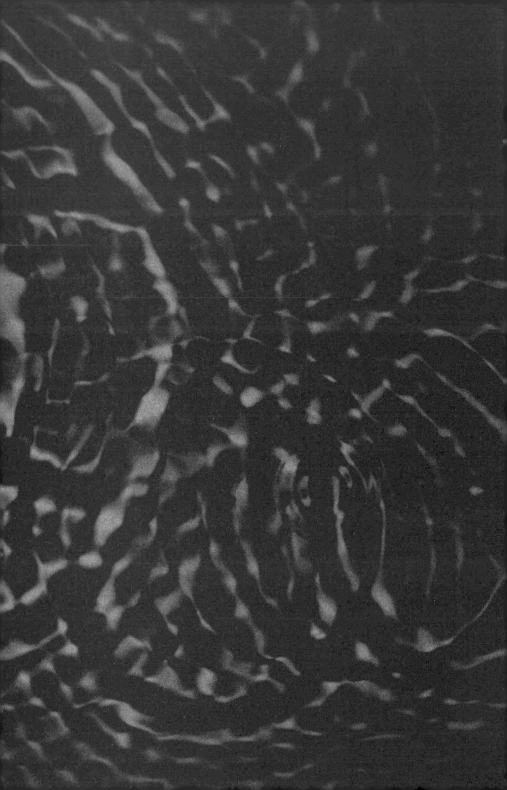

BEAUTIFUL

BROKEN

GIRLS

KIM SAVAGE

Farrar Straus Giroux · New York

Farrar Straus Giroux Books for Young Readers
An imprint of Macmillan Publishing Group, LLC
175 Fifth Avenue, New York 10010

Printed in the United States of America
Designed by Elizabeth H. Clark
First edition, 2017
1   3   5   7   9   10   8   6   4   2

fiercereads.com

Library of Congress Cataloging-in-Publication Data
Names: Savage, Kim, 1969– author.
Title: Beautiful broken girls / Kim Savage.
Description: First edition. | New York : Farrar Straus Giroux, 2017. |
    Summary: Ben learns why the love of his life, Mira, and her sister
    drowned themselves when he receives a postmortem letter from Mira
    challenging him to find and decode notes hidden in the seven places
    where they secretly touched.
Identifiers: LCCN 2016001909 | ISBN 9780374300593 (hardback)
Subjects: | CYAC: Mystery and detective stories. | Death—Fiction. |
    Sisters—Fiction. | BISAC: JUVENILE FICTION / Mysteries &
    Detective Stories. | JUVENILE FICTION / Family / Siblings. |
    JUVENILE FICTION / Social Issues / Death & Dying.
Classification: LCC PZ7.1.S27 Be 2017 | DDC [Fic]—dc23
LC record available at https://lccn.loc.gov/2016001909

Our books may be purchased in bulk for promotional, educational, or business
use. Please contact your local bookseller or the Macmillan Corporate and
Premium Sales Department at (800) 221-7945 ext. 5442 or by e-mail at
MacmillanSpecialMarkets@macmillan.com.

For Charlie, my beautiful dreamer,
whose gifts touch my heart every day

For the eyeing of my scars, there is a charge
For the hearing of my heart——
It really goes.

And there is a charge, a very large charge
For a word or a touch
Or a bit of blood

—*Sylvia Plath,*
from "Lady Lazarus"

PROLOGUE

AUGUST 2016

When they found Mira Cillo at the bottom of the quarry lake, her fingers were shot through the loose weave of her sister Francesca's sweater, at the neck. They were so tangled, jammed through past the knuckles, the coroner had to cut away the yarn to separate them.

Ben kept thinking about that.

Ben heard this from Kyle Kulik, who had graduated that summer from Bismuth High and was training to become an EMT. Kyle's voice shook as he told Ben it was the sight of the Cillo girls as they were lifted from the water, blue and wilted, with hollows around their eyes and, later, froth cones around their lips, that made Kyle realize being an emergency medical technician wasn't for him if it meant plucking hot dead girls out of the quarry.

Ben knew in a hazy way that he was focusing on the wrong thing. It didn't matter that the girls were wearing sweaters in August. Or that pink-tinged foam could appear from dead lips even after it was wiped away. It must be shock that was causing Ben to focus on the little things instead of the big horrible thing right in front of him: that the girls next door dumped their bikes the night before behind Johnny's Foodmaster and hiked three-quarters of a mile through the dark to the highest ledge. And fell.

Frank Cillo noticed his daughters were gone at eleven o'clock bed check. He called the police immediately. At 11:29 p.m., cell phones across the Northeast jumped with a shocking mechanical buzz and read, "AMBER Alert now. Bismuth, MA: Missing," with the girls' names and ages. To get an AMBER Alert that fast meant Frank Cillo knew Someone at the Department of Justice. He also knew Someone at Bismuth High School, Saint Theresa's Church, the Parks Department, and the Bismuth Boat Club. Friends he'd gone to school with, played football with, served in the army with. Fellow football boosters, Lions, and Rotarians; members of the Massachusetts Association of Personal Injury Lawyers, the Workers Injury Law & Advocacy Group, and the Brotherhood of Malpractice Attorneys. Friends who brought macaroni and cases of Budweiser when Francesca and then Mira were born after his wife's miscarriages, and later, after she passed at forty-three. Networks of prematurely grizzled men with yellowing shirts and eyes who owed Frank Cillo, directly and otherwise.

Between 11:29 and 11:36, lights flicked on in bedrooms throughout Ben's neighborhood of compact brick colonials clustered in the throat of Powder Neck. Calls were made among the houses. Mothers panicked and checked their children. Fathers shrugged fleece jackets over undershirts and staggered toward the Cillos' house, the glare of flashing police lights filling their glasses.

The only ones who wouldn't have seen the AMBER Alert would have been the girls themselves, since their shared and heavily monitored cell phone rarely moved from the top of the refrigerator. That technology was barely present in the Cillo household only reinforced for the Bismuth mothers how *healthy* the Cillo girls were, what firm limits Frank Cillo set.

It was around January that the girls started acting weird. By early summer, their weirdness had become a topic among the neighborhood boys. Some argued it made sense, with Connie's accident only a few weeks before. Connie with her helium laugh and her dumb nicknames—Sistah, Sangue, Cuz—the slangy, silly words Mira and Francesca used for Connie, the ones that thrilled Connie as much as they annoyed Ben, bounced around his head.

Ben touched the picture on his phone with his fingertip. The divers had left the sisters attached, removed their pants but left on their panties. The photo was a pocket shot, a quick yank of the camera out of Kyle's pants, a snap-and-stuff. The image ended above the ribs, leaving waists and legs turned inward toward each other, as though they were curled in bed whispering to each other. At that angle, Ben couldn't tell if it was Mira; the oval coffee-colored stain on the back of her right thigh, above where her knee folded, was hidden. Still, he knew them by the lengths of their legs. In the foreground, the shorter set was shadowed, and covered by what Ben thought might be downy fuzz. In the background was a longer set, with the familiar rise of the thigh even at its most lax. The lovely swell.

He told himself that it was another girl. Not Mira.

Ben blinked hard, focusing on their bare feet, small and wrinkled. According to Kyle, the sisters had lined their sneakers side by side on the flat rock, the one the boys called the altar. Ben thought the rock looked more like an old man's throat, its skin loose over tendons, with the tip as its chin. The summer before last, Ben had stood on the chin, showing off for a sunbathing Mira. He pointed at her, turned, and made a clean dive. Seconds before breaking water, he saw the viscous stuff that floated on its surface, iridescent swirls of silver, blue, and purple, and it alarmed him. He'd struggled to surface quickly and didn't bother waiting for the reward of Mira's reaction. Instead, he powered to the wall, scaled it quick, and toweled off hard.

Ben let the sisters' deaths as they had been told to him play once more through his brain: misguided adventure, impulsive spree, deadly escapade. The local bum who stole recyclables after dark told the police he saw them riding their bikes toward the quarry on August 8th at 10:30 p.m. By 5:44 a.m., when the first streaks of purple streamed across the Boston skyline, the entire recovery team had descended, red-and-white trucks screaming, tearing into the quarry, where the first responders in scuba suits had already pulled the girls out, entangled.

It was the parts in between that gave Ben trouble.

Like, why would the girls ever come to the quarry at night?

"It seemed fun," Ben said, his voice hollow.

Why would they fall off a ledge they knew as well as they knew the bedroom they'd shared since birth?

"It was dark."

Ben closed his eyes and tried to imagine the girls who bathed in the sun bathing in moonlight. Catching sight, maybe, of something in the water. Something worth leaning too far over to see. That got Ben to wondering in what order they fell. It made sense to Ben, now that he thought about it, that Francesca and Mira would have reached for each other. According to Kyle, the girls had been in the water for at least six hours, because the blotches on their skin had joined up. Ben opened his eyes and counted on his fingers, from 11:00 p.m. to 5:44 a.m.

The girls must have been quick. Quick to get there, quick to line up, quick to place the rocks that were found in their sweater pockets. Quick to fall off the high ledge into the black water, one after the other.

Not one after the other exactly. If it had been an accident, they would have tried to save each other. They would have done that.

Fingers snarled in wool.

Francesca first, then Mira.

Mira first, then Francesca.

Ben shuddered. Though he knew it was wrong, he preferred to think of them falling at the same time, holding hands. Because, by the start of the summer, they had sealed themselves together and off from the rest of the world.

Ben used two fingers to enlarge the image on his phone, but it blurred into meaningless pixels.

PART 1

Palm

Mira's letter arrived seven days after she died.

Mira. Was. Alive.

The idea hit Ben like a punch to the throat. It grew into a vibrating, ludicrous shiver of hope that he'd seen another girl's body in Kyle's photo. A different beauty with long arms and gold-flecked eyes and a perfectly straight back, another girl had fallen alongside Francesca. Not Mira.

But: the swell of a thigh. He knew that swell tanned in white shorts. He knew it peeking from under the hem of a skirt, sitting at her desk in English, toes curled under, leaning forward. He knew it taut, lying on her back on a towel at the club and the quarry, one knee up.

Of course Mira was dead.

Ben studied the envelope, wondering if it was a sick joke. But there was the handwriting. Benvenuto Lattanzi, 20 Spring-vale Street, spelled out in purple ink on a long white generic business envelope, stained where it had passed through hands. Mira had put the letter through a convoluted dance to be de-livered next door, a dance that made little sense until you realized that arriving too late was the whole idea. A deliberate misspelling of Springdale Street that kept the envelope circulating around the city. That was like Mira: resourceful. Good at sneaking out in the middle of the night to meet Ben.

Good at sneaking out in the middle of the night to die.

Ben moaned. He pressed the curve of his fist into his mouth.

"Ben?" his mother called from her bedroom, her voice threaded with worry.

Overhead, his mother's footsteps quickened. Ben's head snapped. He pulled himself together fast and tore open the envelope, extracting the letter. It fluttered as his hand shook. More of Mira's handwriting, but the words wouldn't come together, and Ben felt like he was reading Spanish, which he sucked at, as if Mira's sentence was a string of cognates at which to guess. Sweat prickled under his arms. He rubbed his forehead with his wrist and held the letter close, his eyes skittering over the words. Finally, the words decoded themselves.

Everyone wanted to touch us. Including you.
So remember the seven places you touched me.
That's where you'll find the truth. In my words.
Start at the beginning.

Ben wiped sweat from his eyes. Mira had left him something. Mira had left him her words. Letters, notes. Something. Where?

Remember the places you touched me.

A whole summer had passed since Mira broke contact with him, after Connie's wake, days after Easter. But Ben remembered those places. Places where Mira had let him stroke, brush, caress, graze, kiss, nuzzle.

Stay.

He couldn't go there, not now.

She had done things with him in those places, innocent things, then more. The parts of Mira that Ben had touched were etched on his soul.

Palm. Hair. Chest. Cheek. Lips. Throat.

Then—

Not now.

Ben shook it off. Mira had given him a puzzle, one that Ben could solve, that would give him answers for the holes that haunted him, the parts of Mira's life between what he saw from his bedroom window and the diluted version he got when they were among friends. For Ben had spent endless hours wondering about the pretty mysteries of Mira's life that seemed far away, but were playing out right next door. Ben drifted again to a place he knew he shouldn't go, and the shame and pleasure was awful.

A creak above. He stuffed Mira's letter in the back waistband of his shorts and looked up as his mother flew down the stairs, slowing at the bottom, attempting to model normalcy. She'd had practice at remaining calm when evil intruded into their lives. Specifically, when it targeted her son. Ben imagined her pacing upstairs moments before, whispering "You've got this" to herself, over and over.

"I heard a strange noise," she said, her hand reaching toward his face, then pulling back. "Are you all right?"

It was like she thought death was contagious. Ben had considered the possibility. First Mrs. Cillo died (ten years back, and Ben barely remembered her); then the Cillos' cousin, Connie Villela, in March; and now the Cillo girls. Was death a germ you could catch, like Mrs. Cillo's depression, and Connie's deadly allergy, and the girls with their . . . what?

Nothing.

Maybe he should call in sick. This would be the fourth day he hadn't gone in to work, and the clubhouse manager had sent word that he was considering replacing him. Ben had been saving his paychecks to get Mira out of Bismuth. The timing worked. If he showed up five days a week for the rest of the summer, the $232.80 in his bank account would grow to $500.00. It was the half grand he needed to buy his father's failing BMW. His father had been on his side since he'd turned sixteen—he was eyeing a new convertible—but that could change with weak grades or another roach and a vial of Visine found in a dirty pants pocket. Mira hadn't known the plan, but she had only needed to say the word, and they would have left Bismuth for foreign highways. Getting out of Bismuth had become an obsession nearly as great as Mira herself.

Ben rammed his nose with the heel of his hand. He hadn't realized he was crying.

"Oh, Ben," his mother said softly, producing a tissue. "Maybe it's too soon to go back to work." She had been "giving space" and "being available"—the things suggested by her friends, who no doubt wished more than anything that this awful story would go away and they could get on with their tennis and low-glycemic diets.

Start at the beginning.

"Can you take me to the boat club *right now?*" Ben begged.

His mother searched his face while Ben took in the sight of her. Her unwashed hair fell in finger-combed rows. One freckled breastbone pointed out of a graying tank. The ends of her eyes drew downward into the soft wince that accompanied the subject of the Cillos. Another person might translate the wince into empathy for the Cillos, but Ben knew better. His father's historic falling-out with Mr. Cillo had been brutal. The intervening years with a scant eight feet between their houses had been strained. Mr. Cillo's daughters dying? That was plain awkward.

"I'm glad you want to go back to work already," she said. "But I want you to be prepared. Have you spoken with Eddie since the incident?"

Connie's brother Eddie, the Cillos' cousin Eddie, his oldest friend Eddie, now steeped in death's perfume. Ben forgot he was going to have to face Eddie, never mind work around him to find more of Mira's "words." Not that he didn't have experience. The Lattanzi-Cillo bad blood had kept his relationship with Mira secret from Eddie, who valued family loyalty and would've seen it as a betrayal from both sides. Though Eddie loved Ben and Mira both, he could not love them together.

Sangue. Cuz.

It was all so stupid.

"Because I imagine you'll see Eddie today," his mother nattered, oblivious to Ben's darkening expression. "Give him our love and support, and let him know we're here to help. You might even tell him about the scholarship Daddy set up in the girls' names."

Eddie had little to fear. After Connie's wake, Mira had dumped Ben cold. Mira's sudden silence was the first thing Ben thought of when he woke, and the last thing he thought of as he drifted off to sleep. In the mornings, he rose and stood at his window, staring at her house. Constantly, he checked his phone, though a text was as unlikely as the idea Mira might one day disappear from the earth. Later, he rationalized that girls were a headache, especially girls you had to see in secret, most especially girls who were complicated puzzles that often left him feeling dumb. He'd convinced himself that no longer having to hide their relationship from Mr. Cillo (and, truth be told, Eddie) was a relief. That the last time he and Mira had been together was sublime, and now it could never be corrupted by lesser, fumbling attempts.

Lie after lie after lie.

"Oh, bud." His mother's hand fluttered, producing another tissue.

Ben kneaded his fist against the spot between his eyes. "I want it on the record that I will not serve as the goodwill ambassador for the Lattanzi household."

"I'm sorry. It was inappropriate. Give me five minutes and we can go," she said. She knew Mira had been something more to Ben, though she was careful to talk about the "loss of his friend" and the "four stages of grief when losing a friend," imagining she was minimizing Ben's devastation by defining their relationship. Though it was only day seven, his mother had suggested there might be value in Ben speaking with someone—Saint Theresa's Spiritual Director Nick Falso, for example—if only because she was running out of things to say.

Ben waited in front of a calendar encased in lucite on the wall. Someone had interpreted August to mean fireflies caught in a mason jar, with moody, Monet swirls, the flies whirring in useless motion. Ben had looked forward to this summer, because it had meant more time around Mira without the distraction of school and sports and *activities* (his; the girls had none). Days swimming at the club and the quarry had their allure, especially for guys who had no real interactions with the girls otherwise, and who planned their days around seeing them in their bathing suits. Ben preferred the early evenings, when the windows were open and the sounds from next door drifted in: upstairs, a shower running overlong, one of the girls washing the metallic funk of quarry water from her hair and skin. Outside, the thrilling vacuum rush of the gas grill, which meant they'd assemble at the picnic table soon, Francesca fussing over her father's plate, Mira indolent from the day's sun.

Ben wondered if summer would always be a tainted season for him now. Before he left, he touched his finger on August 8, leaving a smudge.

Ben made for the gate that led to the clubhouse, through shrieks and lifeguard whistles, and beyond, the tidal roar and squeals of gulls. The wooden shell housed a snack bar and locker rooms. Built around the tired pool and facing the ocean, it captured and amplified the noises of both. The manager, Kenneth Laidlaw, lingered around the entrance, waiting for him to arrive.

"Lattanzi!" he called.

Ben jogged past him with a wave and beelined for the locker room, rank with ammonia over urine. Boys tumbled in, first three, then five. One boy pushed another. Ben glowered at them, waiting until the last one had zipped his fly and left to begin his search for Mira's note.

The manager stuck in his pustuled forehead. "You stroll in twenty minutes late and sit here catching up on your fan mail?" he whined.

Ben slid Mira's letter into his bag. "I'm getting changed."

"Looks like you're dressed. Get behind the counter. The place is jammed and Eddie's been alone for half his shift already. Have some sympathy, Benvenuto. The dude's been fed a tragedy sandwich."

Ben cringed. The manager was an ignorant putz who would never feel empathy for Eddie, but it was a convenient excuse to abuse Ben.

"I'm aware. Thanks though."

"Then help the man!"

Ben knew the note was somewhere inside the clubhouse. Mr. Cillo might have had eyes everywhere, but not between their hands at the snack bar last summer. Ben had sensed Mira coming before he'd seen her, making her way through the kinetic energy of sugared and sunburned kids. Behind her, the sun glared white. It hurt to look at her. She'd worn her father's button-down shirt over her wet bathing suit, and it clung in places. Ben had dreamed of her that morning and felt sure she knew. It seemed possible he was still dreaming and coming to the best part. Water beaded on her eyebrows and lashes. Ben wished he could fold her inside a towel and lead her away, wished he could tell her that's what he would like to do, but the recurring theme between them was Ben sounding stupid, and so he almost always said nothing.

And then she was there.

"Hey," he murmured.

Mira blinked. "Hey."

"A real live mermaid!" Eddie boomed as he came out from the supply room. Ben stiffened, waiting for the cascade of hugs and kisses between cousins, a display that tapped the hollow in his chest. Ben wasn't jealous that Eddie got to touch the girl everyone wanted to touch. It was that Ben had nothing like that in his life. No extended family that acted like every time they bumped into one another was the first time in a year. It was excessive and vulgar and lovely, and Ben ached for it.

"Ever hear of a towel, sweetheart?" Eddie said, pushing past Ben and leaning over the counter to plant a kiss on her cheek.

Over Eddie's shoulder, Mira's eyes fixed on Ben.

"I hate it here," she murmured.

"Look at the bright side. Some of us don't have a choice every day between the club and the quarry; we gotta work for a living. We'll get you a towel. Benny, you seen any extra towels back in the lost and found?"

Ben slunk away for a towel, relieved for the chore. The exquisite pain of Mira's closeness, especially when she looked slightly porny, was more than Ben could bear. He was certain his ears glowed hot.

"Don't!" Mira said suddenly. Ben stopped short. "Don't bother. Francesca wants to leave."

Eddie planted his fists on his hips. "Someone giving you girls trouble?" Eddie's play at being his uncle Frank's surrogate seemed stupid to Ben, the way Eddie pretended Mira needed a protector of her virtue when his own sister fooled around with everyone. Whatever myth Mr. Cillo had created about his daughters, it was contagious, because even the same boys who sneered at the Cillos' untouchability upheld it. Mr. Cillo's no-dating rule was an excellent excuse to avoid the ball-busting fail of asking out his daughters.

"Relax, no one's giving us trouble," Mira said. "Get me a Coke, okay?"

"You got it."

As Eddie's head disappeared inside the cooler, Mira held out a bill. Ben frowned, confused. The Cillo girls never paid at the snack bar. Not unless the manager was hovering, and even he refused Francesca's money.

"You know Eddie won't let me take that," Ben said, low and conspiratorial. She had allowed him to speak that way to her: her gesture required it. He was grateful.

Mira pushed the wet dollar on him. "I want to pay like everyone else."

Mira shifted from hip to hip, tangled in the damp cage of her father's shirt. Ben took the dollar. That's when it happened. Mira's two fingers, reaching past where they should, a stroke on the inside of his palm. So light he thought he'd imagined it, but knew he hadn't, because of Mira's smoldering look after. He'd practically danced away, looked the fool, tacked the dollar right up on the cork board for anyone to ask about. A flash of amusement, a sly smile before she padded away without her Coke, leaving wet footprints on the cement. Ben's elation dissipated into panic, and he sweated the rest of the afternoon, wondering if Eddie had seen any of it go down. Maybe for Mira, the thrill was in the risk of getting caught. Ben knew there were couples who purposely had sex in places like alleys and golf courses and the bathroom stalls at the boat club because it was more exciting. Getting caught became what Ben and Mira feared most. Because that would mean the end.

Ben conjured the feel of Mira's fingertips grazing his palm, and the memory made a stir in his pants, luscious and sad. Around that same time, Mira was changing, all nervy jangle, her limbs spring-loaded. On a towel, her knees sliced at the air, discontented. Listening to her sister, she would thrust her long neck forward; the slightest sound or movement made her head snap. Coiled and constantly alert, it was as though she might leap from her skin, or from this world. In a dream, Ben had watched as Mira launched herself off the altar, her legs flush back, her popped throat bound for the sky.

"Dude!" his manager shouted, ducking in. Ben considered how easy it would be to take off his pimpled head with a swift kick of the door. Instead, he stashed his bag in a locker and picked through a mob of sweaty kids to reach the hinged half gate that led behind the counter. Eddie's back was to Ben, operating the shake machine and pouring Goldfish into tiny cups at the same time.

Ben slapped an apron around his waist and cracked open a fresh mega-sized carton of Goldfish. "Help's here!"

Eddie swung around fast. Always ready for a fight. The cousins and siblings shared the same loosely wired nerves. Where Mira displayed the genetic reactivity throughout her body, and Connie in her hair-trigger laugh, Eddie was known for snapping. He once smacked Steven "Piggy" Pignataro for cupping Connie's butt when he was drunk, and Piggy still had to plug his ears when the T rumbled by.

"Geez, Benny, you took your time. Slap dogs on the turner and help me do drinks."

Ben quickly glanced around the snack bar space, desperate for a flash of white. Would the note be the same size as the first letter? The same color? In an envelope again? He felt Eddie's sharp eyes on him and turned fast, plugging in the relic electric turner. "Laidlaw didn't even warm up the turner for us," Ben mumbled, his face hot.

"Douche," Eddie said, settling, turning away from Ben.

The lunch crowd came in waves, dashing Ben's chance to search. They worked silently until the mob subsided, Eddie at the front end, taking orders and keeping the brats in line, and Ben working the back, pushing out hot dogs, Goldfish, and sugary drinks. Ben wished more than anything that he'd come early and beat Eddie and the crowds. The action seemed to taint the place, making any note Mira might have hidden impossible to find. He began to doubt he was right. Maybe he was reading too much into it, getting too technical: did Mira consider a palm stroke "being together"? Was it even worthy of a memory? What was? Ben snuck a look at Eddie. What if Eddie had found the note before Ben arrived and thrown it away? Or worse: what if he had it? Ben studied the back of Eddie's short neck. He needed to get Eddie talking. He needed to know.

Ben waited until the last customer slapped away in her flip-flops.

"Yo, Ed. Can I ask you a question?" Ben said lightly, washing his hands at the sink to avoid his face.

Eddie turned and slumped against the counter, guarded. "Depends on the question."

Ben dried his hands with a bar towel and softened his voice. "I was just gonna ask you how you were doing, man."

Eddie folded his overdeveloped forearms. Fresh ink circled his bicep. The last time Ben had worked with Eddie, there was one star. Now, two new blue stars connected by swirls circled his arm.

"Three stars," Ben said, pointing.

"Three stars together up in heaven now. Tight as they were in real life. They were saints, my cousins. *Mio sangue.* Don't you believe anything you hear about them being depressed or nothing."

"I don't."

Eddie went on as if he hadn't heard. "They were fine. I mean, they were sad, about Concetta. We all were. Are. Devastated." He rubbed the back of his neck and bulged his eyes. "But not enough to do *that*."

Ben didn't take offense to Eddie getting his back up. He knew there were lots of people interested in the accident for the wrong reasons. He needed Eddie to know he wasn't one of them, but Eddie was too raw to remember that Ben was one of the good ones.

"Anyone who knew them knows it was an accident. It's good your family's got church and all. And Mr. Falso," Ben faltered. "I mean, it's got to help. To have a higher power, to look to, to look *up* to, when terrible things happen . . ."

Eddie pushed off the counter and moved to the electric turner to spin the hot dogs. "What do I know? I ain't been to church since . . . whenever."

Ben knew he meant Connie's funeral. The whole thing had been a shit show, from his own parents' uptight, robotic appearance to Eddie's mom on Xanax propped like a rag doll in a metal folding chair to Eddie's dad smoking on the curb with the men, including his brother-in-law Frank Cillo, cracking knuckles and talking about throwing a Molotov cocktail on the front porch of Connie's doctor's mansion. Half the guys in the neighborhood went just to see the Cillo girls dressed up. Francesca wore a black scoop-neck top with a skirt, like a ballerina. Mira's dress was simple and sheer around the hem, and it whirled when she walked up to the casket and settled in a flutter on her calves when she kneeled down; Ben remembered that. They squared their shoulders toward each other, talking to no one, not even relatives, their faces pale ash. Mira strayed from Francesca's side once, to rearrange a disordered vase of pink-and-yellow-sprayed carnations from the Parks Department, slipping the flowers into different positions with meticulous care. She never acknowledged Ben, which seemed okay—that was how they did things. It was acceptable for a Lattanzi to attend a Villela wake, but grabbing Mira Cillo and crushing her against his chest in front of her father and his parents was not.

Both girls stayed out of the line of relatives that led away from the open casket, in which Connie was perfectly intact, if unrecognizable. Ben's head had throbbed from the masses of stargazer lilies, cheap, since it was Easter season, their gaudy, pink blooms clobbering everyone with a medicinal funk. And though Ben was sure he hadn't brushed against them, he found yellow powder on his sleeve. The second Ben's parents paid their stiff condolences and left, Ben bolted and accepted a hit off Kyle's joint right in the parking lot.

There had been no funeral for Francesca and Mira. Only a private cremation.

Ben wedged hot dog buns into cardboard rectangles. "I wanted to say. I know my dad and your uncle had their differences. But we feel your pain."

"Benny, what are you talking about?" Eddie said, shaking his head.

Ben's stomach tightened.

"Not for nothing, but ain't no one's thinking about the Lattanzi-Cillo feud right now. In fact, maybe it's time all that crap went away," Eddie said, tonging hot dogs aggressively into buns.

Ben agreed gruffly. The unfairness of Mr. Cillo warming to the Lattanzis after Mira's death was too much to think on. "Sorry, man. I didn't mean to make it about that."

Eddie kept his back to Ben, his shoulders relaxing slightly. "I know you didn't. You're one of the good ones. Guys are easier, you know. Uncle Frank's a guy's guy. He didn't know what to do with girls. Feminine protection and mood swings and shit. It had to be hard. You think you're doing the right thing: treat them like glass, keep the dogs away, protect them, hold them real close. And still this happens. Sometimes I think this family's cursed. Like the Kennedys or something."

A kid waved a dollar over the counter. "Can I have a Ring Pop?"

Eddie threw the kid a lollipop. "Suck it." He moved to the fridge and pulled out a mesh bag of lemons and drew a short knife from the drawer under the counter.

"Nah, you're not cursed." Ben pretended to wipe down the sales counter and peeked over the ledge, searching for a note tacked underneath. "The truth will come out," he murmured distractedly.

Eddie froze, his knife hovering over the lemons. He turned his head. "Ain't no truth to come out. They fell."

Ben stepped forward. "God, everything I say keeps coming out wrong. I'm not thinking straight. Tell you the truth, Eddie, I loved them."

Eddie's shoulders fell. "I know you did. Nobody knows why any of this happened." He let the lemon roll away, signed the cross over his chest, and looked up. "Only The Man knows."

Their shift went along predictably, each falling to his own thoughts. Ben was glad for the quiet, scanning his eyes over every nook in the snack bar. If Eddie was paying attention, he might have noticed that Ben was taking unusual care, lifting the rubber dividers in the cutlery drawers, dusting behind massive plastic mayonnaise tubs, and inspecting the back of the money drawer. Eddie sliced more lemons than they would need for ten pitchers of lemonade. Ben enabled his distraction, grabbing a two-pound bag of sugar and three fat plastic pitchers and filling them partway with water from the tap. Eventually, Ben left Eddie with his lemons and tended the dogs. Rolling the dogs on the turner, he meditated on where he'd gone wrong in his calculations. Mira's secret note would not be found; Ben had checked every inch of the space. His mind skipped to the next place they were alone, and wondered when and how fast he could escape the snack bar to get there. His dead ex-girlfriend was watching from somewhere above, he was sure of it, and he was failing this task. As he gazed over the empty counter, his mind played a terrible trick. He saw Mira in her father's shirt, soaked not from the pool but from the quarry lake. Ben shivered. Pretend-Mira smiled and handed him a dripping dollar bill.

The dollar.

Ben dropped the dogs and walked swiftly to the tiny hall that led to the back pantry. On the cork board, among tacked-up messages begging for more hours, mysterious keys, and a coupon for Dunkin' Donuts was Mira's dollar. He had pinned it on the board that day, gotten busted by Mira doing it, and hadn't cared. It seemed right, a secret reminder every day of what he was busting his butt for: eyes on the prize and such. He lifted the corner and found her note underneath, folded into a delicate sliver. His fingers fumbled, and it fell to the ground, light, achingly slow.

Ben snatched it off the sticky floor and cleared his throat. "Eddie, you good?" he called shakily. "I gotta go to the can!"

Eddie grunted over a mountain of chopped lemons. Ben slipped off his apron and sidled from behind the counter, ducked into the locker room. He landed hard on the bench and peeled apart the tiny folds.

Daddy tells Francesca that it's all in her head.
But I've seen it happening with my own eyes for years.
Now, she bleeds.

Ben's face burned. He thought of what Eddie had said about Mr. Cillo living among all that feminine protection. He didn't know what felt worse, reading about Francesca getting her period or the way it made him mad at Mira, like she was trying to shame him from beyond. He set the scrap of paper on the bench, walked to the sink and splashed his face with water. His reflection in the cloudy mirror said defeated, the butt of a bad joke. Francesca was a sore spot for Ben. She knew about him and Mira, and though she never outwardly acknowledged it—its futility made it inconsequential—he knew she didn't approve. That overdeveloped jaw she slid back and forth, a judge-y, clicking noise that sounded like *tsk, tsk*. The idea that Mira would waste a note on Francesca pissed him off.

What was all in Francesca's head, anyway? Ben didn't want to know. He pulled hard at the corners of his eyes as Eddie screamed.

The door swung open and Eddie shouldered in, staring at his hand swathed in a crimson dishrag. Their manager ran behind, yelling, "You may nev-er swear in front of the guests!"

Eddie raised his good hand to slam the door in the manager's face.

His face was the shade of a ping-pong ball. Ben yanked his

shirt over his head and wrapped it around the dishrag, pushing Eddie gently onto the bench. Eddie stared at Ben, his
mouth a tight line.

"Can you speak?" Ben said, squeezing the mass of cloth.

Eddie whispered, "It stings bad."

Ben matched his whisper. "Because of the lemon. You gotta
put pressure on it. I know it hurts. But unless you do, the blood
won't stop."

The manager busted back in. "I called an ambulance, un-
grateful as you are."

Eddie rose to say something and fell backward. Ben caught
him with a hand on his back.

"No way am I taking no ambulance to the hospital," Eddie
gasped. "That's the last thing my mother needs."

"Is an ambulance really necessary?" Ben said.

"Are you gonna drive him there?" the manager spat, his
voice pitched up. "Besides, someone's gotta stay and clean up.
For all I know, Villela left a digit on the cutting board. The
place looks like a slaughterhouse."

"Fine!" Ben yelled. "You man the counter, I'll sit with him
and wait. Stick up the cleaners' sign."

Ben knew he was treading a fine line: nothing was off-limits
for his manager. Just six years older than Ben, he was an im-
mature toad, and the only person in town sadistic enough
to use Ben's status as "touched" to keep him in line. Taunts of
"delicate sensibilities" and "having issues" were whispered for

Eddie to miss, and thus not report to Ben's ad hoc protector, Kyle Kulik, which would ensure a good tire slashing of the manager's Corolla.

The manager blinked. "What. Did you just say to me?"

Something blazed inside Ben. He smiled ferociously, let his eyes loosen and jitter. The manager backed into the door. He tucked his chin into his chest, swearing he would never again hire a messed-up psycho, and left.

Ben watched the door until he heard the scrape of the sign on its hook, then rose.

"You're gonna be all right, Eddie boy," Ben said, flinging open lockers until he found a pile of thin white towels, which he tore into strips that shed dust. He wrapped them around Eddie's wrist, then circled the palm where the knife had made a clean diagonal slice toward the pinkie. He counted Eddie's fingers: 9.5, since the pinkie was severed near-through. He used the strips to tack the finger back together tight. When no blood showed through, he pushed Eddie's head between his knees and rubbed his back, lowering his own head against a wave of nausea. Through the slats, Ben spotted a flash of white. Mira's note had gotten knocked off the bench, and was right under Eddie's nose, if he was looking.

"Close your eyes, man," Ben said.

Eddie groaned.

"The palm's a bad place to get cut, that's all," Ben yammered, eyeing the note. "Like a nose or a lip, it goes and goes.

Might not be using that hand in basketball for a while, but you'll be fine. Maybe keep those eyes closed."

Ben studied the mummified hand to distract himself from the note. He was impressed by his own handiwork. It hadn't been easy to cover the palm in a way that kept the slice closed. Or the finger on. He hoped it would stay on. Maybe he should call Kyle. Where was the stupid ambulance? Ben knew it could be tricky to get across Bismuth in the middle of the summer with the endless construction, and then the long ride out to Powder Neck meant they might be waiting a while. Ben placed his hand over Eddie's and squeezed.

Eddie moaned.

"Gotta stem the bleeding," Ben murmured.

Eddie swooned forward. Ben caught the collar of his polo shirt and righted him, slapping his cheek lightly. "Eddie? Eddie, listen, stay with me!"

"I'm coming, Concetta Marie. It's your big brother, Eddie. I'm coming to take care of you . . ."

"Jesus, Eddie! Listen: Do you remember how funny Connie was? How much she looked up to you, and the girls? Remember that time the three of them had a yard sale and Connie sold your special 1975 Carlton Fisk World Series card to the creepy dude with the handlebar mustache for twenty-five cents?"

He shook his head and laughed anemically. "I wanted to kill her. She didn't know."

"And the girls got mad at you, like you were the one who did something wrong? They were ready to lynch you for yelling at her! All for one, they said. You guys talk about blood. Those girls were Connie's oxygen, man. She wouldn't have wanted to be around if they were gone. It's a terrible thing to say, but Connie loved her cousins so hard, I don't think she could've handled it." Ben could hardly believe what was coming out of his mouth, but it seemed to help, so he kept going.

"Maybe not," Eddie whispered, rocking over his thumb.

"Sometimes stuff happens for a reason. Maybe they're better off in heaven, together."

"Ouch," Eddie whispered.

"Ouch," Ben said. "They're angels looking down on you right now, and you're gonna be fine."

"You hurt one, you hurt all of them. That's what they said." Eddie shifted uncomfortably. "Truth be told though? She could be kind of annoying sometimes."

"Nah. She was a cute kid." Connie had been barely a year younger than either of them, but Ben went with it. "A real cutie."

"She wanted to please people. Delicate, too. Not just her condition. She was sensitive. Easily led and easily hurt, a bad combination, my mom always said." Eddie coughed thickly into his swaddled hand, the signature hacky cough that always made Ben wonder. In basketball, he'd stop and hock a loogie, two or three times a game, into trash barrels in the gym or on the asphalt. He wasn't nearly as bad as Connie, where any real exercise would send her into spasms, but Ben wondered if there was something rogue about the Villela genes, where doing ordinary things made them implode.

Ben shook the image from his brain. "Led?"

Eddie's lips were turning blue, and he trembled. Ben snatched a dirty towel from the warped particleboard shelf and wrapped it around Eddie's shoulders and gave him a loose, one-armed hug. Sirens wailed in the distance. Ben figured they had reached the breakaway stretch and would arrive in less than a minute.

Eddie slumped into Ben. "Connie wouldn't like me saying that."

"Nah, she knows you loved her."

"And she loved those girls. They were the sisters she never had. I shouldn't have said that, about her being led. When she died up there on the hill, they were just having fun."

It seemed to Ben that Mira and Francesca were always leading Connie away from things that could hurt. Like stopping her from heading behind the boathouse with two dudes. Running interference between her and Piggy, both drunk. Just the way she died—running after the girls, forgetting her EpiPen—smacked of Connie's refusal to be left behind, and her recklessness.

Eddie slumped forward.

"They're coming. Hold on, buddy."

"It's like I'm bein pun'shed. You eva feel that way? Like you're bein pun'shed?"

Ben didn't like the way Eddie was slurring his words. "Punched? You're talking gibberish. Try and relax. That siren's for you." Ben tapped his sneaker on the floor, eyes sweeping the locker room desperately. He was starting to think Eddie might be the next Bismuth teen casualty.

"Not punched, knucklehead," Eddie whispered. "Punished. For not having protected them good enough."

"Shh now."

"You. Them." Eddie shook his head hard at the floor. "I could've protected you, too, but I didn't. I didn't tell when I knew."

"That was a million years ago." Ben didn't like where Eddie was heading. Coach Freck had been in jail for seven years. His list of baseball players he touched—and Ben's place on it—was old news; Ben was better now, and Eddie would never have said anything if he wasn't half out of his mind with blood loss.

"You're talking nonsense," Ben said, a little roughly.

Eddie's head tipped up, and he held Ben's eye. The door banged open and a girl and a guy, paramedics not much older than Ben and Eddie, charged in, the guy pushing a wheelchair. The girl was small and pretty and grim looking, with a hard fringe of honey-colored bangs and a turned-up nose. The girl felt Eddie's pulse while her partner kicked out the feet of the wheelchair.

Eddie raised his good hand weakly. "I ain't walking out of here in that."

The guy shoved Ben out of the way and lifted Eddie underneath his shoulders. "You ain't walkin'," the girl said, wrapping a blood pressure cuff around his bicep. Eddie's head lolled. Ben followed them out, suddenly conscious of his own shirtlessness, which seemed disturbing even though they were at a pool. He avoided the eyes of the mothers whispering "Villela" like an answer, or a curse. Little kids stared at Ben's ribs. He looked down and saw blood smears across his torso like war paint. Walking behind the paramedics in their navy pants and white button-down shirts, Ben felt like a savage. He took mental inventory of the gawkers' feet: tan toes, wrinkled toes, fat smooth kid toes. When the ambulance whined away, Ben wandered back into the locker room. Under the bench, Mira's tiny note was speckled with blood. He snatched his nylon bag out of the locker and tucked the note inside, his thoughts flashing to a story where a man sewed a leather bag for a woman who carried her heart outside her body. Ben had found it hard to read—the descriptions of the heart made him gag—but it was exactly the kind of bag in which he could keep Mira's letter (and the notes he would find. Oh, the notes!) protected, near his heart.

His cheeks grew hot at his own familiar dorkiness. Where the Cillo sisters made other guys behave worse than they actually were, Mira made Ben want to commit heroic acts.

Ben slunk back to the snack bar. Because they had no more shirts, the manager ordered Ben home immediately, and he waited for his mother in the parking lot, leaning against the plaster pelican with the Bismuth Boat Club sign in its beak, hugging his elbows to hide the blood.

SEPTEMBER 2015

Mira rolled off the bed and into the bathroom, unwinding her arms, pajama pant cuffs swishing above her ankles. She shifted on her hip and sighed.

Francesca had been scraping for close to an hour. She tore the brush through her hair, ripping from the roots, creating tangles. Mira thought of other times she'd seen her sister in the same trance. Like when their father found the tablet Francesca had borrowed from school, and she'd gone glassy-eyed under his hollering, tearing sheets of skin from the sides of her fingernails. And when he blocked her from getting her driver's permit, biting the insides of both cheeks so hard they swelled, which made her look pouty. Even further back, after their mother died, and Bambi Maggiore appeared in the doorway with a pan of lasagna. They'd sat on the couch watching their father's ears turn red, Bambi's drugstore Vanilla Musk invading the room. Mira had watched Francesca file her fingernails into points and make fists, leaving four purple marks on the heel of each hand.

And though she knew the answer, Mira asked, "What's wrong?"

The black nest of hair in the bristles grew.

"You're going to be bald," Mira warned.

The brush caught a snag. Francesca's mouth twisted as she yanked. Mira eased Francesca's hand from the handle. "Let me," she said, tugging the clump. She cupped her sister's shoulder and skimmed the brush lightly over the tangle.

Francesca stiffened.

"I'm trying to be gentle." Mira set the brush on the slim edge of the pedestal sink. "Here, I'll use my fingers."

Mira weaved her fingers into her sister's hair. Francesca relaxed slightly, her arms falling to her sides, eyes half closed, exhausted. Mira caught a bright red flash, a trick of light in the mirror, she thought, until she saw the tendrils of blood trailing down Francesca's lax fingers.

Mira sucked in her breath. "You cut yourself!" she gasped, pointing into the mirror.

Francesca raised her hands, fingers curled into claws, twisting at the wrists. The blood reversed direction and curled back on itself, past the palm and the wrists and down the blue insides of her arms.

"What did you touch?"

"Nothing! I didn't touch anything!" Francesca bent her elbows and gazed about her waist, as though admiring a pretty dress. "Am I bleeding from anywhere else?"

Mira shook her head. "Just your hands. Let me look at them."

Francesca offered her palms to Mira, who lowered her head over the dark puddles. A thin stream bled from identical holes in her palms and crested the creases of her cocked wrists.

Francesca started to shake. "It keeps coming."

Mira grasped her hands and squinted. She could not place where the bleeding started, or how such a thing could happen without cause, and she blinked to clear her vision, but nothing changed.

"Make it stop!" Francesca cried, her voice warbling.

Mira dropped her hands and shook a towel from its metal hoop with a hollow clang. She pressed it between Francesca's fists, squeezing the tops between hers. As the towel grew bright with blood, a sticky warmth inside Mira's own palms made her pull away.

"What?" Francesca squeaked.

"The blood is coming from both sides," Mira sputtered.

Francesca swayed, her face draining of color.

"I'm getting Daddy!" Mira said.

"He'll think I did it," Francesca said.

Mira's forehead shot up. She hadn't considered what Daddy might think: that Francesca had tried to do what their mother had done, but a nonnarcotic version, messy and overblown. All that was missing were razor blades in the sink.

"Then stick your fingers in the holes," Mira cried. "In the palms. Do it."

Francesca nodded mutely and let the towel fall, dropping her middle fingers delicately to the centers of her palms.

"Press harder," Mira breathed. "It's not going to stop unless you press harder."

Francesca bit on her lip and balled her fists. "There's so much blood. It's not going to stop. You need to plug both sides."

Mira dug her fingers into the pulsing stars on the backs of her sister's hands, taking jackhammer breaths to stem the shock that was catching up with her. "Oh, Francesca." She leaned in until their foreheads touched. "What now?"

Their heads snapped at footbeats on the stairs, slow and reluctant. Their father usually receded from his daughters' before-school manipulations, which were fraught with higher emotions than other times of day. But this morning, there had been no drawers slamming, no rumble of hair dryers, only whispers: Francesca's, harsh; Mira's, pleading. He cleared his throat. More whispers, rushed. He pushed open the door, eyes still cast down.

"Time for school!" he called.

"Daddy!" Mira cried.

He gaped at the sight of his girls attached at the hands, blood between them. Mira was never to see their father in his bathrobe. It was an unwritten rule of their house, one of many bodily-related vagaries, like when he showered, or what he slept in. Mira was surprised by her overwhelming wish that he cover himself, put on his uniform—suit, shiny wingtips, black socks—so that she didn't have to see him in this state. She tried to look away from his body, barrel-chested in his robe, thin legs below. He was her beloved dad, but somehow she was disturbed by his swollen parts. What was it about Mira that gave her weird, out-of-place thoughts? A normal girl didn't hear the T coming and back away from the urge to leap onto the rails. She didn't cradle a baby and consider how easy it would be to hold its nose for a minute, maybe two. Didn't know the smell of gypsy moth caterpillars when they burned in an aluminum watering can filled with lighter fluid. Sometimes the only thing that stopped Mira was her mother's voice in her head, reminding her that where she was, it was quiet.

He pushed past Mira and scooped the towel off the floor, blotting Francesca's hands clumsily. Mira thought it was not like their father, to seem clumsy, but Francesca wasn't making it easy for him, twisting and drawing away.

"Should I call an ambulance?" Mira said, her voice small.

His cheeks flapped as he shook his head. "Why, baby? Why would you do this to yourself? Why?"

"I didn't slit my wrists!" Francesca said. She flipped her hands to expose the backs and threw them under his nose. "I have holes, Daddy! I have holes in my hands!"

He held her hands, turning them over and over, examining them for what seemed like an eternity to Mira.

"I didn't make them," Francesca whimpered. "They were there when I looked down."

He raised his eyes. "Do they hurt?"

Francesca nodded, wincing. As their stare deepened, her wince dissolved until her face was neutral.

"I'm going to ask you again. Do they hurt?" he said.

She shook her head no.

"Good. That's good. Mira: get the long ACE bandages from my bathroom, under the sink," he said, never dropping contact with Francesca's eyes.

Mira ran into her parents' bathroom and dug around the tiny vanity, knocking over old bottles of her mother's hairspray, nozzles encased in amber globules. It was touching that Daddy kept these relics, but it also seemed sort of lazy to Mira. She found the bandages and ran back to find Francesca with her face buried inside their father's shoulder, his big hand cradling the back of her head. Mira felt the familiar sting of envy, and then shame. Francesca was her blood.

"Daddy," Mira whispered.

He released Francesca and unfurled the bandages, wrapping them swiftly around her hands. Francesca cried softly.

"I'm sorry, baby, but we have to stop the flow," he said.

"I can't go to school like this," Francesca cried.

"You're not going anywhere until we sort this out," he replied.

Mira crept closer, breathing in her father's smell of coffee and eggs, aftershave and sleep.

"Are we going to the hospital?" Francesca sniffled.

"No!" he said, catching himself and saying more softly, "No."

"Dr. Amendola, then?" Mira said.

He drew Francesca close to him, shooting Mira a pointed look past her sister's head that meant *yes and stop talking now.* Mira frowned. He pushed Francesca away and held her chin.

"You're going to be okay, do you understand? You're going to go downstairs and Mira is going to make you a nice breakfast. Orange juice, too. I'm going into my office to make some phone calls," he said.

Francesca broke into sobs. "But what if it starts up again?"

"We've got it under control. Don't use your hands for anything for a while." He steered her into the hall and down the stairs. Mira followed. When they got to the bottom landing, he turned before his office door. "It's nowhere else, right?"

Francesca looked back at him, her face blanched. "The blood? No!"

"Good." He shut the door.

Francesca slipped into the red leather banquette. Mira opened the refrigerator and spoke quietly into the sterile space.

She needed to prepare her sister, who hated doctors keenly. "I think he's calling Dr. Amendola."

"Daddy wouldn't," Francesca said sharply.

Mira flinched, tossing her father's cold eggs and toast from his plate into the trash. She dropped fresh slices into the toaster and topped his mug with sludge from the pot, staring at the ombré coffee as it swished inside, catching the light, gradations of black and brown. As she swept away the crumbs from around the toaster, she felt the grainy sharpness of each tiny morsel under the soft side of her pinkie. The toast popped exuberantly, it seemed, and she placed it on a plate, dragging the knife across the rough surface, the butter melting fast into sharply defined crevices. She looked over her shoulder at Francesca, her head bowed above her bandaged hands crossed in front, prayerful. Mira had noticed that in times of shock, life's details became overly distinct, scoring themselves into her memory. She first noticed it the morning after her mother didn't wake up. Her ordinary world took on a surreal quality, with higher colors, textures, and distinctions. It was a cruel trick her mind played, because those moments were the ones she wished to rush past, yet somehow they were made more vivid.

In those times, she'd hear her mother's voice too, commands reminding her of thing she already knew.

You can make it stop, Mira.

Though she heard her mother's voice less often now, which made her relieved and sad at the same time.

She pushed a plate of toast toward Francesca, who shook her hair about her face. "I'm a freak," she said.

Mira exhaled through her teeth. She flicked the gas under the tin teakettle (a gorgeous gust of gas and flame) and disappeared into the dining room. From the built-in china cabinet she chose two teacups and matching saucers. Mira thought she could see the brushstrokes in the gold filigree pattern encircling each cup. She balanced them on top of each other with the saucers in between, china tinkling as she walked.

Francesca sobbed again.

The teakettle whistled. Mira ran to lift the pot and the whistle died. As she poured steaming water into the tiny cups, Mira wished the water would move faster. Anything so that she could finish her pretty tableau and make Francesca feel better. Mira dropped a tea bag into each cup and stepped back swiftly, a small cock of her head. She moved the tag of one cup to the opposite side and stood back again, frowning. She disappeared into the pantry and returned with a box of sugar cubes, which she stacked in a glass bowl, and poured milk into a matching glass creamer. She scanned the kitchen and settled on a cutting board, on which she set the cups, sugar, and milk.

Francesca blotted her nose on the inside of her shoulder and reached for her tea.

"Wait," Mira said. "Let me serve you."

Francesca sniffed. "I can serve myself."

"Let me serve you." Mira used a small gold spoon to deposit two squares of sugar and placed the cup in front of Francesca.

"We're not supposed to have caffeine," said Francesca.

"It's mint tea. It's calming."

"Daddy said I should have juice."

Mira placed the gold spoon in front of her. "There is no juice."

Francesca stirred her tea awkwardly. "Do you think I tried to . . . you know . . . do it, and I don't remember?"

"Of course not," Mira said. "That's crazy. Besides, there were no instruments."

"By instruments you mean razor blades," Francesca said.

"You ought to drink your tea," Mira said, marching to the refrigerator and pulling out a bowl of hard-boiled eggs. She cracked one and peeled it, washed it and set it on a shot glass. Mira wrinkled her nose at the smell. She placed the egg next to the tea. "And eat. Please, Francesca." Mira thought of feeding Francesca, after she found their mother. Right before Dr. Amendola was about to insert the feeding tube, Francesca had allowed her sister to pop a bite of yellow custard into her mouth, for show. Only Mira and Connie understood that Francesca could fast for months and still go on, gaunt and spiny, but herself in most ways.

"Salt?"

"Stop trying to make everything pretty and perfect. What

are we going to tell Connie?" Francesca pushed the egg away. It fell off its perch and rolled across the table.

Mira set the egg back on its perch. "You don't have to explain. I will. She'll want to come over right after school."

"What if I don't want Connie knowing?"

"Connie knows about your episodes. This is just another one."

"She'll make such a big deal out of it. She's my blood, and I love her, but she gets so worked up."

"Connie's in awe of your talents. Besides, your talents make her special by association," Mira said, thinking, *even if no one knows but us.*

But Francesca ignored the gap in Mira's logic. Instead, she snorted. "Special."

"Gifted, then," Mira replied.

Francesca raised her hands. "You can't even call this a gift. A gift is something you use for good. The birds, the languages, the fasting. At least those things aren't horrid. And I can hide them. Seem like a normal sixteen-year-old. Holes in my hands are not something I can hide."

Their father's voice came, rushed and insistent, behind his closed office door. Francesca mashed her cheek against her swathed palm and stared through the kitchen doorway. "Who's he talking to? And why can't he talk in front of us?" she murmured, piqued.

"Eat. Before I go," Mira said.

"Don't leave me home alone. Staying home is so depressing." Francesca covered her head with her hands. "I'm a freak. This will become one more reason for Daddy to keep me locked in the house." She dropped her head to the table with a thump and tented her forearms around her ears, shoulders rising with fresh sobs.

"You are not a freak." Mira came beside her and leaned over, pressing her body over her sister's heaving back, as if to stamp her with her calm. "This new gift only makes you more special."

"Please stop using those two words!" Francesca cried, muffled.

Mira turned her head to the side, her sister's hair cool on her cheek, and thought for a moment. "Touched."

Francesca's body stilled underneath her.

From his office, their father's voice grew excited. Mira straightened and Francesca wiped her tears, both faces to the door.

Francesca straightened her neck. "Shh!"

"I didn't say anything," Mira said.

Francesca slipped from her seat and ran lightly across the linoleum tile to her father's office. She pressed her ear to the door.

"Francesca, get away!" Mira whispered harshly.

Francesca's head snapped, eyes bulged. "He said Nick!"

Mira wasn't sure. It made no sense, that her father should

call Mr. Falso about Francesca's problem that seemed so personal. But she was used to agreeing with her when it was easier. Her best skill was being Francesca's ideal audience, of saying exactly what her older sister needed to hear. It was a talent she had cultivated through years of fielding Francesca's insecurities, nearly always related to the veracity of someone's love for her (this boy, their father, Mira herself). Mira knew the truth: Francesca's heart was so big and she loved so hard that it was nearly impossible for anyone to love her back as fiercely. Mira had often pictured Francesca's heart—overgrown, muscular, pulsing—barely contained inside her narrow chest. So, when they talked, Mira never asked, "Are you certain?" Rather, she asked for details that served to make Francesca's vision more real: the color of his cheeks, the set of his shoulders, the smile on his lips. Anything to keep Francesca calm, anything to keep her near. Because nothing frightened Mira more than when Francesca moved away from her into that space inside herself and went dim.

Mira inched toward Francesca. "Then I'm certain it has to be Mr. Falso." She brushed her older sister's hair behind her ear and whispered inside it. "There's no other Nick."

PART 2

Hair

AUGUST 2016

Ben sat upright in the gray soup of morning. He wasn't sure if he'd slept. He felt as though he hadn't. It was already hot, or it had stayed hot, for days on end. The june bugs buzzed early, or they hadn't stopped. The days without Mira were beginning to run into one another, indistinguishable in their emptiness.

Ben jammed his knuckles into his eyes and smelled Eddie's dried blood on his hands. After arriving home from the boat club, he'd collapsed on the couch watching stupid kids' sitcoms, stuff he hadn't watched in ten years. Each show ran exactly twenty-three minutes and followed the same formula. The flash of trendy clothes and the flip way they spoke to one another and their disdain toward adults was the opposite of the weirdly antiquated Cillo world and so was an antidote to his pain. Ben had let it wash over him.

The green numbers of his clock read 5:58 a.m. He couldn't sleep or lie unsleeping for one more minute. Not when there were still six places where he had touched Mira. Ben swung his legs over the bed. He pulled on a pair of nylon basketball shorts from the floor and a clean shirt from his drawer, and lifted Mira's note and the first letter, fanned and damp, from his underwear drawer, where he'd thrown them the night before. He slipped them back inside the cheap string bag and strapped it over his shoulders, then closed his door with a soft click—his parents wouldn't bother to open it; they'd let him sleep in on his day off. He slid out the back of the house and mounted his bike. The air was heavy with low tide. He pedaled against the early morning traffic, past bland faces in cars, shipyard laborers, garbagemen, and people in suits leaving Powder Neck to commute into Boston, and the people who served sweet muddy doughnut-shop coffee to those people. The road trailed along the edge of the Neck until it merged into busier Route 3. Ben rubbed his eyes every few seconds to clear the ocean mist that settled in them. He remained firmly to the right of the white line, rode through glass and Red Bull cans and sticks, knowing that most people who drove cars at this hour were either rushed or half-asleep. He rode and rode, his shirt pillowing out from his back. He left the Neck with the sun climbing behind him and coasted into the parking lot of Johnny's Foodmaster and around back, where he jammed his front tire into the bike rack and popped the rubber-coated chain lock around the cage.

He looked toward the quarry and beyond, toward the jagged, low skyline of Boston. A haze lay over the familiar string of high-rises, their broken reflections on the ocean beneath.

For a second, Ben was transfixed, sensing he was seeing something special and beautiful.

"Are you watching?" he called to the sky, his voice thin.

The expressway hummed back.

He shifted. The nylon bag felt disproportionately heavy for two scraps of paper. He told himself it was just damp, not trying to get his attention. He tore himself away. If he didn't hurry, kids who couldn't stand the heat would start showing up. And he wanted to be alone with Mira's words when he found them.

Ben switched to a jog. If Mira was watching from heaven, he wanted her to see him running, with purpose, to make things right for her memory. His feet had gone numb riding, and it felt good when his sneakers touched the ground. He allowed himself to imagine he was running through these same woods centuries ago, living peacefully on top of five acres of rock, before a steel company machine-blasted a crater into it and the crater filled with rain and bodies and rusted things. He tired of jogging and took long strides over rock and patches of rough vegetation. Brambles scraped his calves and branches blocked his path. He didn't remember the path being so tough to pass. Maybe the flow of kids had slowed since the accident, and nature crowded in. He shook the idea off. It had been little more than a week, and quarry kids weren't the scared type. You don't jump a hundred feet off a ledge or watch other kids doing it if you don't have some balls. Besides, the quarry was a grave before Francesca and Mira fell. Half the time, when they were looking for one body, they found another, sometimes from decades earlier.

Ben came to the clearing and froze. He knew the quarry held majesty for blue-collar kids who hadn't seen the world's wonders beyond the Internet. For Ben, it had a different aura, the sense that the whole place was alive, rank and pulsing, and the quarry kids were trapped in it, like in movies where the characters got shrunk and injected into the vena cava, or the throat, or tumbled along arterial walls.

Today was entirely different. He had never seen the quarry still. No bodies on the ledges, slick from sunblock, playlists belting the same overlapping songs, a scene at once fun and grotesque. This was closer to what Mira must have seen that night. Underneath the morning mist, the water was silver instead of its usual iridescent patina. Ben's mother had warned him that decades earlier, Bismuth Steel Company had pumped hundreds of gallons of poisonous pickle liquor—waste left over from cleaning metals—into the quarry. If his mother knew Ben swam in the quarry she would have grounded him, and, possibly, called a Realtor to put their little cape on the market. She had been looking for such an excuse. The real danger wasn't poison, but the objects underneath: boulders, old refrigerators, cranes left to rot. High dives had become competitions. That the water was contaminated amped the X factor, but it wasn't something kids talked about.

There would be no diving today. Ben was on a mission.

He used his hands to lower himself down to the altar rock. The pack on his back swung as he climbed. The altar rock was the flattest, best ledge, left empty for the Cillos every day of the summer, and the site of a growing memorial: two stuffed bears, wilted carnations in a plastic cone, a ceramic cross, old ballet slippers, a bottle of Panama Jack suntan lotion, and a plush angel with a halo made of gold pipe cleaner.

Ben looked down into the water. The high-speed ride and hike had left him shredded. Vertigo slammed him, a shift deep in his ear that made the painted quarry walls take on funhouse angles. His eyes fuzzed over, and he backed away from the tip, dropping to his knees and easing himself to the ground. Already, the sun was fierce and open, same as that day when Ben had touched Mira for the second time.

He entered the memory like it was a safe room.

Mira hugged her knees and smiled at Ben behind her arm. Ben could hardly look at her, fixing instead on her rounded back, and the bumps of her vertebrae, and the strings on her bikini top with the metal caps on their ends, and wondered if they got hot in the sun, and if they could burn her. The guys were relentless that day, giddy to be at the quarry with the girls, a non-coincidence involving a slip from Eddie. The shoving and besting was at an all-time high, and Francesca was grave and reserved, barely spoke, flat on her towel with her wrist over her eyes. The special care Connie took not to aggravate her exercise-induced anaphylaxis made the hike from the parking lot of Johnny's take twice as long, and Francesca had barely hidden her irritation. Still, Piggy pressed cold beer cans against her thigh to make her jump, and tried to interest her in videos on his phone. Louis Gentry, in love with love, challenged Ben to dives, over and over again, begging attention from everyone, indiscriminate in his need. Piggy was the last to give up on Francesca, eventually butt-scooting on to Connie, who offered half her towel and a set of earbuds. Unlike Francesca, Connie accepted male attention from any source, even one who wore sweatpants puddled over his sneakers on a ninety-degree day. Usually Francesca's moods infected Mira, but Mira had been playful, flirting with Ben.

Louis's chest lifted and fell. He jumped off and spun, heels over head, and tucked his knees, flipping twice before hitting the water with a slap. Mira sat up as Louis entered the water, her hair clinging to the top of her back. Seconds passed. Colors swirled over the spot, silver, blue, purple. Mira made a low whistle.

Francesca rolled onto her stomach and groaned, burying her face in the bend of her elbow. The muscles in her back bunched up. Mira patted her arm absentmindedly, and Connie asked "Everything copacetic, cuz?" for the twentieth time, but they were rote gestures meant to placate, because their eyes were on Louis—Connie gazing over the lip, Mira five steps back—who finally emerged and shook beads of water from his hair, grown long before the August football shave. Louis swam to the side and climbed to the altar as kids on other ledges hooted and clapped. He was tan from roofing, and, Ben noticed with irritation, more ripped every week.

Louis collapsed into the narrow space between Ben and Mira. "That's what they call throwing down the mic, Benny. Now it's your turn."

Mira lifted her hair off her back with one hand and shaded her eyes with the other, fixing Ben with a smile. "What's your answer to that?"

Piggy murmured in Connie's ear, and she giggled.

"Impressive," Ben said, trying for cool. "Too bad it was one somersault away from the *three*-and-a-half reverse somersault with a tuck, the dive perfected by, oh yeah—me."

"Fine, fancy man. I'm calling it." Louis glanced sideways at Mira before cupping his fishy lips and yelling out to anyone who'd listen: "*Three*-and-a-half reverse somersault with a tuck!"

On other cliffs, heads rose. Mira straightened her back. Ben stood slowly and looked out over the water, then at Mira. She raised her eyebrows. Ben was a good diver, and an even better swimmer, with hollows in front of his broad shoulders and bones like pipes. There was nothing to fear here. He had this.

Ben stepped back and forth like a colt.

Francesca aimed a dark look from under her brows.

Connie gazed at Ben too, all wide expectancy, her closed-mouth smile stretching her eyes even farther apart. Piggy aimed his phone at Ben, ready to record. Now everyone was staring at Ben, waiting for him to plunge into the viscous stuff, like he'd done a hundred times before, but the stakes were higher, heightened and dangerous, a violence against him that he felt, an unconscious but palpable wish for him to fail.

Ben took a deep breath and rose on his toes before stepping out. As he lifted his arms over his head, locked his thumbs and pushed off, he heard the shout—

"Francesca!"

—but he was already spinning backward, heels over head, and tucking in, flipping three times. As he hit the water, he felt a vibration to his right, a seismic underwater shove. It spooked Ben, and he fought not to panic, surfacing fast and gasping. A foot away, a sleek black head popped up. Francesca's eyes bulged as she gulped for air.

"That. Was. Awesome!" Francesca said between pants.

"That was stupid!" Ben said, breathing hard. "You could have killed yourself."

Francesca struggled with her breath. "I'm not afraid to die."

"Then you could have killed me. Why would you do that?"

Francesca fixed on him with a look of barely suppressed hate. "I guess I needed to cool off. You guys get me hot and bothered," Francesca said, mocking, rolling onto her back. Her jawbones formed a perfect heart shape as she pushed away from

Ben, arms rising and falling languorously over her head, trying to tame her own breathing so Ben wouldn't see her struggle. Above, Mira and Louis pointed. The sun was behind them and their faces were blotted out, but Ben thought they were laughing because of the way their shoulders shook.

"You could have killed us both," Ben faltered, Francesca's moon face the only thing visible as she glided in her one-piece bathing suit the color of shiny eggplant. He knew he sounded childish; he knew he was angrier than he had a right to be. He treaded water spastically, too awkward for the swimmer he was, and felt his shout linger, pathetic. He wanted to say something cool to patch it over, make it seem like she hadn't completely freaked him out, but he gave up and swam to the wall. Ahead, Francesca climbed toward Mira, who crouched on her hands and knees at the tip. Ben made out the outline of Piggy, and Connie on a lower ledge, having scrambled down for a better view. Connie couldn't have done that. Ben bobbed for a few minutes, stalling, though more than anything he wanted to get out of the water. Eventually he climbed, arriving first on Connie alone, leaning on one hip, her legs swept to the side like a mermaid. Ben paused to get ahold of himself before reaching the altar rock. He felt dangerously close to crying. Connie handed him a towel, purple and plush, from a bathroom, characteristically inappropriate.

Ben blotted his face. Connie bit her lip.

Ben peeked over the towel. "You're mad that I yelled at her.

Your 'blood.' Well let me tell you something: you would have freaked out, too."

Connie shook her head, still smiling.

"What then?" Ben snapped.

"I know you care about Francesca. That's why you were mad she did something so dangerous." Her eyes filmed over with dopiness. "I understand. We all love her."

"No, Connie." He handed back her towel. "I don't love Francesca."

"I know. You love Mira. But we're one. *Sangue.* You said it yourself." Connie traced her calf with her finger. "If you love one of us, you love all of us."

"Connie."

"Mira would say the same thing. You do something to one of us, you do it to all."

"Connie, listen. It's way hot, and it's probably time we headed back."

"I thought, I mean, if you did like me, too, we might . . ."

"Connie!" Ben's tone was louder than he meant it to be, and his cheeks burned. "Please stop." He checked to see if the others had heard, but the silhouettes had moved away. Even Piggy didn't care if Ben was making the moves on Connie, hangdog now around the eyes and mouth. "Hey, don't sit here by yourself. Come up with me. I'll help you."

Connie shook her head.

"You gotta go up to get out, anyway. Come."

Connie squinted past Ben's legs, as if into the sun, though it was the wrong direction. "I'm gonna lie here alone for a while. You go."

"You sure?"

She nodded hard.

"Your way then." Ben turned and climbed, hand over hand, having trouble feeling for the notches that he knew by heart.

Connie called up to him softly. "She wouldn't have drowned. She's protected, by her gifts."

Ben let Connie's words float away over the lake. When he reached the altar rock, he saw Francesca seated like a queen with a towel draped around her neck, Mira at her feet. He hoisted himself up and collapsed on the bare rock. Mira sprang up and ran to him, planting her hands on both sides of his chest, hovering over his face as though she might kiss him. Ben had no way of knowing her expression: she had eclipsed the sun. If he hadn't known better, he would have sworn she was going to mount him.

"Whoa!" He laughed. Instantly, everything was better. Everything was amazing. This was Mira's gift, he wanted to yell to Connie, dumb, dramatic Connie.

"That dive was sick!" Mira gasped, damp hair spilling onto his chest, light shining through a hundred shades of butter gold, the smell of tropical flowers and coconut. Instinctively, he reached up and touched it; it was sunlight on his fingers.

Louis crawled over, a wicked smile across his face. He leaned and whispered in Ben's ear. "I thought, Benny. I just thought, if you did like me, too, we might . . . you and I might, you know, right here on the ledge . . ." His imitation of Connie was loud enough for Mira to overhear, but it hadn't mattered; nothing mattered. Ben had touched sunlight. All bets were off: Mira would be his.

Ben looked up at the sun. The morning was passing fast. He wasn't here to remember: the memories would only drive him mad. Mira had given him one last job to do. He scanned the ledge. Pockets of trash—cans, Johnny's Foodmaster bags, condoms—were stuffed into crevices. A knot of panic poked the back of his throat. Where would someone leave a note where no one would find it unless they were looking? Where?

Ben took a deep breath and stuck his head back over the side of the ledge where Connie had sat. Behind a weeks-old sapling flashed white. Mira's note, weighted with a rock. The knot in Ben's chest loosened. Ben scrambled down to the shallow ledge and snatched it up. The ledge was skinny and seemed less stable than it was a year ago, when it had held Connie and him, or maybe he was becoming a wimp. He jammed the note in his pocket and pulled himself onto the altar, crab-walking backward, spraying tiny stones.

Ben unfolded the note. When he saw the first word, he let out an anguished groan.

*Francesca wakes every morning with hair soaked
from tears. She cries all night over him and the things
he does to her. She makes excuses, says he can't help himself.
Only I know better.*

Ben swore and threw the note to the ground. Why was Mira wasting her notes to him on her sister's love life? Everyone knew Francesca Cillo had a crush on Mr. Falso. It made sense, the guys rationalized, for her to fall for a dude who was unreachable when she wasn't allowed to date anybody anyway. He was lean, had shoulders that looked good in shirts, and actual dimples. His skin stayed dark in January when everyone else looked like dishwater. Rumor was he spray-tanned. His eyebrows dipped in the middle, making him look angry when he wasn't smiling, which wasn't often. Mr. Falso ("Call me Nick!") didn't shake hands: he hugged. It didn't matter if it was a girl or a guy, he grabbed your shoulders and looked you in the eyes.

Then: "How are you doing?"

Followed by the Meaningful Pause.

Worst thing was, Ben wanted to dismiss Mr. Falso's touchy-feeliness as hokey, but he liked it. Many times Ben had gone to Mr. Falso to talk about games that went south and grade troubles, and once, the fights between his mom and dad. You'd text Mr. Falso, and he'd be in his office waiting for you to arrive.

He'd let you talk, then tell his own thinly related stories, always with a reference to the time he lost the big game, or the girl, or some tale that included a lesson learned. You knew his story didn't match up: the shame of missing a three-pointer two decades ago couldn't sting the same as attempting a behind-the-back fake and having the ball fall out of your pocket last spring. Not the same sting at all. But no one cared. Mr. Falso knew sports, liked girls, and seemed to have a life outside the church. He was never exhausted by the problems of teenagers in his congregation; he got energy from them. More importantly, he fixed things. When Kyle didn't pass the state trooper exam, Mr. Falso was the one who suggested EMT training, then hooked Kyle up with the right people. Mr. Falso was the one who sat with Eddie in the days after Connie died, dispensing lots of advice, mostly centered around helping his mother re-enter reality. Technically, his job wasn't far off from a camp counselor, herding kids onto yellow buses for spiritual retreats, to build houses in the deep South, and to Bible camp in the summer. Also technically, his job was to "counsel the youngest parishioners, particularly about spiritual matters." Since his arrival last fall, Mr. Falso had found fans among the mothers and fathers, too, and as a single young guy, was invited for lasagna dinners and beers with the dads at Black Rock Tavern five nights out of seven.

Mira *had* to be talking about Mr. Falso in her note. Right?

Whatever. He cared so little about Francesca. A tear welled

in the corner of his eye, and he brushed it away roughly. There
was a special cruelty that Mira would feed his lust for her voice
with words about Francesca. The notes were like a drug:
he needed the next one, and the next one. And Ben knew
where the next one was, because after he had touched Mira's
hair on the ledge, it was officially on.

He needed to get to Eddie's house. Soon. He'd text him
later, ask him to shoot hoops like old times. Make an excuse
to go to the bathroom like he had that day last summer, and
find the next note, a note that had to say something more about
Mira. In a cramped hallway, under the Villelas' spoon rack,
half-blind from the sun. Mira had let him know.

But today the sun felt so good.

Ben turned his ear to the woods. He thought he heard
voices. He listened hard, but there was only the muted rush
of the highway. Sure he was imagining things, Ben yawned
and leaned back, feeling the rising sun on his face. He placed
the notes on his chest and folded his hands over them: two
notes now, and he was no closer to knowing anything about
why Mira was gone.

More than once, Ben had suspected the quarry had a hyp-
notic effect. He'd seen it in Mira's eyes as they rolled upward,
the way her foot slid down the towel to meet the other. One
after the other, the girls, their bodies cooled from swimming,
would still. Ben felt heavy. He no longer minded that sharp
points dug into his back, didn't bother to flick away the june

bug that landed among the hairs on his wrist. Ben told himself that it was the sun, settling over him like a blanket, that made him fall asleep at the quarry. Nothing else.

Ben's knee jerked. He settled back again, remembering again the way he had touched Mira for the second time in this exact spot where she had also fallen or maybe leaped but definitely died. He smelled a trace of sulfur, and thought he should stay awake, but the fall from consciousness was delicious. His last thought before sleep was of violet gas rising from the pickle water and himself, flat on the ledge, a stick man, the lines of his body drawn in pencil, clear and colorless, waiting for the gas to meet him. He let himself be heavy as the gas swirled around his head, trunk, and legs, growing a vibrant shade of eggplant as the color filled him.

Scoffs and low whistles mingled with footsteps breaking branches.

"I heard the EMTs had to pry them apart. Long wet hair and purple lips. Like Korean water ghosts," said Louis.

"Ever think of asking me? The one guy who was actually there?" said Kyle.

Voices traveled in the quarry in funny ways. If kids were splashing below, you could have trouble hearing the person next to you, but a conversation three ledges above would sound

crystal clear. It was the main reason Piggy got away with saying he did a chick on one of the ledges, because you knew if
he hit the acoustics right, the whole event could have been
soundless, even if that particular girl had a reputation for being
a screamer.

Ben's eyelids had sunburned into tacky shells. The collar
of his T-shirt dug into his neck. He checked his watch: 12:45
p.m. He'd been asleep for five and a half hours. The voices
threaded through the thin saplings and grew louder as they
made their way up the hill toward Ben.

"Not for nothing, but the quarry's not normal during the
daytime. The way it screws with time. Ghosts from dead bodies
down there. It's got, what do they call it? Bad energy. You ask
me, I think the spirits didn't want those girls messing with their
burial ground, and maybe made sure they knew it," said Piggy.

"Ghosts? You're saying the Ghosts of Quarry Divers Past
pushed them off the ledge?" said Louis.

"I'm saying something got to them, dude," said Piggy.

"It was a waste of hotness, that's what it was," Louis said.

"You should have made your moves faster. Mira was ready,
man," Piggy huffed. "If I had whatever it was she saw in your
sorry mug, I would've been in months ago."

On the ledge, Ben's bowels clenched.

"Instead of having to make moves on the cousin?" said
Louis. A chorus of "hey!"s rose up. It was a fine line, talking

about the Cillo girls and Connie, even when Eddie wasn't around.

"I'm just saying. Those girls were like one big lost opportunity," said Piggy.

"You chuckleheads ever consider Villela might have beat us there? Seriously, shut the f—" Kyle froze, expecting to see Eddie.

Ben rolled up onto his elbow and put his finger to his lips.

Kyle nodded. His widow's peak fell into wings worn long to cover his bad ear, and his mouth belonged to a little boy, with screwed-up, rosebud lips. Kyle was overgrown for his grade, and preferred to hang with guys from his hood, even if they were two years younger. Girls thought Kyle was cute, with his shambling walk, like he was wearing invisible ski boots.

Kyle spun around and disappeared back into the brush, waving his arms, yelling. "No room up here. Let's go jump off the other side!"

"If somebody's squatting, they got no right!" Piggy called.

"That ledge is sacred ground. Tell them to hit the road!" Louis yelled.

Ben shoved Mira's notes into the waistband of his shorts as he crawled close to the edge, turning toward the water and giving them his long back. The boys shoved past Kyle and charged into the clearing. Piggy spotted Ben first and planted his hands on his thick hips.

"Lattanzi?"

The only sound was june bugs whirring to a fever pitch.

Ben cringed, stinging his sunburn. He spoke out over the water. "I want to be alone."

Kyle yelled from his place behind. "The dude's grieving over Mira. Let the man have some peace."

Louis approached. "What's he doing here by himself?"

"What does it look like he's doing here? He's praying," called Kyle.

Piggy snickered. "He ain't praying."

Ben felt Piggy's cool shadow on his neck before he swiped the notes from his waistband. Ben spun around wildly.

Piggy waved the notes out of his reach. "What are these? You writing journal entries up here? Communing with nature?"

Ben tried to swipe them back, but Piggy was quick. He waggled them above his head. "Love notes to a dead girl, maybe?"

Ben felt his ears fill with blood. Everything around Piggy turned shimmery and fragmented. Ben shoved Piggy backward.

"Dude, relax! Not for nothin', but you and Mira Cillo were over way before this all went down," Piggy said.

Ben pounced on Piggy, taking him to the ground and slamming his skull against the rock, and then sat on his chest. Piggy rolled and Ben fell off, groped his way back on and shook his head like a dog. His fists sank into Piggy's jowls, the meat of his chest, and the softness of his belly, and every punch was better and better, like Piggy's body welcomed Ben's fists, begged to be pummeled and shaped. Piggy had at least twenty pounds on Ben, but he covered his face with his hands. Ben smelled imaginary Old Spice deodorant and stale breath, cigars and Scotch; saw hairs in his opponent's nose and ears not there as he drove his head back with jabs to his jaw, which had grown from the Pignataro chin that folded up on itself into something sculpted. Piggy raised a knee to Ben's balls, and Ben rolled off, nearing the edge of the ledge.

"Christ, don't fall!" yelled Louis.

Ben rolled away from the edge and snapped to his feet, charging at a half-risen Piggy and knocking him to the ground a second time. He loomed and swayed over him, then fell to one knee.

"Lattanzi, that's it!" said Kyle.

"You're even!" said Louis.

Ben cupped the back of Piggy's head as though he might kiss him. The head in Ben's hand didn't wear a shaved fade, but was streaked with silver and slick with drugstore hair oil. It was Mr. Cillo he wanted to kill for keeping him and Mira apart. Because Ben could have made things right with her; he was sure he could have.

The old man was to blame for all of it.

Ben head-butted Piggy with his forehead. Piggy's head

snapped back and hit the ground. Ben staggered away, pressing his wrist into his mouth. He dropped to his knees and fell forward to his hands. Vomited.

Kyle dragged the towel from around his neck and handed it to Ben. "Dude, you cracked him with your skull. A freaking Glasgow kiss. Who *does* that?"

Ben's ears rang, and the nausea caused by Piggy's one good hit got worse in waves. The quarry grew dark. Ben blinked, thinking he was losing consciousness, but it was only a cloud passing over the sun. He felt the absence in his waistband, a cold settling at the small of his back. He scanned the ground. The notes had settled, miraculously, ink-side down. They could have been receipts or Kleenex or trash. He fell to his side and lay still.

The rest of the guys kneeled around Piggy, whose eyes were slits.

"Is he alive?" called Kyle.

Louis leaned into his ear. "Can you speak, Piggy?"

Piggy muttered, "Ucker." His reptilian eyes fluttered and rolled back, white gel flashing.

Kyle rubbed his hands together and bent on one knee to flick up Piggy's eyelid, listening to him breathe. He looked at Ben. "You gave him a nice concussion, Lattanzi. I never would've guessed you had it in you."

Louis held his head. "He's gotta weigh 190 pounds! Who's gonna carry him out of here?"

"We'll take turns carrying him," said Kyle. "One at the head, one at the feet."

"What happens when we get him home?" said Louis. "I don't know about you, but I don't want to be the one to face Mr. Pignataro."

"Piggy's playing you with that mob talk. Besides, the only person who's ever home at that house is Nana P., and she'll be cooking in the basement," said Kyle.

"I got it. We say he got jumped by kids from Germantown," Louis said. "I got a cousin who has a score to settle. I can get some names."

Kyle cuffed his shoulder. "Don't be a moron. We can't get away with pinning this on someone else. Besides, he's the one who'll have to worry when his dad finds out who clocked him." Kyle smiled over at Ben, who closed his eyes and held his groin.

Louis gave Kyle a cold stare. "Always sticking up for Lattanzi, no matter how much of a nutter he acts like." Rubbing his shoulder, he scraped up the notes and dumped them at Ben's nose. "Whatever these are, I hope they're worth the way you're gonna feel when you wake up tomorrow."

"What the hell happened here?" Eddie stood in the clearing, staring at Piggy on the ground.

Kyle sprang up. "Nothing, man. Lattanzi decided to use some of those new big muscles on Piggy 'cause he was getting out of line about his mother. The usual Piggy trash talk. Ben got in a lucky punch and Piggy's milking it. Right, Piggy?" Kyle kicked Piggy in the side and he groaned.

"Mother-ucker," Piggy moaned.

Eddie grunted and moved past Piggy like he no longer saw him. From the ground, Ben watched Eddie with his big bandaged hand, eyes clouded, dragging his feet. The idea of stopping by the Villela manse to shoot hoops suddenly seemed whack.

Still, Ben tried. He spit blood and brushed his knuckles across his lips. "Ed. You wanna get out of here and shoot some hoops at your place?"

Eddie looked at Ben like he didn't recognize him. He dropped his towel and rifled through his gym bag until he found a plastic bag, which he tented over his hand and secured with duct tape. Ben doubted it would keep the bandages dry, but no one else said anything, nor did Kyle offer any professional medical advice. Eddie moved past the boys like they were ghosts, stood at the top of the ledge of the altar rock and raised his hands above his head as if in salute. Then, he was gone.

SEPTEMBER 2015

Francesca let out a pained sigh.

Mira looked toward her sister's bed. There was no hint of pale, no lighter darkness, nothing that suggested a form. She raised her hand in front of her face, expecting to see a shimmer of movement, but blackness saturated the room, and Mira had lost the most familiar parts of her body to it. She scrambled upright and swatted at the lamp, which fell to the floor with a soft filament *pop*.

Mira waited for Francesca to startle. Nothing but darkness.

"Francesca?" Mira's voice was small. "What's wrong?"

Nothing.

Mira threw off her covers and righted herself. "You've been groaning. Are you sick?"

She was used to Francesca's unresponsiveness. Though eighteen months younger, Mira often felt like the older sister. She slipped off her mattress and felt for the cord, pulling the blinds up in a shriek. It was later than she'd thought: the sky was already the color of a raincloud. A flutter as Francesca's birds rose and dipped low, landing on the branch outside the window again, one higher than the other. Not just any birds, but the same two that had lived outside their window since Mira was a little girl, that followed Francesca everywhere. They were a complicated mix of green and purple, with white breasts and garlands of deeper purple around their necks, so ubiquitous and with Francesca since such a young age that no one spoke of them anymore. Except for Connie, who still nearly squealed every time she saw them, and probably wished there were three, because then they could say they were *their* birds, one for each girl, instead of simply "Francesca's birds" (kinder, to ignore the "two": Mira's idea).

One bird shrugged and cocked its head, puffing snowy under-feathers at Mira.

"Shoo!" Mira whispered. The birds stomped their insect legs, uncomfortable.

Mira navigated to Francesca's bedside, leaning in close. Her sister's face was slick with tears and waxy, as though her blood had drained away. Mira touched her hair. It was soaked, by sweat or tears. Mira thought she might have a fever. Francesca spiked fevers constantly, ran hotter than her body's limits. Mira skidded in socked feet to the door, easing it open and listening for her father, considering if she should wake him. Snores crescendoed into a choke.

Francesca moaned again, arching her back, pointing her chest to the ceiling.

Mira returned and stood over her sister. Her thoughts went to their mother, in her bed on a different morning ten years ago, after an après-dinner Ambien/vodka cocktail cured her insomnia forever.

Mira grabbed Francesca's shoulders and shook them roughly. Francesca's chest rose and fell. Mira hovered her ear over Francesca's mouth, and heard her slow, wet breath. Satisfied, she hissed, "Francesca, stop this, now!"

A room away, their father mumbled in his sleep.

Francesca's eyes flew open. Her black pupils were vast. Mira jumped.

"You scared me! " Mira nearly shouted.

"I'm in so much pain," Francesca squeaked, her lids lowering.

"Oh no. Your hands again?" Mira asked, more softly.

Francesca yanked the sheet tight under her chin. "It's not my hands."

"I'm getting Daddy," Mira said, moving away.

Francesca released the wad of sheet and clamped onto Mira's arm. "Don't!"

Mira jerked her arm. Francesca's power crouched inside her and popped out at unexpected moments. She held on with that strength that always blindsided Mira.

"Let go," Mira said, twisting. "You need help."

"The pain is in my heart," Francesca said.

Mira pried Francesca's nails from her arm. "You could have a virus. Food poisoning. We don't know." Mira's random diagnoses hid what she really feared: that this was one more out-of-control thing happening to Francesca's body.

"It's not like that. My heart *aches*. It feels like it's been stabbed, through my side; it's the worst pain I've ever felt. It's hopeless." Francesca's voice was ragged.

Mira perched on the edge of the mattress and pushed hair from her sister's face in wet clumps. Her pillow sagged under the weight of tears. "What's hopeless?"

"Loving him."

An extra-loud snore, followed by silence. Mira shot a wary look toward the door before whispering the question whose answer she already knew. "Who?"

Francesca closed her eyes and rolled over onto her side, hair stuck like kelp to her cheek. "Mr. Falso."

"I know, love," Mira said, pulling her hands to her lap, relief mingled with a new fear. Things with Mr. Falso had been building. Mira imagined a growing tower of white china plates, wobbling with each plate added. "I know."

Francesca rose slowly. "I can't go on like this. I need to tell him how I feel. Once I show him the holes"—she held up her bandaged hands—"he'll see what makes me special. It will change everything."

Mira twisted her ring. "It will. But in the way you want it to?"

Francesca threw a sharp look over her shoulder. She peeled off her nightshirt and snatched a dress from over the back of a chair. Weeks earlier, Francesca had excavated an old white lace dress from their mother's closet. Mira assumed the dress was an attempt to look older; mostly, Francesca looked out of time. Filmy, dingy, and overlaid with appliqué daisies, its front draped to reveal twin hollows nested inside a sharp collarbone. It hung away from her narrow middle and ended at mid-calf, where the hem bunched in spots. The effect was of an ill-fitting shroud.

"You can't go to him. It's too early in the morning. He won't even be awake."

"So I'll wake him." Francesca stomped into the bathroom and returned with her paddle brush. She flicked the lamp switch over and over again, frowning. "I'll be the first thing he sees."

Mira shivered at the raking sound as Francesca brushed her hair. "You'll have to ride your bike. It'll be awkward in that dress."

"Suffering puts me closer to God." She drew hair behind both ears. "Let him see me naked and vulnerable."

Naked? Connie would have yelled, Mira knew. But Mira was accustomed to Francesca's extreme word choices. Instead, she asked simply, "What about Daddy?"

"Tell him I'm sleeping late. I'll slip back in through the kitchen slider."

Francesca checked her bandages and slid a pair of old black leather gloves over them before facing Mira. The dusky glow of morning fell on and around her.

Mira touched her throat. "Oh."

It wasn't beauty, though there was that. Barefaced and shoeless, with her damp hair drawn severely behind her ears and her body hidden in milky folds, Francesca had transformed herself into someone timeless. There was nothing to pin her to the year, or her actual age, to the Cillo family, or to any of the things that defined her. She had erased herself and become a canvas on which Mr. Falso could project anything.

"How do I look?" Francesca asked.

Mira swallowed. "Not like yourself."

Francesca clasped her hands to her chest. "That's exactly right! You see? It's absolutely perfect! Because I'm not myself anymore! I'm a vehicle chosen by God to do his work on Earth!" Francesca sprang toward Mira and squeezed her.

"Your pain," Mira said softly.

"You know I can absorb my suffering. And soon, it will end."

Mira buried her nose in her damp hair, breathing deep. "Francesca."

Francesca held her away, studying her face. Mira didn't like the feel of her dead mother's old hard gloves tightening on her bare arms.

"What is it?" Francesca asked.

Mira honeyed her voice. "I'm sure it won't be the case, but what if telling Mr. Falso about your gift has the *opposite* effect?"

Francesca's eyes went hot. "I should have known." She dropped Mira's arms and strode to the mirror, smoothing her hair one last time, her sharp movements carving the air. She slid into worn ballet flats, working her jaw, her most awful angry habit, that suck-click noise that signaled a shutdown was imminent. *I could wake up Daddy,* Mira thought, *make a loud noise right now that so that he will stop her as she leaves.* There was still hope.

Francesca tugged at the dead woman's gloves. "If you can find it in your heart of hearts, wish me luck. You're not the only one who can make a boy love her."

Mr. Falso's not a boy, Mira thought, staring at the floor. Francesca could be so cruel. So often Francesca reminded her that blood was thick and binding, that they were part of each other, that this shared blood transcended anything. But Francesca's blood was shifting, turbulent. It wasn't like Mira's. It left Francesca in a constant state of discontent. Perhaps this idea was a good thing: if Mr. Falso believed she had a higher purpose, it would calm her. Mira believed her, though it no longer seemed to make a difference. And Connie believed. If only they two were enough.

Francesca disappeared down the stairs. Mira felt her heart in her mouth, as hard and full as if there had been a death. They never left without saying "I love you." Snores trailed in through the door. Mira ran to the window and scraped her fingers forcing the grimy screen locks. It squealed open. She leaned out as Ben Lattanzi walked out his own front door in pajama bottoms, dragging his ancient shaggy terrier on a leash. Ben sensed Mira and turned his face. From ten feet above, she watched Ben's spine straighten as his eyes met hers. Mira felt the familiar rush of warmth and sadness and desire to touch away the auric pain that burned bright around him.

The dog grew rigid and barked. A *whiz* of bike tires on asphalt: Francesca, tearing from their garage out into the street, her bare calves circling below the bunched silk hem. The dog lunged at her.

"Francesca!" Mira yelled, as her sister sped past Ben and the dog. Mira winced, knowing their father may have heard her call and hell could break loose. She stared at her sister's misshapen figure for as long as she was in sight. It wasn't unusual for the Cillo girls to ride bikes like they were twelve, not when they weren't allowed in hardly anybody's car, and neither had applied for their junior license. Anyone who saw Francesca would think she'd lost it: a bag lady tearing along the highway down Powder Neck before seven a.m. Mira wondered, had she lost it?

Ben gave a half wave up to Mira, straining against the dog pulling toward Francesca's leftover dust.

"Hey!" he called, unsure.

More importantly, would Mr. Falso think she'd lost it? And if he did, would he tell their father? Mira was fairly sure Daddy never noticed when Francesca went dim; she hid her withdrawals, citing girl problems, or lack of sleep. Mira helped, backing up the same excuses, even claiming the same ones sometimes, to make them seem more likely. What would happen if there was some adult consensus that Francesca needed help?

Above, the crayon-colored birds held Mira with their eyes, wobbling on their branches. They crouched one by one, then rose together on silent wingbeats, toward the ocean and Francesca, up and out of sight.

The dog yanked Ben's arm. He planted his legs.

"Girls?" her father called crustily from inside.

Mira dragged the window shut.

Francesca rounded the tip of Powder Neck, riding close to the ocean. She tried to ignore the cooler air gripping her chest and her runny nose. She rode slowly past identical bungalows until she spotted the cherry Miata parked in front of a white house with a porch layered in jalousie windows like a glass cake. The garage door mawed open. Anxious thoughts skidded through Francesca's mind: Had someone broken in? It was so early. She slid from her bicycle and walked it, taking baby steps alongside. Mr. Falso's fancy European racing bike lay on its side with its parts strewn around on the garage floor. Her heart pounded: he was already awake. More toys lay about, in the garage and the driveway, and on the lawn. They included a second bike, for off-roading, which he did in the nearby conservation area; a moped, for cruising Powder Neck Beach at night; a small speedboat for fishing off the boat club dock; rappelling hooks and harnesses, for climbing in the quarry; and an eerie man-sized scuba suit hanging from a hook, for dives into the harbor. Francesca knew precisely how Mr. Falso used each of these things from scraps of overheard conversations.

She slipped her hand through the armpit of her mother's

dress and felt her breast. The muscle was pleasingly thin over her sternum. Saints starved themselves so that others could see their heart beating for love of Jesus underneath their skin: this she knew.

"Francesca?"

Mr. Falso's voice came from the dark back half of the garage. He emerged in a thin T-shirt and jeans stained with grease. Francesca stared at his arms—how hadn't she known about the tattoos?—and shivered.

"You rode out here on your bike? It's barely seven in the morning!" His words were stern, but his face exploded with happy surprise, the signature Mr. Falso look: eyebrows spiked upward, white teeth bared.

Francesca snapped to attention. "I don't drive."

"You could have asked your dad to drive you out here. Or I could have met you somewhere! You didn't have to come out all this way . . ." He wiped his hands on a cloth and stepped toward her, his smile tightening. "What did you come out all this way about, anyway?"

Francesca held her elbows. Rehearsing them at night, the words seemed easy and right. Now in the harsh light of morning, they seemed impossible.

So she lied. "I want to talk to you about a friend."

Mr. Falso pocketed his thumbs. "Then this isn't a spiritual matter?"

Francesca cleared her throat. "It is, in a way. My friend's spirit. I care about her deeply, you see. And I'm afraid she's in trouble."

"I see. Remember, talking to me isn't like confessing to Father Ernesto. If someone in your family is in trouble, I'm obliged to tell an adult."

"Whatever," Francesca said quickly, then scolded herself: *stupid Cesca!* Her flip "whatever" made her sound like a dumb teenager. She felt a tide rolling back, sand moving back under her feet, everything in reverse. His face assumed its professional mask. She stumbled for lost ground.

"What I mean is, I don't care, because you're the right person to tell. Father Ernesto is—God forgive me for saying this—a little out of touch when it comes to stuff of *young people*"—*Young people, NOT teenagers. I am a young person,* Francesca thought hard, willing him, telepathically, to understand. She cleared her throat—"stuff *young people* have to deal with. I would never be comfortable telling Father Ernesto that a friend is acting . . . inappropriate. With boys."

Mr. Falso's mask dissolved, she thought. It had softened around the eyes and mouth, she was sure.

"I'm touched that you came to me," he said.

Francesca's blood pounded hot in her ears. It was going to be okay. And her story about Connie wasn't untrue; her behavior around boys lately was appalling. The kind of person Francesca wanted Mr. Falso to think she was—the kind of person she was-was—would care about Connie's self-respect. She couldn't ignore the problem. Her concern was based in love.

"She's been letting boys touch her for the attention. And they've been using her, terribly," she whispered.

She saw a tiny flicker, a blaze in his eyes. It was a protective fire, anger born of gallantry. She might have been talking about someone else, but he seemed to be thinking of her. And he wanted to protect her.

"Go on." He matched her whisper.

"Not just any boys: awful boys. Of course, all boys our age are awful. It's always been this way for us."

He leaned forward. "Us?"

"We attract boys we want nothing to do with. It's like we give off some vibe. But the ones we want don't seem to see us." Francesca bit her lip as she watched the muscles in his arms shift under his shirt. She trained her eyes on his faith charm. "Of course, we're talking about my friend. Not my sister and me."

"Of course. But, Francesca . . ."

"Yes?"

"There's only so much you can do. You can give advice to a friend who's making a fool of herself, but you likely won't be able to change her ways, at least not right away."

"But I've got to!"

"Oh?"

"You see, I've been inspired to help her by the life of Saint Gemma Galgani."

Mr. Falso coughed. "A saint?"

"You know, the story of Saint Gemma and the prostitute."

"Why don't you remind me?"

"When Saint Gemma was ill, as she was a lot during her excruciatingly painful life, a prostitute offered to take care of her for extra money. Saint Gemma's aunt tried to turn the prostitute away, but Gemma wouldn't allow it. She knew it was her soul mission to convert sinners to God."

"I see."

"Chastity is the custodian of authentic love. Isn't that right, Mr. Falso?"

"That's a very mature thing, to look to the saints' lives. Hard to live up to, though."

"But anything worth doing is. Wouldn't you say, Mr. Falso? Some people might say your chosen path is tough. Listening to young people's problems every day. You could have probably been anything you wanted after college. A businessman. A doctor. A lawyer. But you chose to work for the church. I believe many of us are called to higher purposes. But not everyone listens. Don't you think, Mr. Falso?"

"Call me Nick."

"Nick." She said it softly, and it sounded sweet.

"You know, Francesca, you're an unusual girl. Mature. It's

admirable that you want to help put your friend on a better path. I'm glad to speak with her, too, if you wish."

"That won't be necessary," she rushed. "Connie will be fine." Francesca slapped her cheek in horror.

His eyebrows shot up again. "Whoa. No need for names."

"I mean, I can be the one to stop Connie—to stop my friend—from looking to boys for . . . fulfillment." *Too much. Too much, Francesca. Scale back.*

Mr. Falso looked behind himself and into the garage. "Perhaps we could step inside and say a prayer for Concetta." He stifled a yawn and rubbed his arms. "And maybe I'll have some more coffee. Have you had breakfast yet?" For the first time, she noticed his hair was adorably ruffled, as though he'd gotten out of bed and gone immediately to work in his garage. Industrious.

Francesca felt herself smile. "That would be lovely."

Suddenly Francesca felt the wet warmth in her palms. *Not yet,* she told herself. She tried pressing her middle fingers upon the holes, but the gloves were stiff with age, and her fingers wouldn't bend to reach. She forced her hands into claws, but it was futile.

Mr. Falso glanced at her fists. "Oh, hang on. You're upset."

Francesca stared at her hands like they were unfamiliar, letting them fall to her sides.

"Of course you are. This is your cousin we're talking about."

"Mio sangue," Francesca whispered.

"Your blood. Come inside." Mr. Falso vanished into the back of the garage as the garage door rattled down behind her. She blinked to adjust her eyes as a hand snaked around her arm. "This way," he said gently, leading her up a set of rickety stairs into his kitchen. "Gloves in September, huh? You must run cold. Take them for you?"

Francesca blinked. The kitchen was painted neutral beige. The appliances were stainless steel and entirely unused. Above a generic granite countertop were cheap blond cabinets with brushed steel hardware. To her, it looked modern and sparkling, though she knew it was what Connie's dad would call a contractor's special. A scratched George Foreman Grill in the center of the counter appeared to be the only thing used in the whole kitchen. She imagined how much Mr. Falso would appreciate her cooking homemade gravy at the stove.

"Of course you can leave them on, if you're cold," he said.

"Oh! Yes, I'm cold. I mean I'm warm. Here, Mr. Falso." She turned her back to him before gently tugging off each glove. The bandages were intact and stuck where she bled. She turned and handed the gloves to him, leaving her hand dangling in the air. This would be a perfect time for him to ask her about the bandages. It would be a relief to stop talking about Connie; already, guilt about throwing her beloved cousin under the bus crept in at the edges, tainting their special time together.

He took the gloves and pretended to snatch her nose

between two fingers. "Oh, come on now! How many times am I gonna say it? Nick to you!"

"Nick," Francesca said, another soft cluck. She could see too much of his chest through his shirt; not really, not see-through-like, but the rise of his pecs and where his biceps strained the sleeve, and she was embarrassed. She dropped her eyes. He grabbed a plaid button-down shirt from a hanger in the back closet with a cold clink, and slipped it over his shoulders, smiling mildly. She rubbed at the sharp goose bumps that ran up her slender forearms and watched as his eyes grazed her jaw, which tipped up slightly, knowing it was her best feature, and then his eyes pulled away and searched the counter for something, though it was bare.

"Francesca?" he said, still looking away.

"Yes?"

"Does your father know you're here?"

Francesca winced. Her father was Bismuth royalty, and tough: not a guy you messed with. Mr. Lattanzi next door, that weaselly, whistle-blowing CPA, had learned as much. Until now, Francesca had only benefited from her father's chilling effect, keeping away the creeps. Now, it was backfiring on her.

She had no choice but to lie. "Yes."

His shoulders loosened, and he turned to face her. "Good. Can I make you some eggs?"

Eating in front of Mr. Falso seemed vulgar, though she

couldn't place why. But saying no felt rude. "Water for now, please."

He opened a cabinet stacked with canisters of vanilla protein powder and bottles of ready-to-drink Muscle Milk, also vanilla. It took him two tries to find the cabinet with the glasses. He rinsed the glass of dust, dragged a stool out for Francesca, and sat opposite, leaning forward. Francesca smelled the bike chain grease on his jeans, and that he'd popped a mint when she wasn't looking.

Francesca sipped her water with closed eyes, trying to remember her lines as she'd rehearsed them.

I have something of the utmost importance to show you.

Because I respect your opinion, I wish for you to examine . . .

There are few people in this world I trust and admire more than you. Because of that . . .

But the words sounded silly and formal. She set her glass on the table with a dull thud and flexed her fists.

Mr. Falso tempered his smile. "Now, is this the only thing you came to talk to me about?" he said gently.

Francesca's words came in a torrent. "I'm so scared I don't understand why this new thing is happening to me Daddy says it means I'm special but that I shouldn't tell anyone because hardly anyone believes in this stuff anymore so one half of the world will think I'm a crazy attention-seeker—"

"Hold on!"

Francesca stood then, wild-eyed, the stool scraping behind.

"And the other half of the world will stick me up on a pedestal and never leave me alone and treat me like I'm some kind of sideshow act—"

Mr. Falso grabbed Francesca's arms, his stained fingertips meeting around them. "You're so thin," he whispered.

She kept babbling.

"But I'm not freaky. I'm special. I know this. I've known it for a long time. I'm scared. I'm so scared." Her eyes cut up and to the side toward an unseen voice.

He released his grip on her arms, afraid she might bruise, floated his hands to her shoulders, and eased her to the stool.

Her back jumped.

"There now," he said, taking her hands into his own. "Breathe. Go slow, and start at the beginning."

Joan was sixteen when she led France out of English rule and was martyred. Agatha, fifteen, rejected the advances of a lower-born and had her breasts sliced off. Maria Goretti got stabbed to death for the same. Lucy lost her eyes. How dare she be so afraid when her sisters had gone before her and showed bravery in the face of true danger? This was nothing. *Have courage, Francesca!* She said this to herself, but maybe it was someone else who said it. She couldn't be sure.

"Francesca?"

Francesca shuddered and gazed up through her lashes. "This isn't about Connie."

"I got that. Then what is it about?"

She held Mr. Falso's eyes as she spread open her palms slowly, white flowers blooming with blood. He looked down and gasped. Francesca's wounds had bled through her bandages.

"Did you do this to yourself?"

Francesca shook her head and smiled gloriously. "It just came."

He dropped his head again and stared. Francesca studied the swirls in his hair, admired their pattern and gloss. A minute passed. It was wonderful, to be held like this. It felt right. She breathed in soap and scalp and something woodsy. He closed her fists and disappeared, and her heart skipped faster until he returned with cotton, a brown medicinal bottle, a clean rag and fresh bandages, setting them on the table and turning to wash his hands in the sink. The only sound was the tight whine of the still-new faucet and his hands as they rubbed together vigorously, like a doctor, Francesca thought. He dried them with a paper towel and sat in his chair, straight-backed, his thighs flexed aggressively.

He drew her right hand to his chest. "May I?"

Francesca felt a liquid rush. She knew it was love. Not the kind that Connie declared for boy bands. Or the hidden kind that Mira felt for the damaged boy next door. This was real love, the kind grownups felt for one another. Francesca knew the difference now, and at the same time, a desperate pang struck her belly, and she sensed that this love she felt was a one-shot deal.

Francesca whispered yes and tried to still herself. Mr. Falso squared his shoulders before he pinched the edge of the bandage, peeling slowly. Francesca could barely sit still.

He froze. "Am I hurting you?"

The effort to remain still drove her to tears. Smiling, doll-eyed, she shook her head.

He blew pufferfish lips. "Good. Okay, here I go." One bandage came off, then the other, fast. The exposed wounds felt wet and vulnerable, and she pulled away, but Mr. Falso held her wrists firm, his dark head tipped over the perfectly formed holes. Francesca's stomach twisted and she closed her eyes, calming herself with his mossy scent.

"Amazing," Mr. Falso whispered. He turned them over, front to back. "How long ago did you say it started?"

"Three weeks ago. Yesterday. Three weeks ago yesterday."

"There isn't the slightest clotting or scabbing over. Is it always fresh like this?"

"Some days it bleeds more than others. It depends on what's happening."

"How so?"

"It changes with how I'm feeling. I guess. At least it seems that way."

He looked up, a wrinkle in his brow. "Does it hurt?"

Francesca broke into a febrile smile. "Not now."

Mr. Falso scowled at the pile of bandages. "You need to be careful. You're at constant risk for infection." Francesca nodded obediently. He set her hands on the counter and poured disinfectant from a brown bottle onto a cotton square, staining it mustard. "You need to see a doctor."

"My father won't let me," she said. "He says they'll think I did it to myself."

He dabbed the cotton square on her wounds. It was heavenly, having him hold her hands in his own, treating her as though she were made of glass. She nearly sighed.

"Your father's instincts are right," he said, though he didn't sound sure.

Francesca cleared her throat lightly. "Have you ever seen anything like it?"

"Never," he rasped. "It's breathtaking."

Her eyes flashed and met his.

"What I mean to say is, I know that there are people who have things like this happen. Who things like this happen *to*. But I've never met one."

"Until now," she rushed to say.

"Yes."

"'Things,' like a miracle?"

"That's not entirely clear." He grimaced, took a long look, then unwrapped a plastic-backed gauze pad and covered the wound. Over that he added Steri-Strips. Francesca changed her own bandages every day, but she simply copied the way her father had dressed them that first morning the wounds had appeared. She liked the purposeful way Mr. Falso was redoing what her father had done. Rectifying something wrong: making it different. Making it right.

A tingle at the base of her throat. She felt the rush of speeding headlong toward some critical point. It was time to make Mr. Falso understand.

"Of all the girls in the world, why did God choose me?"

He looked up. His eyes were warm and sad. Why was he sad?

"All I can guess is that you've been—touched—by something very special."

Francesca looked down at the table, her entire body charged. She wondered if she should tell him about the other talents that had shown themselves over the years: the birds that followed her everywhere. The ancient languages she inexplicably knew. The way she could read other people's hearts by pressing ear to chest.

Instead, Francesca said, "You think so?" Because she wanted to hear it from him.

Mr. Falso finished taping the second palm and held both hands inside his. "I do."

His face was inches from hers.

"What happens now?" Her voice was a shredded whisper.

"I guess we wait for the next miracle."

PART 3

Chest

If Ben didn't get inside Eddie's house, he would lose his mind.

Karmic payback, since he only wanted to get in to find Mira's next note. A true bro would be more concerned with checking on his buddy who nearly lost a digit and had since dropped off the planet. For weeks, Eddie hadn't responded to Ben's texts. After Labor Day, the pool would close, and if Eddie kept up his self-imposed exile and blew off school, Ben might not see him at all.

He could just show up on Eddie's doorstep, of course. But rumor had it the whole Villela family was spiraling—both parents now zombies—and Ben was afraid of what he might find.

Ben left the Closed sign on the snack bar counter and turned his back to the growing noises outside the clubhouse door. He pulled the bag from under his shirt, drew its strings apart, and dumped the notes in a clump onto the stainless steel counter. They seemed heavier every time he looked at them, as though they were contracting and hardening with age, which worried Ben vaguely. A flash of yellow caught his eye. He reached behind a steel canister of sugar and pulled out a shriveled lemon smudged with a brown thumbprint. He set the lemon down as the text arrived with a bright chirp:

Heading out this morning to visit Eddie V.
He seems to be having a hard time. Come with?
Your mom says it's ok. Nick Falso

The fixer. Mr. Falso was his ticket in. What was it to him if Mr. Falso had a thing going on with Francesca Cillo? It wasn't Ben's business. Besides, Mira hadn't actually named Mr. Falso. He'd been dying to help Ben, so let him. His mother had told Mr. Falso where he was, probably orchestrated the whole thing as a goodwill gesture.

Ben typed:

I'd like to come. Please pick me up from the boat club.
Thank you.

He paused over the phone, realizing he would probably be fired for leaving before his shift began, with the pool opening and families starting to arrive. It didn't matter: he didn't need the money anymore anyway, and his mother obviously didn't care if he had a job. Ben shot off a second text to his manager citing a vague "family emergency" (did it matter it wasn't *his* family?) and hit Send.

Mr. Falso's overlapping reply read:

On my way!

He lived on the other side of Powder Neck, which gave him approximately nine minutes to get there if he was coming from home, which Ben assumed he was.

Here!

Kid voices cheered, "Mr. F!"

In the frosted door window to the pool, Mr. Falso's shadow flickered as he bent to give hugs and high fives. Ben quickly scooped the notes and stuffed them into his waistband. He tossed the empty nylon bag into the mouth of the trash can, wiped his hands down his shirt, and started toward the door, grimacing as the notes scraped him in sensitive places. The door's bar latch squealed as it released him into the daylight.

Ben was dazzled. The sun off the sea behind Mr. Falso framed him and the children around him. His face was tan and his teeth shone, white and even, the crests of the ocean waves behind giving the scene a commercial quality. He wore shorts and loafers, and a lavender button-down shirt rolled at the sleeves and unbuttoned to underneath his gold chain, which ended in two charms: a dog tag and a black enameled cross. He'd held the charms under Ben's nose once, telling him they symbolized faith's many layers. Ben had thought it looked like something Piggy's older brother wore clubbing.

Mr. Falso looked up. "Ben!" He stretched his arms wide, palms up, biceps peeking below his cuffs.

Ben rubbed the back of his neck and looked down. "Nah, Mr. F. You don't want to hug me. I'm sweaty." The kids snickered. Ben noticed they were mostly girls, and not that little. The hard edge of a note nudged his pubic bone.

"Don't you have a sailing lesson?" Ben's voice hitched as he spoke to the girls, and he hated himself for it.

"Don't you have to pour Goldfish?" said one, all sass and short shorts.

"I'm here on a mission with my boy Ben," Mr. Falso said. He pointed at Ben. "You set, big guy?"

A girl fixed on Mr. Falso and bounced, bending her knees. "Oh-wa! Why do you have to leave so soon? You just got here!" she whined.

Mr. Falso looked past the girls, scanning the parents filtering in, sleepy eyed behind sunglasses and under baseball hats. Most would come back hours later from dropping those same kids at the next activity, more awake, more put together, but for now, they looked weathered, and served to make Mr. Falso's showered manliness more dazzling. He tipped his head toward the whining girl: "Come to youth group this Sunday if you need more Mr. F. time." He cupped Ben's shoulder and steered him toward the parking lot. From behind, Ben heard the girl call, "Buh-bye, Mr. Falso!" He kept his hand that way until they reached the exit gate, where Ben turned to face him.

"Thanks for thinking of me. I'd been meaning to go see Eddie, check on how he's doing."

Mr. Falso squinted, the sides of his eyes crinkling. "I'm not helping you break any rules, am I?"

"Nah. They don't need me." It occurred to Ben that he would have no job next summer. But who said he needed to be in Bismuth next summer? The thought invigorated him. Mira's notes were sparking that same feeling of purpose, of moving toward an end point that she gave Ben when she was living. A gift. He squinted at the sky for a second, wondering if she was up there, watching him find her notes, cheering him on.

"It's more important I go see Eddie," Ben murmured.

They entered the parking lot, bare under the sun. Mr. Falso walked slower than Ben as he slipped on a pair of rose gold-rimmed aviators. "You know, I was really glad when your mom told me you'd be open to visiting Ed. Gives you some time to chat with old Nick here."

"Yeah, well. Between you and me, I'm a little worried about him." Ben turned and jammed his fists into his pockets, walking backward. Not exactly a lie. He was worried about Eddie. "And you're the expert on this kind of stuff."

"A real man knows when to ask for help."

Eddie's the one who needs help, far as you know, Ben thought. "Right, Mr. Falso."

"Nick to you, Ben."

They arrived at Mr. Falso's car (small, red), in which he'd stuffed five seniors last May to drive down to Tennessee to build houses for families living in cardboard lean-tos. As Ben slid into the sunbaked seat, the smell of musk air freshener overcame him. He pressed his curved finger beneath his nose, pretending to scratch an itch.

"So, you're just gonna talk to Eddie, or his parents, or . . . ," Ben started. He needed to know if he'd be alone in that house in the way that he needed to be.

"Let's talk about you for a second. You're a special kid, Ben. Your mother is worried about how you're taking all of this."

Ben cringed. *Special.* He hated that word more than he could hate the man who saddled him with it. Mr. Falso's mention of his special status was a buzz kill. Ancient history that had no bearing. As he told his parents, and the police, and everyone who would listen, he didn't even remember the old coach messing with him, and it was better that way. Mira, on the other hand. Mira was real to him, maybe more so in death. He fed on her notes like sugar: they kept him high until he crashed and needed more. His blood was abuzz with finding Mira's next answer for him, and he would not be stopped.

"I am one hundred percent okay," he replied.

Mr. Falso wrapped his hands around the steering wheel in a practiced way that popped his triceps. He smiled at the road ahead. "I gotta tell you, Ben. I have seen many things. But this"—he puffed his lips and blew staccato noises through them—"this was like nothing else. You can't expect to recover from an event like this too quickly. Everything you hear, see, and do in the next year, maybe years, will be colored by this terrible event. But know in your heart, Ben, that everything happens for a reason, and where one door closes . . ."

"Another opens."

"Right. Some good always comes."

"God has a plan. We have to remember that, even when it doesn't seem to make sense."

"Exactly."

Ben thought of Mr. Cillo alone in his Barcalounger in that house once filled with the fumes of flowery hairspray and astringent and scorched microwave popcorn. The girls' yells, too, across the house, from any room, calls that always ended in "uh" because their names ended with the same letter. Ben imagined it smelling now of arnica, boiled water, and instant coffee; the only music the drone of the Golf Channel. Something told Ben he should pity the old man whose only two daughters were now dead, though he'd felt no pity toward him when they were alive. First, because he'd turned so many people in town against his dad, but then because he'd kept him and Mira apart. He thought Mr. Cillo should want to end his own life right about now, if he hadn't considered it already. Surely something potent was still tucked in the back of the medicine cabinet. He'd learned from his wife's example exactly which cocktail would stop your heart, painless and clean.

Ben realized he was smiling maniacally and looked over at Mr. Falso, who seemed to be reciting something in his head and appreciating how it sounded. Ben wondered if Mr. Cillo was too religious to kill himself, though evidence ran to the contrary. He'd overheard his own father say—with snark, it was unmistakable—Mr. Cillo opened his law office back up two days after the girls fell. It would take an epic event to shake Mr. Cillo's work ethic; apparently one greater than his only children exiting the earth.

Ben was surprised to see Eddie's dad's truck parked at the end of the driveway. He flushed, thinking about the days he made extra cash roofing for Mr. Villela, and that one particular day he'd been sent home early. He glanced over to find Mr. Falso giving him a strange look, and swore to himself no more smiling.

Mr. Falso pulled over a block before Eddie's house.

"Oh, Eddie's house is that one." Ben pointed, wondering why he was telling Mr. Falso something he already knew.

"I'm pulling over here so we can talk," Mr. Falso said. He

removed his sunglasses and tucked them in a compartment above the mirror. "Tell me how you're feeling."

Ben sat straighter, notes poking his soft spots.

Mr. Falso pushed the ignition button and buzzed down the windows. Waited. Seemed to be able to wait a long time.

Ben treaded carefully. Mr. Falso was still the object of Francesca's misery. As grateful as he was for Mira's notes, he was not enjoying this secret knowledge about her sister. "I guess I wonder sometimes. About the last month of Mira and Francesca's lives, and what was happening with them. Like, behind closed doors."

"It's natural to wonder what you might have done differently to prevent a tragedy," Mr. Falso said.

Ben shifted uncomfortably. Sitting here in this car steeped in roasted musk wasn't getting him any closer to Mira. Ben needed to get Mr. Falso to back off. "I'm not wondering about what I could have done. I'm wondering about the stuff we couldn't see. Things that might have . . . changed them."

"Changed them?" Mr. Falso stiffened around the shoulders. "I think I see. Was Mira different in the weeks leading up to the event?"

Mira's name on Mr. Falso's lips jolted Ben. "Mira? Well, yeah. She definitely closed me off. Stopped talking to me, I guess"—*They both stopped talking. To all the boys. Not just Mira*—"and she—they—stopped going out. Leaving the house at all. I mean, it was summer"—*No quarry. No boat club. No anything*—"they—both of them—stayed in the house. In the few weeks before they did what they did. They didn't even have AC"—*which meant the windows were open*—"which meant it was so hot. That's not natural, right?"

Mr. Falso held up his hand. "I think I get it."

"You do?"

"It must be difficult to think about Mira in those last days. But you need to stop. It won't help Mira, and it won't help you. Mira is with God now."

"I'm talking about both of them."

Mr. Falso reached over and clasped Ben's knee. "Of course. We *both* loved *both* of them." He poked the ignition button and the car purred awake, rolling the block to the Villelas' tiny cape before they stopped. "Now, you're a good-looking boy, Ben. I mean, you're lucky to look the way you do."

Ben looked away.

"I mean it now!" Mr. Falso punched Ben's shoulder across the console. "Look, you're blushing! Aw, I didn't mean to embarrass you." Ben felt his cheek as Mr. Falso pointed his finger to his own ear. "Hey, look at this ugly mug! Can you imagine these ears on a sixteen-year-old boy?" Ben couldn't see anything wrong with Mr. Falso's ears, but he nodded anyway. "If I'd have looked the way you look at sixteen, I would've had a lot more girls in my day."

Ben smiled despite himself.

"What I'm trying to say, Ben, is that you had a crush on a good girl, but there will be other good girls. Lots of them. You'll see, I promise." He climbed from the car, unfolding like a giant, as though it was too small to contain him, when really it was Ben's head that grazed the roof. "Let's do this."

Ben gripped the door handle. It was going to be tough to look for Mira's note. Mr. Falso banged on the hood open-handed, and Ben jumped.

He smiled hard. "You daydreaming about those girls?"

Ben ran his hand through his hair and climbed out of the car. He met Mr. Falso on the flagstone walkway lined with Mrs. Villela's rosebushes. Only a few flowers bloomed, and of those, only halfway. The rest were tight buds, their leaves curled under and sucked dry by aphids. Abandoned staging rested against the front of the house, exposing red paint underneath the gray that had been half stripped when the job was aborted last spring. Mr. Falso squinted up at the house, pale lines spraying from the edges of his eyes.

"I thought they'd have finished painting by now," Mr. Falso said.

Ben pressed the buzzer, and they waited seconds, then minutes.

Mr. Falso turned to Ben, rocking on his heels. "You know you can talk to me anytime about Mira."

Ben swore he emphasized *Mira*. "Sure, Mr. F. Thanks for coming."

"You sure you pressed hard enough, big guy?" Mr. Falso leaned over Ben and gave the buzzer a long, hard press. Ben had grown that summer. At five eleven, he could see the top of Mr. Falso's head where the hair was getting thin. It felt disrespectful, so he turned his gaze to the straw wreath hanging on the outer door, with its pastel foam eggs the sun had faded, their bric-a-brac dangling in places. Mr. Falso opened the outer door with a whine and tried the inner door, which opened easily. Ben followed him into the tiny alcove before the kitchen that served as a mudroom and was hit by a rush of cool air and cat urine. The house vibrated from the AC. From a peg rack hung Connie's coat, a cheetah-patterned parka with a fur-lined hood. Forever April, Ben thought.

Mr. Falso called out as he moved through the kitchen. "Hello? Anybody home? It's Nick Falso, and I have Ben Lattanzi with me!"

The coat creeped Ben out, and for a moment, he was glad that he was the kid and Mr. Falso was the adult and that he wasn't alone.

"Ma!" Eddie yelled from the back of the house. He entered the kitchen blinking, in a threadbare Bruins T-shirt and basketball shorts that fell too long, and his hair was mashed up in the back, his hand now expertly bandaged. "Oh, hey, Mr. F. Didn't know you were coming."

Mr. Falso moved fast to embrace Eddie, who looked at Ben

over Mr. Falso's shoulder, his eyes blank. "My parents must not have heard the doorbell. TV's too loud, and the AC makes them deaf." Canned laughter roared from the back of the house. Eddie's parents were too young to be holed up watching game shows, Ben thought uneasily. Mr. Falso had a lot of work in store. "You want some, uh, coffee?"

"First things first, my man!" Mr. Falso released his hug and took hold of Eddie's shoulders. "How are you?"

Ben had eaten many meals at the Villelas' and never could have imagined the kitchen in the state in which they found it. Someone had given up on the mountain of crusted plates and placed a package of paper plates beside the sink. Tall bags from Johnny's Foodmaster covered the counter. It looked to Ben like Eddie had been eating directly out of them. Connie's cat slinked behind him and curled around his leg, her ribs brushing his calf above the sock. On the floor was a double cat bowl with both sides empty.

Eddie's eyes welled with tears, and he stepped backward, waving his bandaged claw.

"I'm good. Better than you might think, with this mitten on my hand. Now I can get a job as toll collector on the Mass Pike. I'll fit right in. You ever see one of those guys with all ten fingers? Good money, they say."

Mr. Falso slapped Eddie on the back—a little hard, Ben thought. "That's the Eddie I know. Did you say your mom and dad are in the back? Mind if I say hello?"

"Knock yourself out, Mr. F. Remind them it's time to eat soon, okay?"

Ben felt his stomach drop. He'd known Mrs. Villela had taken Connie's death hard. But the fact that Eddie's dad wasn't doing well pained Ben. Big Jimmy Villela (who was not big, but compact) had coached Ben in three different sports as a kid. He was the dad who shot hoops with the neighborhood kids and gave everybody day jobs in his roofing company, including guys no one else would hire. He was the first guy on the roof well into his fifties, scurrying up ladders like a goat, planting himself on the steepest pitches to show his boys they could do it. Mr. Villela was old-school, kind under his gruff exterior, like Eddie—and like Eddie, devastated when their precious Connie's throat closed for good.

Connie was diagnosed with her life-threatening exercise-induced allergy at age nine. It shouldn't have taken that long for the doctors to figure it out, with her periodic fainting spells in gym. For a while, it gave her kind of a Victorian heroine chic, and she lapped it up. At fifteen, she carried around an EpiPen, and seemed to enjoy the status her perceived fragility provided. Put simply, Connie needed an edge with people, and her unusual condition provided one. Where the Cillos were all sex and unknowability, Connie was easy to know, to the point of transparency.

Ben heard Mr. Falso straining to talk with the Villelas above the air conditioner and the Wheel of Fortune ticking on its axis. Eddie leaned heavily against the counter, his bandaged paw resting in the crook of the opposite elbow.

"Aren't you supposed to be working today?"

"I gave myself the day off," Ben said. Connie's cat appeared and licked the tips of Ben's fingers, which hung at his side. Ben snatched his hand away in disgust, then felt rude. He rushed to say something about the cat still being able to smell his dead dog on him, but he caught himself in time. Today was not a day to mention the dead. The cat meowed defiantly, glaring from its one good eye, the other a milky cataract.

"C'm'ere, cat. I'll give you some food." Eddie moved to a lone bag on the kitchen table and reached in, pulling out a can. Ben was impressed that Eddie knew exactly where it was, then realized he was the one doing the shopping. Eddie razored the can using the side of his bandaged forearm to hold it in place.

"You're good at working around that," Ben said. "Does it hurt?"

A briny smell permeated the kitchen. The cat screamed. Eddie dumped the can into the bowl on the floor with a liquid plop and shrugged. "It hurts for a while. Then you live with it. Hard part is when it gets knocked around. Hurts fresh all over again, like it just happened."

"Maybe you shouldn't swim with it," Ben ventured, thinking of Eddie diving over and over again like an automaton.

"It's the only thing that helps."

Ben leaned against the opposite counter, his butt knocking

over a line of plastic prescription bottles labeled for Mrs. Villela and an orange EpiPen. As he tried to right the bottles, they skittered from his hands and bounced off the floor. The ones he managed to place back on the counter fell over and rolled away again. He chased one bottle toward the dining room, past the hanging rack of miniature spoons from places like Las Vegas and Lake George. He looked fast over his shoulder; Eddie's head was stuck in the fridge, his square butt shining in his basketball shorts. Ben quickly tipped the rack away from the wall and out dropped a white note, folded fat and tight as an origami star.

YES!

Ben stuffed it into his shirt pocket and hustled into the dining room, scooping the runaway pill bottle off the floor. As he rose, he came level with four Easter baskets filled with plastic grass on the dining room table. He hustled back to the kitchen and spied the last bottle on the floor next to the cat food. As Ben reached for it, the cat swiped at his nose, and Ben yelped.

Eddie cocked his head.

Ben rose, rubbing his nose and mumbling about having too much caffeine, maybe. His words trailed off with every passing second of Eddie's silence until all that was left were the canny strains of Mr. Falso. It felt rude for Ben to comment on the prescription bottles and the Easter baskets; it felt rude to say anything. Mira's note burned a hole in his pocket. The fact was, Ben hadn't set foot in Eddie's house since right after

Connie's funeral, but now that the girls were gone, here he was, presumably checking in, but really looking for secret messages from Eddie's cousin. That the girls were favored even in mourning was a final insult to Connie that Eddie would not bear.

The unfairness of Ben's visit flickered between them, hard and bright.

"So why are you here, Benny?" Eddie said with a cold edge.

"Checking in on you. That's all."

"I saw you at the quarry."

"That was weeks ago. 'Sides, you weren't exactly yourself that day. I just wanted to make sure   "

"I hadn't killed myself?" Eddie smirked darkly, considering Ben. "Nah, you wouldn'ta been dumb enough to say that. You know, Benny, if you were really concerned, you woulda sent me a pretty get-well-soon card with a nice note inside."

A nice note inside.

The rounds of Ben's ears grew warm. He felt sure Eddie could see the white-hot tips of Mira's notes in the places he'd tucked them. He thought of an old movie he'd seen too young—*The Cook, The Thief, His Wife, Her* . . . something, where a guy killed his wife's lover by forcing him to eat pages from his own books. He'd had nightmares for years. That Mira's notes might someday end up in his belly did not seem altogether impossible. But Eddie's eyes weren't on Ben's pockets.

"I was worried about you, Eddie. Not for nothing, but you were acting weird at the quarry."

"Not for nothing, but from what I saw, you're the one who went batshit crazy on Piggy."

"I mean, it has to suck losing half a finger."

Eddie laughed, first through his back teeth, then from his throat and belly, shaking his head at the floor, his one good hand on the counter to steady him. Ben thought he might be going nuts, in this house that would always be painted half-red and where Easter stayed. Finally, he held up his papered claw.

"This?" He staggered as if drunk, and waved it in Ben's face. "This is nothin'."

Mr. Villela shouted from the living room, and Eddie's head snapped. He started toward the back of the house but Ben caught his good wrist.

"You gotta give Mr. Falso time to do his thing," Ben said.

Eddie stared at Ben's hand. "He's wasting his time. The old man's mad at God."

Ben let his hand fall. "He's got a right. Let's go outside." Ben headed out the front door and to the driveway, betting that Eddie would follow. He felt underneath a bush and pulled out a basketball with his fingertips. When he rose, Eddie was standing in the driveway. He tossed it to Eddie, who caught it with his good hand.

Ben grinned. "How you gonna do me now?"

"Fool, I could beat you with no arms and one leg using my nose," Eddie muttered, managing a perfect layup with his good hand. Eddie's height belied the fact that he was springy and nimble, like his dad scrambling across rooftops in the summer. They were opposites on the court, Eddie's scrappiness next to Ben's elegance, his shooting arm resembling a swan's neck arched elegantly toward the basket. When they played together, they burned through everybody. One on one, they were well matched, taking turns dunking on each other until sweat blinded them. It felt good to run and grunt and sweat and not have to talk. Eddie was explosive, coiling and then shooting up like a spring, and he had the advantage the entire game. They went at it for forty minutes before Ben collapsed on the front lawn near the ceramic Mary on the half shell. Mrs. Villela repainted her every year, and added extras, like red lips and cheeks. Ben knew it wouldn't be long until Mary was abandoned, like the house and the roses.

Eddie flopped beside Ben and lay in the clover that flourished across the overgrown lawn.

"Nicely played. And yet—"

"And yet?"

"I'm thinking pick-up hoops isn't part of the chopped-off-baby-finger protocol. How's your hand?"

"It itches."

"Sorry, man. Stitches are the worst."

"Not the stitches. My finger itches."

"Can you stick a chopstick down past the bandages, you know, to scratch it?"

"No, knucklehead. It's the missing half of my finger. It's called phantom limb syndrome. You feel a part of your body that's missing because the nerves are still firing. It's your body fooling itself into thinking it's still there, and you can fix it."

Ben blinked into the sun. "I dunno. Maybe if you scratch it, it'll go away."

"That'd be a waste of time." Eddie sat up on his elbow. He plucked a piece of clover and chewed on its stem, considering the darkening edges of his bandage. "Can't fix something that isn't there anymore. Besides, it bleeds whenever I try to do anything."

"I'm really sorry. About your finger. And Connie. Connie, too. I'm really sorry about all of it."

Eddie spit the clover to the side and gave Ben a shove. He had an endorphin flush to his face and verged on smiling. "I know you are, man. You're one of the good ones."

Ben bit his lip. A sound came from inside the house, aluminum clanking, kitchen noises.

"I wish things had been different between your uncle and my dad."

"Nah. What you don't get is that my uncle didn't want those girls getting any extra attention, for anything, period. Can't say I blame him. You saw the way the guys in the hood treated them, slobbered over them. Uncle Frank couldn't stand it. It was getting outta control."

"True that."

Eddie fell backward and rested his claw over his eyes. "I'm probably the only guy in Bismuth who didn't wax the dolphin for the first time thinking about them."

"Ed . . ."

"Louis acting like an after-hours door-to-door salesman? Piggy breaking his toes?"

Ben laughed. "All right. You got me."

Eddie peered at Ben from underneath his hand. "So tell me something, Benny. If they were your girls, would you give people more reasons to be talking about them?"

Ben felt the note in his pocket. He shimmied slightly on the grass. "I guess not."

"So I think we put talk of them to rest. Starting now." He sat up and stood slowly, suddenly aged, and wandered, slope-shouldered, back into the house.

"You all right?" Ben called.

"Hand hurts," Eddie said, barely audible over the wheeze and slam of the screen door.

Ben sat, frozen. He could tell Eddie didn't want him to follow, but Mr. Falso could be in there for hours. There was only one thing he wanted to do, was dying to do, but he couldn't. He busied himself by checking his armpit stink. He grabbed a bit of clover and stuck it in his mouth as Eddie had, then spit it out. He looked over his shoulder at the house. Finally he grew sure Eddie wasn't looking out the window. He knew that he'd been swallowed by the bowels of the house, the forever-Easter house, and wouldn't emerge again anytime soon.

Ben hunched his shoulders and slipped the new note from his frontmost pocket. He unfolded it on the grass between his legs in the shadow made by his growing body. But before he read it, he made himself remember. Because if the note was going to be about Francesca, he wanted first to think about Mira.

"Let me feel it," Mira had whispered, insistent.

Ben's febrile brain had flashed on the guys' catcalls, had they heard. But that wasn't what was going on. This wasn't some backseat, copping-a-feel scenario. It happened on an Indian summer day the October before, tearing out shingles and shooting in nails. Eighty degrees in Powder Neck, but closer to a hundred on the roof that Villela and Son had been working on that week, twelve of them up there. By one p.m., Ben couldn't say his own name. Mr. Villela was worried enough that he took Ben home early himself, to sit in his cool linoleum kitchen with a jelly glass of Eddie's mom's lemonade. When Ben excused himself to use the toilet, it wasn't because he needed to pee, but because he thought he might puke, and he didn't want to embarrass himself in front of his friend's father. He'd heard the music of the girls' voices in the living room as soon as he left the kitchen: Connie's hyena laugh, Francesca's pious insistence of something. Mira quizzical, excited. Ben slipped in the bathroom, pale and miserable, and stood over the sink for a time. When he came out, Mira was there, standing under the spoon rack. She pushed him against the wall and dragged up his sweaty shirt.

"Mira!" Ben gasped.

Mira pressed her finger to his lip. Then she pressed her ear over his heart. Hard.

Ben forgot to breathe. When he remembered, he choked.

"Shh!" Mira whispered. He gazed down into coarse, dark gold waves of hair, at the pink shell of her hand resting against the inside of his shoulder. The press of the fine bones of her ear into his bare chest was delicious and disturbing, and he needed to move, but moving might have ended it, so he stood, tense, immobile, arms by his sides. He emptied his brain, should his thoughts distract her.

It was the first time Ben felt his own blazing fear that Mira would leave him.

"Mira," he started.

"Francesca has the gift of reading hearts." She pressed her ear against him harder, hot and sharp. "She says it won't work for me. But I still want to try."

"I can tell you how I feel about you right now," he gasped.

He felt her cheek rise against his chest in a smile. "Shh." Her breath blew against his skin. "Not from your mouth. I want to hear it from your soul."

For a moment, she stayed against him. Ben was so turned on he thought he might die. He shut his eyes and pressed the back of his head against rows of dusty trinket spoons. When she finally drew away, the space between her eyes crinkled in a deep frown. Ben's soul had answered her with silence. Her chest heaved and her eyes grew wide; she looked close to crying. Her vulnerability made her even more beautiful. Ben reached down with a tinkle of the spoons and cupped her breast. It was ballsy of him, but she looked so good in that tank top, and for Christ's sake, she'd had her whole head up his shirt. He didn't care. He wanted her. And now that he knew, clear and hot, the terror of her leaving, he wasn't wasting any more time.

Mira moved closer. Ben bent his neck to kiss her as the call came.

"Mira!"

It wasn't Eddie's dad, but Francesca calling her back to the living room. Mira's eyes bored into his: she didn't want to leave. Ben had pushed her away gently; in an instant, he regretted it. Mira looked at him ruefully and started for the living room.

He had called to her back, "You know, Mira Cillo!"

She stopped without turning. Ben's heart skipped. She had looked back at him then, over her shoulder with a half smile that told Ben she knew, and that she was not done with him yet.

Ben pursed his lips and blew hard. He opened the note. Her handwriting was precise and tense.

I see bones through Francesca's chest. She's stopped eating.

Of course. Francesca.

The grass swayed in a sudden, hot wind.

One more year and he'd have had his full license, and there would have been no stopping them. They'd start over, in New York, he figured, where she wasn't the sheltered daughter of an overprotective father and he wasn't the son of the man the jerk hated. Where he wasn't known as a boy who'd been touched. Why couldn't Mira have waited? What could have been so bad that she had to leave this earth before they had a chance to leave together?

Ben mashed the note with his hand and crumpled it into a tiny ball.

"Ready for a ride home?" Mr. Falso called over the wheeze of the screen door. A foam egg bounced off the front step and into a bush. Ben jammed the note in his pocket and rose, walked over to the bush and snatched up the egg, setting it down on the front step. Mr. Falso kept walking to his car, talking as if Ben followed close behind.

"What've you got, a few more months before you're behind

the wheel? That'll open up a whole new world for you, Ben. You wait and see!"

"I'm already six . . . Never mind," Ben muttered, rising slowly under the weight of the realization that he and Mr. Falso would be spending a lot of time together. Because the next place he'd touched Mira was in Mr. Falso's bedroom.

JANUARY 2016

Francesca adjusted her shirt for the third time waiting for Mr. Falso to come downstairs. He'd been on his cell phone, and raised his hand when he saw her at his door. He ushered her in soundlessly, and she was careful not to speak, lest the person on the other line hear her. As he wandered to another part of the house, she decided to sit on the chair she knew was his, in his living room. It was a bold move: for months now, during their wound checks, they'd sat in the same kitchen chairs as the first time she had revealed her true, changed self to him. He had snapped pictures and taken notes on a legal pad, and then they talked of lighter things, him always trying to steer the conversation to this boy or that crush, as if reminding them both that she was still a teenage girl. At the end, he cupped her hands gently from underneath and they closed their eyes and prayed for this inconceivable, unknowable miracle to explain itself to them. The week before, she'd forced his promise not to tell Father Anthony or Father Ernesto, or anyone else. She wasn't ready, she said. She would tell him when she was.

The recliner was the sole chair in a living room with one flat-screen television, a bicycle, a workout bench, a set of dumb-bells, and a retro Pac-Man pinball machine in the corner. She knew there was nowhere for him to sit, but throwing him off-kilter seemed right somehow. This was to be a special day.

As his murmurs grew louder, she slipped one hand under her shirt, pressing the skin over her left breast. A month ago, muscle would have pressed back. Now, the skin was thinner. She closed her eyes and envisioned his face, the curve of his brow over his dark eyes. Her chest was still. She breathed deeply and imagined him holding the back of her hand, mar-veling over her wounds, calling her special and gifted and touched. Her heart beat harder. She felt the pump and the rush, felt the papery skin moving under its pulse. Her stom-ach growled at the exertion. It had been twenty-eight hours since she'd allowed herself a cup of broth. Saints starved them-selves so that the flesh would melt away and their hearts would be left beating behind racks of ribs for God to see. Her father had barely noticed at first; when he had, she'd argued back, expounding long and hard on how fat Americans under-stand self-indulgence, but are disturbed by self-denial. It was an argument worthy of a seasoned trial lawyer. Eventually he gave up, waved her away, swearing, and stormed off to the club.

Francesca arranged her shirt again so that Mr. Falso could see her heart beating for him. She lowered her eyes to a focal point to keep from blacking out, set a weak smile on her lips, and waited.

Mr. Falso bounded down the stairs apologizing and stopped short at the sight of Francesca. In her mind, he was startled by the vision of her, made purer by her fasting. She was certain he could see her heart as it rose and fell, glowing beneath her paper-white skin.

"Are you sick?" he asked, drawing closer in the dim light. He reached underneath the shade of a floor lamp and flicked it on.

"I'm fine," she said, suddenly conscious of her chapped lips. "I thought we might talk in here for a change."

Mr. Falso searched for a place to sit. Francesca closed her eyes and placed her palms on her knees, facing upward. Mr. Falso froze, then realized what she expected. He kneeled on the floor in front of her and took her hands in his. Francesca took a deep breath, her chest rising, inside, her heart like a bird banging against a cage. She could hardly contain her joy, that he had so willingly assumed his position—a supplicant in front of the divine. For the first time, she sensed she was capable of making him do what she wanted.

He peeled away the right bandage.

"You're certain it doesn't hurt?" he said quietly.

Francesca smiled serenely. "You ask me every time. And every time, I say no."

Mr. Falso repeated his examination on the other side. He took pictures with his phone, then scribbled notes. Francesca relaxed into the calm space hunger made for her once she had passed the point of anxiousness. Finally he sat back on the rug. He seemed pensive. Francesca crawled off the chair and sat next to him, smiling benignly, something she had perfected and taken to applying when she sensed Mr. Falso moving away.

She adjusted her shirt. "What are you thinking about?"

"I wonder. Do you have any other signs like these, or is this the only one?"

Francesca felt as though someone had hit a Pause button. "What do you mean?"

"I wondered if anything else unusual was happening in your life, that's all. I'm trying to put it into context. For my research."

Francesca licked her lips. The birds proved nothing. Her ability to speak in tongues was the equivalent of a party trick. And reading someone's heart? Girly-sounding drivel that she wasn't willing to risk.

"Unusual like what?" she asked.

"You know, things you can't help. Have you seen anything unusual, for example?"

Francesca scuttled back an inch. "You mean, have I had visions? No. Not yet. I mean, I don't think I have. Why?"

"No reason. I wanted to know if this is happening in isolation from other miraculous events. That's all."

"What is it that you want me to do?" She flipped through her mental Rolodex of research she'd done on saints, looking for guidance. The lives of the Italian saints were particularly unhelpful, if not downright revolting. Saint Maria Maddalena de' Pazzi lay naked on thorns. Saint Catherine of Siena drank pus from a cancerous sore. Veronica Giuliani cleaned the walls and floor of her cell with her tongue, swallowing spiders and their webs. Francesca pressed her palms into the floor to remain steady.

"There's nothing I want you to do." He reached out to touch her face, caught himself, and pulled back. "I wondered if anything else had happened to you, that's all. Historically speaking, certain things have happened to individuals like you, things common to their stories."

"You mean to saints. Things that have happened to saints."

"Now, no one said saints. I don't think it's helpful to label what's happening to you. Our job is to gather information and let the Church make sense of it. If and when you decide you're ready, that is."

Francesca gathered her skirt around her knees and stood too quickly. The room went white and a tinny buzz filled her ears. She felt around, stumbling, and there were Mr. Falso's arms, steadying her.

"You're faint!" he exclaimed.

She was about to wave him off, uncomplaining, like she always did. Like she imagined the saints did. Yet something stopped her. As her eyes filled in, sparkles reformed into shapes, and she leaned her head against his chest. She was shocked at the way it felt under her cheek, firm and soft, and warm through his T-shirt. She closed her eyes and whispered against his chest.

"I'm not ready."

Mr. Falso drove Francesca home that afternoon. He wouldn't allow her to ride her bike: it was absurd, the sidewalks were slush, and she seemed to be coming down with something. His car smelled manly, and he seemed happy to have her there with him. She imagined he was getting used to the idea of her by his side. Yet every time she allowed herself to relax and enjoy his presence, she felt an overwhelming sense that something was ending. He commented on which Christmas lights he liked best

(The old fashioned ones, big like eggs.)

and the packed parking lot at Johnny's Foodmaster

(Never sets foot in a supermarket himself. Gets it delivered.)

and the traffic visible on the Southeast expressway

(Rush hour already? Who knew? Lucky man he was, getting to work in his own neighborhood!).

Yet Francesca heard only, "Do you have any other signs, or is this the only one?"

When they pulled up in front of the house, Francesca sprang from the car. Mr. Falso called to her.

"What's your rush?" he asked, laughing nervously. Surprise in his eyes first, then worry. As if he didn't like Francesca getting away from him, she thought. For the first time in years, she felt sated.

Francesca smiled as mildly as possible. "I have homework."

Something in the Pignataros' driveway caught Mira's eye: a flicker of reflected glass on top of the Winnebago. She squinted out the window, the candle in her hand poised above the sill. Beyond the Pignataros' house was a white fluorescent mess of strip malls and skeletal light poles illuminating empty parking lots. Farther to the west lay the vast black swath that was the quarry. If Piggy Pignataro was peeping into her bedroom from the roof of his RV, she wouldn't be surprised. Tonight's madness was right up his alley, with his special interest in succubi and sexy blue girl aliens, and any sort of fantastical intrigue involving half-dressed girls.

Behind Mira, in the darkened bedroom, a rustle. The sharp drag of sheets across a mattress.

Mira shivered in her thin nightgown and placed the candle on the sill. She should be attending to Francesca, but she stared out the window a moment more. The thought of a boy out there, even a boy who disgusted her, was a minor comfort. She felt so alone. Before her sister had slipped into her current state—what Francesca called ecstasy but what Mira thought might be a seizure—Francesca had forbidden her to call Connie, whom Mira needed most. Instead, Mira had betrayed her sister in the worst way possible: by telling their father. And at any moment, things were going to get embarrassing.

Francesca moaned.

Mira turned and rushed back to Francesca in her drenched nightgown, twisting atop her bed, feet caught to the ankles in a miasmic tangle of bed linens. Mira had placed votives in a line on the floor, and the flames cast shadows as Francesca arched and writhed, possessed by what infected her. Her eyes were closed and her mouth parted slightly. Not infected: that wasn't the right word. Francesca's trance, or whatever she had slipped into, didn't seem unpleasant. Parts of Mira felt hot, stirred to feel what Francesca was feeling. She couldn't watch, nor could she stop watching.

If Mira closed her eyes, she could put herself on the bed in Francesca's place. She envisioned Ben over her, waves of desire inside her building. Her nightgown against her body teased her skin. He was a beautiful boy, broken, angular, and sharp as a blade, with long muscles in the bones of his hands, curving around his scapula, cording his neck. When he gazed at her, his eyes welled with hunger and fear. Mira loved him more for the damage inflicted on him, the kind of damage that her touch might heal. Mira imagined that the bad coach had hollowed out parts of Ben for Mira to fill. A co-mingling that might suffocate Mira's own wrong urges.

Francesca's head whipped from side to side in an unnatural, fast rhythm, her cheek thumping the pillow.

Selfish thoughts. Francesca needed her. Before she had become insensible, Francesca had told her to pray. So Mira dropped to her knees, her forehead touching folded hands.

The crunch of crushed stone under tires.

"Thank you, God," Mira whispered into her fingers.

It was the sound of the red Miata pulling deep into the Cillos' driveway. Mira imagined the driver running to the front door, compact under winter cashmere, propelled by purpose and heroic delusion. At her father's voice, Mira's face tipped upward and caught the moonlight. He barked flat commands before pulling the visitor inside.

Mira stood, wobbly. Soon Mr. Falso would run up the stairs and take control. He would see what Francesca was. Perhaps not the way she wanted, but she could convince her sister that it was to her advantage. She was practiced at this.

Back at the window, Mira plucked at her gown, letting the winter air off glass cool her. The distant rumblings within her own body were unmistakable. Something was growing inside her, a volcano that would run and run and take everything with it.

She ripped the drape shut.

PART 4

Cheek

Ben's knowledge of what had gone down between Mr. Falso and Francesca was becoming a presence, detectable to Ben, something smutty sharing the space between them in the cramped front seat of the red Miata. He couldn't stop animating Mira's notes in his head, starring an actressy Francesca refusing to eat for heartache, and Mr. Falso, saying he couldn't help himself (from what? Kissing her? Making love to her?), bemoaning their forbidden love. Even secondhand, and removed by time, it was too much.

He hated knowing these things about Mr. Falso. And now he had another note in his pocket—

Despite all he's done, Francesca says she'll forgive
him and turn the other cheek.

—one that implicated Mr. Falso in real wrongdoing, at least in the girls' eyes. The note, which he only peeked at after finding it in Mr. Falso's bedroom, was vague yet pointed: *despite all he's done.* Ben stared at the extra folds of skin in front of Mr. Falso's ear.

What did he do?

Now everything Mr. Falso did seemed suspect to Ben. Parking his car illegally behind Johnny's Foodmaster to hike up the quarry. The whole idea of rock climbing, something Ben tried to quash but Mr. Falso had insisted on, wouldn't have been a bad way of knocking Ben off, so his secret affair with Francesca would never be discovered. Ben suddenly wished he'd told Kyle where he was going, in case he never came out.

"You're awfully quiet. Aw, you still tired, Benny?" Mr. Falso said.

"No sir."

"Because you know real men sleep when they're dead."

Ben almost didn't get Mira's note. He'd had to beg Mr. Falso to let him use his bathroom, which was humiliating. But it had been worth it, because there in Mr. Falso's dark bedroom that smelled like sleep and socks, into which they'd slipped during a youth group meeting because it was on the way to the bathroom, somehow, Mira Cillo had taped a tiny fourth note to Ben underneath the bottom of a Citizen of the Year trophy.

This was the first note that rang of true danger in leaving it. Though the fact that the trophy was dusty was not something Mira was likely to have overlooked. They'd knocked it over when Ben had lifted her to sit on Falso's dresser. Ben understood its significance, and wouldn't have taken long to find it. He hadn't even flinched when he read Francesca's name. By now, he was almost wondering what Francesca would do next. Ben knew vaguely that there was irony to the love of his life relegating herself to the sidelines in retelling her own story. But she wasn't really, was she? Because it was Mira's cheek that he'd touched in that bedroom. An unplanned and reckless dash into a dark room on the first floor, not entirely out of earshot of the other kids. She'd gotten up and signaled for him to follow, eye to eye, and he left a few seconds later. Mr. Falso had been on fire that day, high on his own healing, making everyone hold hands and pray *a lot*. When Ben and Mira finally escaped into the bedroom together, they were afraid to speak, and hiding in a grown man's bedroom was maybe a turn-on. Mira's eyes skittered across his face, unsteady, and she bit the side of her lip in hot concentration. Ben pushed her hair away from her right temple, where a vein pulsed softly. He stared at the vein, then a voice in his mind's ear told him he had no time. He grasped Mira's waist, which felt soft between his hands, and lifted her atop Mr. Falso's bureau, loaded with manly elixirs, phallic awards, and the small things he pulled from his pockets every evening. A lucite trapezoid inscribed *Citizen of the Year 2008* fell to the floor and thudded onto carpet. Mira gulped. Ben stared at the door, staying it with his vigilance. The act of lifting Mira by the waist had sparked something primal, and it made him powerful. He liked it.

"I need you to understand something," Mira whispered. "I can't help myself."

Ben turned back to her and smiled like a cat. "I can't either."

"Ever."

"It's okay," he murmured, shaking his head softly. In the shadows, her upturned face was the color of candle wax, and impossibly sad. Ben needed to change that. He drew his fingers across the planes of Mira's cheeks, sculpting change. Underneath Ben's fingertips, Mira's face grew warm. The downturns at the corners of her eyes lifted, her cheeks filled with blood, the ends of her lips rose. He stroked the contours of her face until the last traces of mysterious sadness were gone.

"You are the most beautiful girl," Ben said, his thoughts careening ahead: future Ben and Mira cruising down the Mass Pike and farther, on foreign highways, top down and Mira's hair tangled, Mira righting his befouled life just by filling the space beside him.

Mira had made a gruff noise and buried her face in his chest: self-conscious, Ben figured. The truly beautiful ones always were. Mira pushed off Ben and slipped from the dresser without a word. They needed to leave separately, stagger their reentry into the living room by minutes. Ben had stared at his fingertips, warm with the knowledge that he could make Mira Cillo happy.

Ben wondered if Francesca had ever been in Falso's

bedroom. Ben felt a prickle across the middle of his back as Mr. Falso banged on his window.

"You daydreaming again, big guy?"

"No sir," Ben said miserably.

They mounted bikes—Falso's souped-up mountain bike, a lesser one on loan to Ben—and rode on the same path Mira and Francesca had traveled, but headed to Little Q, a smaller, stand-alone pool blasted out thirty years after the original chasm, and the only part of the quarry, declared a Superfund site, that the government had successfully emptied. Newer blasting methods meant the walls of Little Q were smoother than the walls of its big cousin, with the same poison gases but none of the craggy footholds and ledges that marked the main hole. Climbers flocked from everywhere, rappelling up and down anchor points on its steep walls with their harnesses and their climber-speak ("Belay! Belay on!"). Their Ironman calls could be heard from the main hole. Like most of the kids who swam the quarry, Ben found them pretentious as well as a threat, since they could call the cops on the kids carrying their coolers full of beer if they bumped into them on the path.

They came to the spot where the path forked. To their right, the trail led to Little Q; forward, they would end up at the main water hole. To the left, they could hear voices and music carrying a half mile ahead. Ben wondered if anyone was on the Cillos' ledge. Mr. Falso pulled ahead and spun his tires hard right, racing ahead toward the hollow, clipped yelps of the climbers. He felt conspicuous and lame showing up in shorts and a Red Sox hat, with the fat pack that Mr. Falso had thrown on his back. Mr. Falso had carried the larger bag of the two, which made Ben feel grateful and wimpy at the same time. The chain-link fence that traced the edge of the main hole had been ripped down at Little Q, and the edge of the cliff came fast. Ben dropped his bike and looked down. Climbers dotted the walls like colored spiders.

"Benvenuto!" Mr. Falso called from a tiny ledge twenty paces to Ben's left and ten feet below. He had already scrambled down and was changing into clownish neon slippers. Next to his brown legs was a pile of ropes, harnesses, and helmets, along with the pack it came in. He smiled wide and pointed to an ancient rusty ladder bolted into the rock. "Only one way down, my friend!"

Ben smiled weakly. He knew he'd look like a putz if he made a big deal out of climbing down a ladder, the easiest climb he'd see today. He walked the twenty paces with a forced bounce and crouched, shaking the ladder to test it. It didn't move.

Mr. Falso laughed from below. "If it held my weight, it'll hold yours, skinny boy!"

Ben winced at that. It pissed him off, the way Mr. Falso was always showing off his muscles. Some guys thought he might shoot gear, but Ben thought his neck looked fine, and he didn't exactly have zits or mood issues. Ben put his growing anger aside and descended, flakes of rust loosening under his hands. When he stepped off the last rung, Mr. Falso slapped his back so hard he nearly tumbled off the ledge.

Ben rubbed the back of his neck. "Do you do this alone?"

Mr. Falso grunted as he gathered up the harness, a coil of rope wound around one arm. "Can't lie, Benny boy. I do come out here sometimes on my own. Helps clear my head. There are plenty of other climbers out here, usually, but you can't rely on them to save you if you get into trouble. How does it go? Do as I say . . ."

"Not as I do."

"Right. Have I told you how glad I am that you wanted to hang out today? I've been asking your parents if you'd like to hang with the F Man, just to talk, you know. They said you weren't interested yet, but I won't hold that against you. Drop you too fast, for example." He smiled crookedly, showing a flash of wet teeth.

Ben cast his glance over Little Q and the rock he was about to rappel down. Some ancient machine had carved thick vertical grooves like an accordion pleat, and another machine hauled the rock out in refrigerator-sized bricks. Piles of bricks still littered the land around both quarries, with tufts of goldenrod and rooted saplings between.

"You'll be needing these." Mr. Falso tossed Ben a pair of cowhide gloves. "You've got the easy part. All you've gotta do is say 'belay on' when you're ready to keep climbing down."

Ben tucked his chin at the word.

"I say, belay? And you say . . . go ahead, say it!"

"Belay on," Ben mumbled into his chest.

"You gotta say it louder, so I can hear you." Mr. Falso pointed to the bottom of the chasm, at least one hundred feet down. "I'm gonna be way down there, remember?"

"You mean you're not gonna be right next to me?" Ben choked.

"Of course not. Who's gonna work the ropes?" Mr. Falso said. "Next thing, you're going to ask me why the rock's not plastic."

"I envisioned us being able to, you know, talk. Mano a mano," Ben said, aiming for Mr. Falso's sweet spot.

"Climbing requires absolute focus. Especially when you're new. You work hard, someday maybe you'll earn these, my man." Mr. Falso opened the inside of his flak vest and flashed a bunch of patches that looked to Ben like Boy Scout badges. Ben hadn't even noticed him changing into it. Suddenly Ben had a terrified thought: that he'd been in the house when Ben was nosing around his bedroom, and that this was his punishment. It didn't make any sense, but Ben still shuddered.

"We'll chat over lunch. Now get in!"

Ben climbed obediently into the harness Mr. Falso held out for him, allowing himself to be trussed and buckled like a child. The process took a couple of minutes, with Mr. Falso explaining each step in detail. Ben felt the note in his pocket every time the harness shifted. Finally, Mr. Falso took a short step back, cocking his head.

"There! Exactly how I want you!"

The ease with which Mr. Falso had complete control of his life washed over Ben. One slippery knot or broken buckle could leave him broken on the quarry floor. He shot out a tight laugh that sounded more like a bark. "Good thing for me you know what you're doing."

"Indeed I do. Did you say your parents knew where you were going?"

Ben lied. "Yes! Yes, they do. They know I left the boat club with you to see Eddie at approximately 7:50 a.m. And that we went rock climbing after. And I'm expected home at four. I have to be somewhere. At four. So they'll be looking for me, right away, if I'm even a minute late."

"Good to know!" Mr. Falso called, already disappearing over the edge of the cliff, scrambling like an insect, rappelling down the slope with ease and speed. Ben thought of Mr. Villela scurrying across rooftops. Ben bet he'd be good at this kind of thing, but he was of a different generation: men who got exercise from physical labor that paid bills and put food on their tables, not muscles on their arms, or to kill time in an otherwise lonely existence.

Ben looked to the sky. There were no clouds, nothing that looked like heaven, only cold blue and more cold blue.

"Belay!" Mr. Falso yelled, his voice tiny and echoing.

Ben crossed himself. "Belay on!" he yelled, securing his first foothold, and lowering himself down.

Within minutes, Ben got into a groove. It was a relief not to think about Mira. The rhythm of finding footholds and releasing himself down, hand over hand, was consuming, a mental game. Sometimes he needed to focus on his feet, other times, his core. He needed to rely on Mr. Falso, and so they became partners. By the time he reached the bottom, he almost felt relaxed and happy.

Mr. Falso stabbed his finger into the air at Ben. "Look at that smile! You see? You've caught the bug! Isn't it awesome?"

"It is pretty awesome," Ben admitted.

Ben allowed himself to be tossed around, a dopey smile on his face, as Mr. Falso yanked at his waist, releasing his ropes and buckles and harness. Other climbers milled about them, nodding, like they'd drunk the same Kool-Aid, and acknowledged one another's high. When Ben was free from his gear he collapsed to the ground. Mr. Falso handed him a canteen of cold water. It was delicious.

Mr. Falso collapsed next to Ben. He was surprised when Mr. Falso pulled out a beer and cracked it. He guzzled it and kicked back, stretching his hairy legs in the sun, saying nothing. Ben leaned on bent elbows and drank more water. He hadn't given Mr. Falso a chance, he realized. He wasn't a bad guy to hang with. It was a relief not to have to pose and act cool like he did with his friends. And Mr. Falso was ten times cooler than his own dad.

"This is nice. Thanks for inviting me, Mr. F."

"I'm glad you came, Ben. You're a great kid. I like spending time with you."

"I gotta tell you though: I'm a little surprised." Ben pointed to the beer. "I thought you were a health nut."

"This?" Mr. Falso held up his bottle. "I allow myself one. A man's body is his temple. Once in a while, I despoil the temple. My prerogative, I guess."

"Right," Ben said.

"I tell you, Ben. Climbing, scuba diving, heli-skiing—I do it all. Some people would call me crazy. But it's my life, and I'm in my prime. I accept the risk. I do what I want. I figure, it's my body, and I control what I do with it."

Ben wiped his mouth. "That sounds pretty good."

"No risk, no reward. You want something, you go for it. That goes for the ladies, too. You ever need girl advice? You come to me, Ben. And obviously anything you tell me won't go anywhere." He leaned over. "That goes the same for anything I tell you, in the spirit of sharing."

Ben cleared his throat. He might want to talk about Francesca. He seemed like he wanted to. They were buds. Maybe the notes were just girl drama, Francesca mooning over an older guy. It would be good to know that. It would be good to hear it from Mr. Falso.

"Actually, Mr. Falso, I wanted to talk with you about the girls. The Cillo sisters." Ben cleared his throat. "I'm trying to get a sense of what was going on in the months before they died."

"I see." Mr. Falso chugged the dregs of his beer and paused, looking off into the distance. "Now why is that?"

"I think . . . getting a better understanding will help give me closure."

"Closure is a tough thing. Some people never find it, no matter how hard they search for answers." Mr. Falso set to tucking away the trash in his pack. "Carry in, carry out!"

"If everyone could understand why they did it, they would be able to—we would all be able to—find peace. Don't you think?"

Mr. Falso put his hand on Ben's knee. "Peace comes from knowing that God has a plan, and that everything happens for a reason."

"I think Francesca was in love. But Mr. Cillo locked her away like a princess in a tower."

Mr. Falso drew his hand away as if he'd touched a hot stove. "And that's why they fell. You must be a pretty amazing kid, to have figured out something their father, their teachers, their relatives, their priest, and their spiritual director didn't know."

"They didn't have a normal life," Ben said, his courage building. Mr. Falso's mood was tanking, but the relief of releasing the things he'd been carrying was great, and the words came tumbling out. "Something bad happened around the time Connie died."

"It did. Connie died."

"Something made them unravel, mentally. Something bad that no one knew."

"Think carefully about what you're saying, Ben."

"I'm not making this up. I have proof. Mira complained to me." Ben felt himself going out on a limb, but he couldn't stop. "She said Francesca was having problems. Not eating. Crying a lot. That Mr. Cillo said her issues were in her head."

Mr. Falso folded his hands over his knees and squinted up at the sky, as if in pain. "For someone who's only ever climbed on plastic rocks in a gym, you did a good job today."

"I'm sorry?" Ben said.

"Thing is, I did everything for you. Did you make sure the rope was threaded correctly through the belay device, and that the locking carabiners were actually locked? Did you double-check to see if your own knot was tied correctly? Tightened? Threaded through the harness, even? Was the tail long enough? Was my knot tied correctly? You didn't look or ask."

Ben's mouth twisted.

"You stood there like a toddler and let me do those things for you. If you'd come out here and tried that descent yourself, you'd have dislocated a finger, shaved the skin off your palms, or cracked your pretty head against a wall."

"I figured you knew enough for both of us."

"Rock climbing is a risky activity, and many mistakes are unavoidable. If you're lucky, your mistakes result in close calls that help keep you vigilant. If you're not, the results can be tragic."

The tops of Ben's cheeks burned. He staggered to his feet, trying to gain height, perspective, something. "You're saying I'm reading too much into what Mira told me."

Mr. Falso turned away from the sun and gazed up at Ben with a terrifying calmness Ben had never seen in an older man—not in his father, not in his teachers, not in his coaches. Though Ben towered over him, Mr. Falso was the one in control.

"I'm saying that when you engage in a risky activity, you have to be absolutely sure you know what you're doing. Maybe it's not so much a matter of reading too much into something as reading incorrectly."

Ben turned to storm away, tripped over his harness, and stumbled. He swore and spun around. When he turned, Mr. Falso was directly behind him.

"Did Mira come right out and tell you what was bothering Francesca?"

The note felt alive in Ben's pocket. "Not exactly."

"See, Ben. Here's the thing. We can't understand what was

going on in that household. If Francesca was sad and with-drawn over something done to her, and her father was saying it was in her head, well, there are many documented cases of abuse where the abuser convinces the victim it's in their head. To the point where it's almost—God forgive me for saying this—a cliché."

Ben felt as though someone had sucker punched him. Mr. Cillo had been abusing Francesca? She would have to have told this to Mr. Falso. And what did that mean for Mira? Even though the foundations of their homes were barely eight feet apart, he and Mira had escaped her father's scrutiny a total of seven times. Seven times Ben had touched parts of Mira Cillo. Never more than seven. Not a lot. What did he really know about what went on behind closed doors? What did anyone know? Ben's face burned. He thought of what Eddie had said about Mr. Cillo living among those girls, not knowing what to do with them.

What did he do with them?

"Ben? I asked you a question," Mr. Falso said, his voice a low growl.

Ben looked up, startled. "What?"

"Have you spoken with anyone else about this?"

"No," Ben whispered.

"That's good. That's very good." He felt Mr. Falso rise to his feet, and watched as his long shadow overtook Ben's own.

"Mr. Falso, Mira trusted me with information. I can't look the other away."

Mr. Falso pointed over Ben's shoulder to a man taking an overhang, his partner belaying below. "See that climber over there?"

"Yeah, so?"

"Anytime you go out on an overhang, you're in danger of putting your leg on the uphill side of your rope." He pointed at the climber's legs. "If you fall with your leg in the wrong position, you're in danger of flipping upside down. Smack your skull right off the side of a cliff."

Ben sniffed. "He doesn't look like he's going to flip." He hated how childish he sounded, but he also couldn't pull himself out of it.

"He's not. Because what he's doing, it's subtle. He's developed a sixth sense about when his leg has moved across the line too far. If it does, he corrects it."

"How?"

"He pulls back. Immediately. Even if it changes his course."

Ben folded his arms around himself and walked away, despite the fact that there was nowhere to go.

Mr. Falso called to him. "Did you know, Ben, that at one time, Bismuth was a town with no old men?"

Ben stopped and beat his upper arms. The sun had slipped behind a cloud, and the temperature at the bottom of Little Q dropped fast. "What does that mean?"

"Silicosis. Clouds of dust containing crystalline silica stirred up by drilling in the quarries. Exposure to silica dust killed off the men who operated drills and their helpers. Entered their lungs every time they breathed. Silicosis causes lungs to stiffen, making breathing more and more difficult. It makes you susceptible to infections, like tuberculosis. Most of the guys who worked in these quarries half a century ago never made it past age forty."

"Sounds like a lousy way to die." Ben no longer cared if he offended Mr. Falso. He wasn't in the mood for a history lesson. He wanted to go home and reread every one of Mira's notes and reconsider what they meant. Mr. Cillo touching Francesca. Her crying over it.

Mira knowing better.

Ben looked up at the wall he'd climbed down, a pleasant hour colored by endorphins and a single-minded focus on where to put his hands and feet. How could he, of all people, not have seen it? He, with his unique vantage. He, with his special knowledge. The deep grooves in the walls suddenly seemed unscalable. He felt a tightness in his chest. Mira knew better. She knew better because whatever Mr. Cillo was doing to Francesca, it was happening to her, too.

Ben leaned over and vomited. Instead of comforting him, Mr. Falso kept talking.

"My point isn't that they died a terrible death, which they did. My point is, Frank Cillo was the lawyer who helped many of those families sue for lost income after their husbands died. He's a hero to many of these families. It was decades ago—way before you were born—but they remember."

At that moment, Ben realized there was only one way out, and to get out, he was going to have to rely on his belaying partner.

"So you can understand your father's unpopularity when he squealed on Frank Cillo for not reporting everything to the IRS. Frank Cillo is a hero in this town. You don't cross him. You especially don't cross him if you're Paul Lattanzi's kid."

Ben dragged his wrist across his mouth hard.

Mr. Falso leaned over. "And you definitely don't cross him if you were schtupping his dead daughter."

Ben scanned the other climbers, in stages of resting, or making their way back up or down. He wondered if they would help him, if it came to that. More than anything, he wanted to get out of Little Q. He tried to make eye contact with the closest climber, a guy with wraparound sunglasses who seemed to be watching them. Ben struggled to see exactly where his eyes were. Suddenly the man waved. Ben's stomach sank as Mr. Falso came from behind Ben and greeted the man by name.

As Mr. Falso passed, he leaned into Ben, his breath yeasty at Ben's neck. "You need to leave this alone, Benvenuto."

JANUARY 2016

Francesca's eyes narrowed as she stood alone in the far corner pretending to survey for tables that needed salt and pepper. Usually when she served meals at the soup kitchen, she felt good about what she was doing. Almost noble. Today, she felt cynical, finding fault with everything. She had served the poor, shown compassion to the vulnerable. It had even made her feel virtuous, like Saint Clare, whom she was into lately. Saint Clare, who said to Saint Francis, "Dispose of me as you please. I am yours." The website said that Saint Clare became more radiant as she served, and Francesca imagined herself becoming more beautiful to Mr. Falso with every globule she scraped into the steel sink.

It should have been the perfect time to confront Mr. Falso about what he'd witnessed. But so much had gone wrong. First: Francesca felt disgusting. Much as she tried to channel the glorious piety of Saint Clare, dish duty sucked. Her nose was shiny. Steam hung in her hair. Her jeans were crusty with white sauce from the chicken tetrazzini, gelatinous gunk heaped on plates that the busboys tossed in plastic bins shoved through the window to the dish room. Dishwater had seeped through her plastic gloves and mixed with the powder inside, and her bandages smelled funky. Second: Connie had insisted on coming. Francesca had tried to tell her the people who came to the soup kitchen for their free meals stank. They chewed with their mouths open. Didn't have teeth. Sometimes, they even groped. Connie should stay home. Francesca's issue with Connie was her potential for distraction. It wasn't that Connie attracted men; not like Mira, whose cool incandescence drew boys like moths. In fact, Connie suffered (unjustly) in comparison to her cousins, always battling something (a zit, a bad-hair day). Connie knew this, but she didn't believe for a moment that she couldn't change her lot. The key lay in studying her cousins' ways—Francesca's fiery dignity and Mira's airy detachment, neither of which Connie was capable of attaining. Francesca knew Connie's habit of observing her every interaction with boys would make conversation with Mr. Falso nearly impossible.

Francesca scanned the room with barely veiled disgust. The overweight man with the undersized Boston College varsity sweater forever asking for seconds was a fraud, she was sure. She didn't feel sorry for the weary couple with their premature baby making kitten noises. The baby needed its milk warmed, and if they didn't know enough to warm it, well, she wasn't going to tell them. She didn't identify with the strung-out junkies who might have been her age, ignoring their table, and they ignored her, pushing powdery dinner rolls around their plates. Beyond the main dining room, the smell of warm dishwater and powerful detergents was repulsive and alluring, and the laughter that slipped out over the mechanical chug in the back room pricked her nerves.

Mr. Falso was laughing at her. Remembering the way she'd rolled around on her sheets, like she was having a seizure, caught in some sort of trance. She'd embarrassed herself, she was sure of it. But there was a word for what she'd experienced; she heard him use the word to her father as she lay on her back drenched with sweat—*ecstasy*—a word he wouldn't have used unless he thought that was what was happening to her. He had labeled it, and she had heard him.

Francesca twirled the apron string around her finger and smiled. The night wasn't over yet.

"What are you standing there for?" Mira said. "The five stoned guys in the corner are asking for more bread. It's your turn, I think."

Francesca looked at her sister, who, instead of folding her apron down like everyone else, wore hers over her chest and tied neatly beneath her chin. Mira approached soup kitchen service with genuine fear, locking her purse in the director's desk and covering her body so nothing was left exposed, as if the patrons were going to gang rape her rather than get a meal.

Not saintly at all. Not Christian.

Francesca untangled her finger and spoke in a harsh whisper. "Nick hasn't spoken to me. Not once. And the fact that Connie's in there with him makes it ten times worse."

Mira frowned. "Connie's not interested in Mr. Falso."

"Connie likes men," Francesca said.

Mira moved closer, looking over her shoulder. "You actually think Connie would betray her blood that way?"

Francesca sighed. "Of course not. I'm worried about the fact that he hasn't spoken to me since he came to our house during my ecstasy. He's blown off our check-in meetings, and my hands are drying up." She showed both sides. The bandages, smaller now, were four pristine, nude circles. Across the room, the man in the BC sweater bellowed for more pudding. The girls looked up in sync. Mira grabbed Francesca by the arm and pulled her to the small room off the main dining area where the furry-faced woman with cataracts sat folding napkins. Privately, the girls called her Catwoman because of her resemblance to Connie's cat, but her real name was Donata. They had never served the poor without Donata in the background. She was already in her seat when they came, and still there when they left, folding and unseeing. Francesca felt sorry for her; Mira thought she was terrifying. Every third or fourth napkin Donata would stop and flex her gnarled hands and rub her thumb along the grain of her palms, massaging. Mira speculated Donata's presence at the soup kitchen was a mercy job, since she only ever folded about twenty-five napkins in the entire five hours the St. Theresa's kids worked there.

They huddled and whispered.

"Consider this: the ecstasy takes it to a whole new level. Out of his hands, maybe. So, perhaps he's paralyzed. He simply doesn't know what to do next," said Mira.

"It's true that I've told him I'm not ready to share it with anyone. It's our secret," Francesca said. "His and mine."

"That's right. Your special secret," said Mira.

"But what if it's too much for him to bear alone?" said Francesca.

"Then you tell him I know. Not Connie, though. Just me. Four makes it . . . less special," Mira replied.

Francesca's eyes filled with tears. She blinked them away and focused on the old woman's hands, painfully slow. Fold, flex, knead. Fold, flex, knead. Francesca shook off her annoyance and came back to Mira. "But what if my ecstasy is some kind of turnoff?"

"But that's his thing. I mean, it's his 'field of interest.' It's precisely what makes you special to him."

"He needs more proof. He doesn't yet believe." Francesca's voice was coarsened by the tears burning the back of her throat. Her eyes cut to Donata. "Oh for God's sake. You're never going to finish at that rate. Let us do it." Francesca spread her fingers over the old woman's gnarled knuckles. Confused, Donata raised her head slowly, her baleful milk-eyes searching Francesca's face. Francesca snatched the green napkin from Donata's hand and took over folding. "We'll never get done otherwise," she said sharply.

Mira folded napkins absently, ignoring Francesca's angry mutterings and watching Donata. The old woman stared wondrously at the backs of her hands, opening and closing them easily, *almost elegantly*, Mira thought. *Like a younger woman.* Donata looked up, sparse eyebrows stretched high, beseeching Mira for an explanation that Mira didn't have. She searched Mira's face wordlessly, though as always, Mira doubted that she saw her, the woman's eyes swimming in their murky pools. As she opened her mouth to speak, Mr. Falso stuck his head in the door.

"Sorry to bother you, ladies. But the kids at the front of the house need your help." He retreated quickly, almost desperately, and Francesca beelined after him. Mira tried to follow, the dish-room door slamming before her nose.

Mr. Falso didn't realize Francesca was on his heels until he stopped short. She crashed into his back, a face-plant into a patch of back sweat. She straightened herself out, undignified and doubly pissy.

"Whoa! I didn't know you were there!" Mr. Falso said.

Francesca threw her hair defiantly over one shoulder. "Can we talk?"

Mr. Falso backed away from Francesca with raised hands. "It's a tough time, don't you think? The last shift of patrons comes in five minutes, and we're way behind in the dish room."

"You said you're always available to talk, Nick." Francesca said his name like it was a swear, and it felt right. The director of the soup kitchen, a heavy-bottomed woman with a severe bob, walked past and looked them up and down.

Mr. Falso slipped his hands out of the plastic gloves, stuffed them in his apron pocket, and snapped off his hairnet. "Come with me," he said, leading her to the closet that housed brooms, mops, buckets, and trash barrels, along with bottles of disinfectants and cleaners meant to tidy after the perpetually unclean. Francesca breathed in the antiseptic smell. She thought of Saint Veronica Giuliani, whose confessor ordered her to clean the walls and floor of her prison cell with her tongue, swallowing the spiders and their webs. She thought of Angela of Foligno, who drank water contaminated by the putrefying flesh of a leper.

It helped her refocus.

"I wanted to thank you for bringing me here. It means so much to me to be able to toil for people who need it most."

Mr. Falso raised his eyebrows. "It's one of the most special parts of youth ministry, the experience of being in service to others."

"I want to devote my whole entire life to making restitution for the sins of others. By performing works of charity. Like this."

"The sins of others?"

"That's right."

"I see. Like Jesus, then?"

"Exactly."

"That's a . . . that's a noble undertaking. A *big* undertaking." He clapped his hands loudly in front of his waist. "Those plates must be piling up out there! Let's save this good talk for dinner at the restaurant. After the work is done."

"You haven't talked to me since you came to my bedroom that night."

Mr. Falso's head snapped to the dish room. He closed the door halfway and leaned in to Francesca. "At your father's request."

"My father requested your expert opinion. Now it's only fair that you share it with me."

Mr. Falso looked at Francesca sideways. "Only you know what happened."

"I know that I was filled with light and peace and satisfaction. It was incredible. And when it was done, I was more spent than if I'd run a marathon. Yet I wanted to experience it again and again."

It felt like what I think sex is supposed to feel like, she thought. *With you.*

Francesca wondered if she had spoken out loud, as Mr. Falso squeezed the back of his neck with one hand, his eyes sweeping the tiny room. Finally, he faltered, "It's beyond my scope."

"I heard you tell my father what you thought it was. I heard you call it an 'ecstasy.' "

"An ecstasy," he repeated, clamping his mouth in distaste.

"You can't tell me you didn't say it."

"Your father was looking for answers. I was postulating."

"You think I'm on the path to becoming a saint. Admit it!"

"I'm not going to 'admit' anything."

"How many sixteen-year-old girls bleed from their hands?"

The bobbed director gave a darting glance as she passed the utility room. Mr. Falso's face darkened. He popped his head to the side like a boxer.

"There are other things," she said breathlessly. "There have been for years. When I was five years old, I spoke in tongues. Do you know what that means? Ancient languages. Birds follow me. I've woken up every morning with the same birds at my window for sixteen years. You can ask my sister. Like Saint Francis of Assisi. It was documented on numerous occasions how the birds flocked to him, and landed on his arms and shoulders, singing sweetly all the while. This happens to me. I'm freaking Snow White!"

"Honestly, I don't know what you are," he huffed.

Francesca weaved slightly. His words echoed in her head, banging against the sides of her skull. She stepped backward, and her cheeks grew cold.

"Oh, Francesca." He reached out and held her shoulders, restraint flung away. "That didn't come out right. You are a beautiful girl with a beautiful heart. But I'm just a spiritual director in a church. I have my talents, but not the scholarly background, no expertise. Until you allow us to share what's happening to you with the true Catholic scholars, we can't begin to understand. Are you hearing me?"

"I p-prefer to keep it between us." She stammered, feeling an unraveling.

"I know you do. Let me see your hands." Francesca let him

take them. "May I?" He peeled off one bandage, then the other, to reveal pink marks. "You asked what I think?"

She nodded.

"I think last Thursday night I saw an overwrought girl faced with enormous pressures over the last few weeks. I think what I saw was those pressures coming to a head. I think—correction, I hope—that this strange, fluky, magical chapter in your life is coming to a close. And soon, you'll be able to get back to living life like a normal teenage girl. With much to look forward to."

Francesca turned to the side as if he'd smacked her across the jaw. "What do I need to do to prove to you I'm special?" she whispered.

Connie peeked around the half-open door. "We're getting super backed up. Are you coming soon? Oh, hey, cuz! What are you two talking about?"

Mr. Falso cupped Francesca on the shoulder. It was the same move she'd seen him do to a hundred guys. "We're chatting about developments in her life. Good developments." He dipped past Connie and disappeared through the door.

Connie shrugged and gave a dopey grin. "Hope I wasn't interrupting anything."

At that moment, Francesca hated Connie. More than her father when, as a child, she'd heard him call her schizophrenic when it was proven by a Biblical scholar that she spoke languages used during the time of Christ: Aramaic, Greek, Hebrew, and Latin. She hated Connie more than the neighborhood leeches, who treated her like an alien creature to ogle and wonder at. More than her mother, who left her too young and clueless as to how to deal with her gifts. Pain wormed through her chest, looking for a way out, but it was trapped there, nesting.

Francesca blasted from the utility closet and headed for the front door. A line of hungry people waited to get inside. Their stark differences made no sense to her: the mumbling man wrapped in a filthy blanket; the tidy family of four who could have lived in Francesca's neighborhood; the skinny girl in the bleached jean jacket licking her teeth. She felt their confusion that she was dressed to serve, yet leaving. Their eyes wandered all over her, not in a dirty way, but to wonder what could be so bad that she would leave a warm, dry place with food. She spun in circles, untying her apron and dashing it to the ground.

"You want to be fed?" she screamed. "*He* can feed you. I'm done!"

Francesca felt a papery hand on her arm and froze. She looked down at Donata. She had never seen the woman leave the tiny alcove where she folded napkins. It scared Francesca to see Donata mobile. And that she had come for her.

Donata's mouth moved, a web of spittle wavering. Francesca stooped to hear. The woman opened and closed her hand in front of Francesca's face.

"You fix," Donata said, a gleam in her frosted eyes.

PART 5

Lips

The day after the climb with Mr. Falso, Ben found Kyle at the quarry, sitting on the lip of the ledge, smiling dully. Every so often, a gust moved the wings of his hair, or he shifted, vertebral nubs snaking up and down his back.

Taking over the Cillos' ledge was a symbolic move. It came from a primeval place, something laced into the boys' DNA that made staking out the altar seem a noble thing. The stories had filtered beyond Bismuth, and kids from other towns started coming to the quarry even though it was off-season now, to check out the spot where the girls had jumped. When a pack of boys, maybe twelve or thirteen years old, came out of the clearing laughing, Piggy stood wordless and slapped his palm with the baseball bat he'd packed for the occasion. The encroachers looked at one another and moved away, to a lower, lamer ledge that barely fit them, and sulked.

Louis whispered to Ben. "Did Kulik get stoned while we weren't looking?"

Ben sat cross-legged on his towel. He had the jitters, a nervousness that had started the moment they chained their bikes behind Johnny's Foodmaster and begun the mostly silent hike. Besides Eddie, Ben hadn't seen any of them since the day he knocked Piggy unconscious. Their fight had become mythic: Piggy didn't remember, and no one was about to remind him that Ben Lattanzi, with his rack-of-bones chest and bulbous Adam's apple, had taken him down. The quarry did mind-erasing stuff like that, so you were never sure if something had actually happened or it was just one more quarry story.

But that wasn't the reason for his nerves. Ben had to make his case, and the guys weren't making it easy. Piggy, hungover and rank with beer, kept trying to nap, and now Louis was climbing down two ledges to talk to some younger girls he knew, only one of whom was a shade over plain.

Worst of all, Eddie had joined them at the last minute.

Piggy pointed his chin toward Eddie at the tip of the ledge getting ready to leap for the nth time. "And that one. That one's like a robot, jumping and climbing, jumping and climbing. He's making me tired just watching him."

Eddie leaped over and over. He had fixed a plastic bag over his hand with rubber bands and duct tape at the wrist, the bag blooming with condensation. Ben understood why Eddie punished his body: it was no different from Ben revisiting the places he had touched Mira. Their answers would be found in pain, and they welcomed it.

Piggy yawned. "This is boring. There's nothing to look at."

From the ledge below, the girls giggled at Louis.

"Anything worth looking at is dead," Piggy added.

Ben hooked his thumb toward where Eddie would momentarily rise. "You might tone it down a little."

"It's true. My eyes are actually bored. That's what Kyle's thinking. Right, Kyle?" Piggy said.

Kyle stared out over the water. The warm fall was finally turning, and so no one else dove but Eddie. The water was smoked glass. Rumors about hordes of gawkers hadn't proved exactly true: there were about half of the usual number of kids from whom to protect the altar rock from desecration, but that was a lot, given the season. Even they were subdued, their dull murmur broken by the periodic plunge of a sad boy.

"So, Benny, you got us here. Talk," Piggy said.

Louis reappeared from below wearing a guilty grin. Ben wouldn't have minded if Louis hadn't come, but there he was, along with Eddie, whom Ben would have to work around. Louis flashed a look toward Kyle before joining the rest. "Somebody decide to smoke and not share?"

"He's been spacey like that the whole time," Piggy explained, not bothering to hush on account of Kyle's bad ear. "Swear to God, between him and Michael Phelps over there, and then this one calling emergency meetings? I think the whole town's gone freaking nuts."

Louis shoved Piggy off his blanket and, after a scuffle, Piggy gave him a scrap to sit on. They fell silent as Eddie climbed up, positioned himself, and dove again.

Piggy lifted his watch, an old-man steel Timex wrapped around the meat of his hand. "I've been timing him. It takes one-point-six minutes to execute the dive, and eleven minutes to climb back up here. He'll start tiring soon, and with that bad hand, we can assume fifteen."

"You got fifteen minutes, Benvenuto," Louis said. "Make your case."

"I'm saying that something obviously drove the Cillo girls to become the way they became. Because it was sudden. Like, in a matter of months, they went from being sheltered but wanting a normal life to sheltering themselves and becoming shut-ins. That doesn't happen for no reason."

"I can tell you the day Francesca switched to granny panties," said Piggy.

"How would you know that?" asked Ben.

Piggy fell back on his towel and smiled behind his sunglasses. "I'm a detail man."

"He sat behind her in every class. Don't give him too much credit," said Louis.

Ben made a face, then looked at Piggy's watch. "How well do you guys know Frank Cillo?"

"As in Eddie's uncle? Jesus, Benny," Piggy said.

"There were no other guys in that house. No other guys to protect them. Eddie himself said his uncle was ready to lose it, with those girls hitting puberty at the same time." Ben's words didn't sound like he imagined, like some revelatory statement that everyone would be wowed by. They sounded seedy, and sick. Like they came from a diseased mind. He could hardly believe they were coming from his mouth. Then again, neither could he believe that he'd spent two hours excising a glued-down six-by-six-inch square of his bedroom carpet and the pad underneath before tucking Mira's notes inside and patching it up again.

"You think he smacked them around?" Piggy said.

"I'm asking what you guys think," Ben said.

"You're the one who was the closest to them. The only one who got anywhere close to—" Piggy said.

"Okay, okay," Ben interrupted.

"You if anyone should know," Piggy said.

"She shut me out, all right?" Ben realized he was yelling, but he didn't care. "She shut me out like she shut out every single one of you. She stopped talking to me at school, she stopped sneaking out and seeing me. She cut me off dry after Connie's wake, but you know something? Piggy was right: something happened in January that changed those girls, and I'm gonna find out what it was."

Kyle whistled, long and loud. The boys froze.

"That was a keeper, Eddie man," Kyle called.

Eddie climbed onto the ledge and turned away from them. He was boxy, a straight line from his sloped shoulders to his hips. With his cylindrical torso, he reminded Ben of the Tin Man. Steam coated the plastic bag that encased his hand, and water puddled at the bottom.

"Give the hand a rest, dude," Louis said.

Eddie flapped his arms at his sides, the bag slapping his hip. He pointed his feet and dove again.

Louis checked his own watch. "Fifteen minutes starting now. And by the looks of that bandage, this might be his last dive. Go!"

Ben began to speak, but Piggy cut him off. "I know the night the drapes closed and never opened again. It was January twenty-first."

The boys crowded Piggy's towel.

"I was on the top of the Winnebago with my Bushnells," Piggy started.

They made disgusted noises.

"Aw listen! It was Thursday night; it was what I did!" Piggy said.

"Fourteen minutes," Ben said.

"Don't judge. I have to watch the chicks in my father's bar 'dance' while I bust my butt busing tables. Can't talk to them, can't touch them. What else am I supposed to do?" Piggy said.

"I can suggest what else you might do," Louis said, grinning over his shoulder for Kyle's approval. A sulfurous crosswind kicked up Kyle's hair, along with the dying ferns that grew between the cracks.

"Anyways," Piggy said, rolling his eyes at Ben. "Something big was going down in the bedroom. They'd lit candles, red, yellow, and green ones, the kind with the webbing on the out-side that you light on the patio to keep away mosquitos?"

"Who cares what kind of candles they lit?" said Louis.

"Go on," said Ben.

"Point being, I could see everything. Right inside. The candles were set around the bed, even on the floor," said Piggy.

"Go on," said Louis, nudging Piggy's leg.

"Francesca was lying on the bed in a white nightgown. Nothing hot: long, prairie-like."

Louis made a scoffing noise.

"Even through the binoculars, I could tell she didn't look good," said Piggy.

"Because of the granny jammies?" Louis said.

"Nah, I don't mean like that. I meant, she didn't look healthy," said Piggy.

Ben shifted closer. "You mean, she was pale?"

Piggy held up his hand. "I'm getting to that. At first I thought she was sick. I even wondered if I should tell some-one, but then I'd have to explain how I saw."

"Good call," said Louis.

"Mira kneeled next to the bed, praying," said Piggy.

"Like an exorcism," said Louis.

"What was Francesca doing?" said Ben.

"That was the freakiest part. She was tossing her head back forth, and arching her back," Piggy said.

"It was an exorcism!" said Louis.

"It wasn't an exorcism, knuckle job. She had a big smile on her face. Whatever was going on"—Piggy paused for effect—"she was liking it."

Piggy and Louis smirked at each other. Five feet away, Kyle was still but for his hair moving in the breeze.

"Then Mira went to the window and stood there for what felt like hours, but it must have been less than a minute. Scared the crap out of me, if you want the truth. Then just like that, bam! She shuts the shade. Then she goes room to room, flicking off lights, and yanking down more shades and pulling drapes together round the whole house! Swear to God: after that night, they were always shut."

"He's right," Ben said quietly. "By February, the shades were always drawn."

"What time was it?" Ben said.

"After I got outta work. So late—one in the morning? Maybe one fifteen?" Piggy replied.

"Was Mr. Cillo's car there?" Ben said.

"'Course it was there. It was the middle of the night. But guess where it was before that?" Piggy grinned.

"His office?" Louis said.

"My dad's bar," Piggy said.

Ben stood and paced. "So you get home from the bar and you're jazzed so you go to peep at the Cillo girls 'cause you got something on your mind. How hard is it to imagine that

Mr. Cillo goes to your dad's bar, gets himself worked up, and goes home to that house? Who knows what happens."

Louis's face contorted, chiseled angles wrong. "What are you saying?"

Piggy stood, clenching and unclenching his fists. "Yeah, what are you sayin'?"

Ben stood, turning fast to face every boy. "I'm saying nothing. I'm saying the girls got weird, fast. I'm saying something happened to them *inside that house.*"

"Jesus, Ben," said Louis. "I wouldn't go there."

Piggy tore his hand through his hair. "Mr. Cillo and my father are friends. You can't libel the man."

"You mean slander. If you wrote 'Mr. Cillo was twiddling his daughters' in the newspaper, that would be libel," Louis said.

Piggy flicked Louis's temple.

"Does it matter?" Kyle called into the chasm.

The boys stared at Kyle's back. The cicadas had gone silent, and the air fell thick between them.

"I believe it matters," Ben said.

Kyle turned, his face in profile, hooked nose dipping down, lips curled up into a smile.

"If Mr. Cillo caused pain, enough pain to make his own daughters kill themselves?" Ben said. "I think something needs to be done."

"Done about what?" Eddie stood dripping behind them. He

had scaled up at a sharp angle and climbed up unseen from a skinny ledge behind.

Ben dropped his eyes; the others looked down and away. Kyle rose, shaking out his bones like an older man, tore his towel from the ground, and approached Eddie, whose square chest heaved from the climb. He handed him the towel. "We were saying something needs to be done about this place. It ought to be memorialized. It's sacred ground."

"You think so, huh?" Eddie panted. "I don't agree. I think it's crap."

"But it feels wrong for people to be getting their kicks out of this place," Ben rushed, hating himself for acting like they weren't talking about what they were talking about. "And we can't be here every day, like guards, can we?"

Eddie blotted his bad hand with the towel. The plastic bag was gone, and the bandages hung like the end of a soggy Q-tip. He dropped the towel to the ground and lined up for another dive. The sun broke violently through the haze and left them exposed; everyone but Eddie shaded their eyes and drew on baseball hats.

Eddie faced the water. "I suppose that depends on whether you guys feel like you owe them something or not."

Piggy waited for the splash before charging toward Ben, his finger pointed. "You know what we don't owe them? Dragging their father's good name through the mud. I don't want nothing to do with that. I'm outta here." Piggy scraped up his blanket, hooked his fingers inside the plastic loops on his personal six-pack, and headed for the clearing. Louis stood behind, working his lips like he was trying to swallow something bitter.

"Go ahead, say what you have to say," Ben said.

"Piggy's right. You've got to give up this idea. It's just"—Louis shook his head—"sick." He threw his pack on his back and stalked away.

Ben turned to face Kyle. "You leaving too?"

Kyle shook his shaggy head. "No place else I need to be." He swept up his towel from where Eddie had dropped it, returned to the tip, and spread it on the ground. He settled, facing out at the water, his long legs dangling over the side. He patted the towel beside him.

Ben eased himself down carefully next to Kyle, tucking his legs beneath him. The tip had never bothered Ben before; heights didn't get to Ben, though he never hung out for very long at the tip, always dove fast, like something was at his back (after the time Francesca followed him in, it was always like that). Clouds appeared and cast a black pall on the surface, and Ben shivered. Together they watched Eddie do a compact backstroke, the water around him swirling, melted crayon wax, purple and black.

Eddie's backstroke turned into a free-float. Kyle pointed. "You see that? He looks natural. Peaceful even."

Ben wanted to say there was nothing natural about diving over and over like a robot with a banged-up hand. Ben tried to look more closely. He thought maybe he could see Eddie's eyes, fixed on the sky, not slitted mean, like when he talked to Ben and the other boys on the ledge, but wide and searching, trying to find Connie among the clouds. For a second, Ben could tell himself that Eddie was fine, they were all fine.

"He does look peaceful," Ben said.

"Don't be fooled. There's nothing peaceful about him. He's in hell, dude."

Ben frowned. "Obviously. I was just saying."

"And he'll be in hell a lot longer if you keep calling his uncle Chester the Molester."

"But what if it's true?"

Kyle gazed at Eddie, floating on his back, his hand a white blur at his side. "Those girls did something incredibly stupid and dangerous. And they had a terrible accident. And from that, you get that their father was abusing them?"

"I'm saying something was so bad in that house those girls decided to creep off in the middle of the night to do something they had to know might get them killed."

Kyle made a scoffing noise.

"Think about it. Even if it was an accident—" said Ben.

"*Was* an accident?" Kyle said.

"Even if it was. You don't play fast and loose with your life like that unless you don't have much to live for," Ben said.

"How about the fact that their cousin keeled?" Kyle asked.

"People die." Ben waved to Eddie. "It happens. It doesn't mean you decide you don't want to live anymore either."

"You ever hear of depression?"

"This is different. I know their father had something to do with it."

"But you don't know what that something was."

Ben shifted and faced Kyle, sending shards of mica over the side and floating down to the water. "What else could be that bad?"

"Have you ever considered that we may never know?"

Ben clawed the ground, scraping for something to throw into the water, hard. The rock cut his fingers, and he wiped streaks of blood on his bathing suit, resentful. Usually Kyle was solid. He was close with Eddie, too, but their families' bad blood was like an invisible barrier that kept them from getting too close. Kyle had been Ben's protector, was the one he could count on to clock anyone who mentioned Coach Freck and Ben in the same sentence. Less so now, since Ben had gotten so big and his shame had faded, but he knew Kyle still had his back, if he needed him. Yet here he was, staying behind to give him a lesson.

"Maybe we won't know," Ben said finally, jamming his towel and a baseball hat hard into his nylon sack. "But if I could prove they were being abused, and if everyone knew they weren't crazy, or stupid, it would make a difference."

"It sure would." Kyle stood, waving his arms in a lazy X over his head down to Eddie. "It would cast a pox on Eddie, and his parents. But for the Cillo girls? They're gone. Least in the way you knew them. For them, it won't change anything."

Ben stood. "I gotta go. I got somewhere to be."

Kyle stood. "You do what you gotta do."

Ben walked down the side of the mountain through the sparse, ugly trees and rode his bike home. He'd never felt so alone in his life. Kyle-as-Yoda was right in line with his personality, but Ben didn't need his closest ally to be preachy right now. He needed him on his side. The whole world seemed to be turning against him, but maybe that was what happened when you spoke truth to power. Ben pulled into his driveway with a hard scrape, and instead of going into the shed, where he knew he'd find Mira's next note, he went directly into the house. It was time for him to stop screwing around. Mira had been trying to tell him what was happening to her and Francesca and he had missed it, had to have Mr. Falso point it out for him. But that wasn't the only reason he wasn't ready to go to the shed. He wasn't sure how much he could handle. So he went into the house, through the front door, because formality seemed to make sense at this moment.

Normally, he would never consider talking to his parents. Unless he wanted his mother to reacquire the twitch that forced her to tape down her eyelid to sleep. The list of nine-year-old baseball players uncovered in a footlocker in Coach Freck's basement, that included the words "B. Lattanzi: strawberry blond/dimples," was the first clue that Ben had been among the touched. It yoked Ben with an imaginary sandwich board printed with words like "twiddled" and "broken," and, worst of all, "special," because that had been Freck's word. His mother's tears evolved into a hypervigilance that would last seven years.

Ben could not bring his suspicion to his parents. It would hit too close to home.

He took the center stairs in three giant steps, ignoring his mother's calls from the kitchen asking if he wanted Vietnamese takeout. He was starving, but not for food. He ducked into his bedroom and hollered, "Pho, please!" as he locked his bedroom door and walked to the corner of his room. He strained to lift the end of the dresser. Something in his back popped, but he ignored it, shifting his weight into his thighs to lift the gleaming wooden hulk. Finally it budged. He dropped to his knees and peeled back the square of blue carpet, then the section of wood he had sawed with a tiny hacksaw. He slipped his fingers between the cracks and lifted the wood like a puzzle piece from the floor and set it aside.

The wad of notes felt heavy in his hand. Substantive, Real. He placed the rug back over the spot and lifted the bureau into place. His back did a painful, snaky thing as he sat leaning against the wall, holding the notes close to his face, trying to breathe in the scent of Mira, the hint of strawberry on her lips he remembered (or made up. He allowed for that). He wanted to reread Mira's notes, get his facts straight before he made the case to his parents that Mr. Cillo needed to be arrested.

As he read, every note took on new meaning. An

illumination. And when he overlaid the notes with Mira and Francesca's behaviors, it became clear. The pain was sharp. Ben felt the old anger swell up again. Didn't they always say that girls in these kinds of "situations" have intimacy issues? Mira with her push and pull, Mira with her erratic meet-ups, months apart, was classic abused. Mira who was obsessed with unlocking Ben's heart—and his own pain, she whispered once—was projecting what had happened to her onto what had happened to Ben.

An ugly thought surfaced. Was that what she saw in him? *Stuff it away. Stuff it away.*

If he could talk to his mother, she would agree. She saw twiddlers around every corner: mall Santas, school custodians, the dude that films every lacrosse practice but isn't related to any player. She might believe Ben, but telling could send her into lockdown mode. And Ben could not become a prisoner again. Not when things were finally close to normal. The dreams about the flattened nose and orange-peel skin, the dip-stained fingers had ended years ago.

He placed the notes facedown and closed his eyes, resolving not to say anything. He would handle it himself.

"Buddy, it's time we had a talk." Ben's father leaned in the doorway, holding the key to his bedroom between two fingers.

He covered the notes with his palm and froze. Ben knew

the key existed, but it had never been used. And by the look on his dad's face, his parents had been concerned about his behavior. Maybe even talked to Mr. Falso about it. Ben wondered what parts of yesterday's chat Mr. Falso would leave out.

"Yeah, Dad?"

"Mr. Falso is worried about you. And so am I." His father flicked on the light. "Why are you sitting on the floor?"

Ben hadn't noticed that the room had grown dark. Some part of his brain had heard the buzz of dinner conversation, his mother's and father's voices overlapping with Mr. Falso's. They had invited him to stay for dinner, and hadn't worked too hard when Ben had refused to come down, faking a stomachache. He was deep into his thoughts when the conversation had dipped, voices gone low so they wouldn't be heard upstairs.

"I must have fallen asleep." Ben raised his head off the wall. "Is Mr. Falso gone?"

"Yes, Ben. He left a few minutes ago. You must have had a pretty exhausting afternoon for you to fall asleep sitting up."

Behind his father, his mother appeared. Even from far away, Ben could see the smudged mascara under her eyes, and the vertical streaks in her makeup that meant she'd been crying.

"May we come in?" she said softly.

Ben nodded. They exchanged looks, each waiting their cue to say their line, as if they were staging a play for the first time and not sure of their blocking.

"You don't look comfortable," his father said. "Why don't you come off the floor?"

"I'm fine." His voice sounded small, he thought. Weak. He had the feeling he was going to be doing battle, and he didn't want to feel weak. What he needed was to feel Mira near him, to remind him to stick to his guns. He cleared his throat. "What were you guys talking about with Mr. Falso?"

His dad folded his hands and sat on the bed, easing into the role of good cop. Ben wished he'd thought to put his earbuds in, or spread some magazines out around him, or done something that didn't make him look so tragic, there on the floor. He drew his knees up and pulled them in tight, suddenly angry at Mr. Falso. He should have said something to him, like *let's keep this between us bros*. Ben exhaled hard and looked up. His mother was shattered, and his father was trying to hide how pissed off at him he was.

He was in trouble.

"That's what we're here to talk with you about, Benvenuto." His father never called him by his first name, given in honor of his uncle he'd never known, who'd died in a car crash in the eighties. All Ben knew was that it involved speeding on the expressway, probably booze, but mostly being reckless and sixteen, Ben's age now. "Mr. Falso is concerned about you. And so are we. Carla, do you want to begin?"

His mom scanned the room like she detected something different.

"Yeah, Mom?" Ben said. She was making him nervous, the way she kept staring at the pale indentations in the rug. Ben hadn't placed the bureau back exactly right. He wondered if she could see the seam where he'd made the cut in the rug. She'd have to be crawling on the floor to see it, Ben told himself.

Still.

"Mr. Falso said you were talking about the Cillo sisters, next door," she said finally.

"Not the ones down the street? You mean the ones right next door? I want to make sure we're talking about the same Cillo sisters," Ben said.

"This is not a time for sarcasm," his dad said.

"The ones I've known my whole life? Those are the ones you mean, right?"

"Ben," his mom whispered.

"Because they're the ones who are dead. You know that, right?"

"You're upset. But that does not give you the right to be disrespectful to your mother."

"I want to make sure we're talking about the same girls."

His mom sank to the edge of the bed and trailed her hand along the crumpled sheet, smoothing it.

His father planted his legs wide. "This conversation is not about what your mother and I did or did not do right in your mind. This is about what you told Mr. Falso."

"Aren't I supposed to talk with Mr. Falso about stuff? Isn't it his job to listen?"

His dad folded and refolded his soft hands. "We know you think Frank Cillo is to blame for Francesca and Mira's accident."

Ben's eyes popped.

"We understand why you are looking for answers," his dad said. "But you're going down the wrong path."

"A bad path," his mom said.

His dad raised his palm in the air toward his mom, a now-slow-down move meant to gain Ben's trust. "Why don't you tell us in your words what you think Mr. Cillo did."

Ben squirmed. This was worse than he'd imagined. Mr. Falso had mixed things up. Or maybe Ben was the one who came to the conclusion? What exactly had Mr. Falso said?

He picked a spot on the rug and stared at it. "If he told you, why do I need to tell you?"

His parents stood together. "Honey, Mr. Falso is concerned that you aren't thinking clearly. He said you think Mr. Cillo drove the girls to take their own lives because he was abusing them. That's a very strong accusation. How did you come to this conclusion?"

"How did *I* come to this conclusion?" Ben yelled, aghast.

"You must have some evidence," his dad said.

"What, like I *saw* him?" Ben said, shifting on the floor.

"For starters!" his dad shouted.

"Paul!" his mother said, looking at the window.

"What, are you afraid he can hear us? The window's closed, Mom."

"Why don't you try to treat your mother with more respect?" his father said.

Ben scrambled to his feet. "Why don't you say what you really mean? That I'm making things between you and Mr. Cillo even more awkward. That you don't want any more ugliness between you and a man who might have twiddled his daughters so much they went crazy and decided it was better to die than live in that house!" Ben pointed out the window.

"That is not what this is about!" his mother said. "We simply asked you what evidence you had to make the accusation. And you still haven't answered us."

Ben stuck his palms over his eyelids and dragged his hands down over his face. He wanted to say *Mr. Falso told me*, but even if they did believe him, that wasn't exactly the truth, was it?

"She told me," he said softly.

His mother approached him. "She who, Ben?"

"Yes, she who, Ben? Because if you think we're asking too many questions, you can't imagine what it will be like when you get grilled by the police, most of whom are related to or indebted to Frank Cillo," his dad said.

His mother looked over her shoulder in horror. "Paul! This is not what we agreed to."

"Yeah, Dad," Ben said. "Why are you so afraid of Mr. Cillo anyway?"

For a second, Ben thought his father might slap him. Instead, he turned his back to them and placed his hands behind his head, elbows pointing out at both sides. "Who told you they were being abused?" he said quietly.

"Mira told me." Ben closed his eyes, not to shut out the horror on their faces, but to envision the words, her words, their sweet girly curlicues belying their meaning. *She makes excuses, says he can't help himself. Only I know better.* He couldn't repeat Mira's words: he'd have to show them the note, and then he'd have to show them all of the notes. He had looked up "signs and symptoms of sexual abuse," and it was like he was reading about the Cillo girls in those last few months of their lives. He threw open the desk drawer, grabbing a sheaf of computer printouts. "Gradual and/or sudden withdrawal or isolation? Check! Change or loss of appetite? They had clothes hanging off their bodies! Check! Speaking of which, wearing many layers of clothing? Check! Francesca looked like a bag lady at the end!"

"What is that?" his dad said.

His mom grabbed the piece of paper from Ben's hand. "Signs and symptoms of child sexual abuse."

"Cruelty to pets? Everyone says Mira killed her kitten! That's a big fat check!" Ben said.

"The Cillos are a tight family with connections all over this town. Why wouldn't Mira tell anyone but you?" his dad said.

Ben snatched the paper back and read, line by line. "Sexual predators use dominance, fear, manipulation . . ."

"Ben," his mom said softly.

"Seductive behavior? Uh, skip that one. Unhealthy/odd attachment to an older person? That would be Daddy! Check!" Ben cried.

"Those girls *loved* their father," his mom said.

"Brainwashing!" Ben screamed, pointing at the page. "Look, it says right here: sexual predators brainwash their victims into thinking they're doing it because they're special, and they love them!"

"Ben," his dad said.

"Anxiety, mood swings, eating disorders—"

"Ben," his mom said.

"Sudden changes in behavior! Excessive paranoia? Delinquent behavior? Always acting like you have something to prove! This one time, at the quarry—"

"You could be describing yourself!" his mom shouted.

Ben swung around. "What?"

His dad stepped forward. "You gave Steven Pignataro a concussion. Mr. Falso said you seemed afraid he was going to drop you at Little Q."

"Acting like you have something to prove," his mom whispered.

"What are you saying? Are you saying I'm projecting what happened to me?" Ben smeared the back of his hand across his eyes. He hadn't realized he was crying.

"Now, Ben. We're not saying *that*. That chapter is over." Her face contracted and hardened. "Closed."

"What your mother is saying is that those descriptions could apply to anyone going through some kind of trauma." His dad's shoulders jerked. He looked as though he might run from the room. "Your mother and I are making an appointment for you to see someone tomorrow. In the meantime, there are medicines you can take to help you sleep and make you feel less anxious."

"Drugs!" Ben laughed hysterically. "My parents, of all people, want to put me on drugs?"

"Lots of people get anxious or depressed when someone they loved dies. It's not cowardly to admit that you need help," his mom said.

"So you want me like Mrs. Villela at Connie's funeral? Whacked-out and spacey, so I don't have to feel anything?" Ben said, tears streaming down his face. "So I can forget what I know?"

His mom wrapped her arms around Ben in an awkward tent-hug. "No one is asking you to forget Mira Cillo."

Ben broke away and charged to the corner of his room. "You're asking me to abandon her."

"You're not abandoning her by trying to get back on track and live your life," his dad said.

If that was what she wanted, she wouldn't have given me the notes, Ben wanted to say. He caught his parents locking eyes. A familiar sense came over him. He'd been here before, come up against their tag-team interrogation. The logic and strategy that kept him off balance, that seven years before had got him to say what they'd never wanted to hear.

A sullen resolve rose in Ben. He took a deep breath and looked each of his parents in the eye. This time he'd give them the answer they wanted.

He dropped his hands at his sides. "I'll do whatever it takes," he said.

His mom descended upon Ben, drawing him from the corner to the middle of the room, where his dad joined them, fluffing his hair like a dog. Ben allowed his mom to squeeze him while he stared over her head, out into the night at Francesca and Mira's bedroom window. Their reflection bounced back, a fractured slurry of streetlight and aluminum siding and something shadowy inside that Ben could not see.

Ben had to wait until their bedroom murmurs subsided and they were both asleep for a full three hours before slipping from his room and tiptoeing down the stairs and out the slider, through the backyard and into the shed.

The smells of WD-40, loam, and musty metal were un-changed. The streetlights seeped into the long cracks where the walls met, same as the night Mira and Ben had met alone. Ben scanned the shelves and saw hammers hanging upside down from hooks. Rakes and hoes leaned in corners. Tackle boxes full of things that stuck. No note.

It had been around the same time as now: past two in the morning. They'd agreed at school to sneak out when Ben ran a flashlight beam over Mira's window. It was early November, so not only could they not go far, they ran the risk of freezing to death. Mira with a chilly red nose, parka zipped beneath her chin and over her pajamas, doing a hopping dance, stripes of bright hair blown across her face. He'd pulled her by the wrist, both of them laughing too loud, into the shed, their breaths blooming between them. Ben had lifted his father's heavy plaid work shirt from its nail and slipped it over her arms for another layer. Ben's goal that night was to kiss Mira: he couldn't wait any longer, and was convinced she'd been disap-pointed that he hadn't tried in Falso's bedroom. When Mira fi-nally stopped laughing, he tipped her chin and leaned in to kiss her, lightly, and lips-only. Her mouth was hot when everything else was cold, and Ben wanted to get farther inside and probe where the heat was coming from. More and more, he found himself thinking about the insides of Mira, healthy, pink organs and long, smooth muscle wall. The parts of Mira no one saw, whose actions were involuntary and unguarded. He imagined glistening blood cells, villi waving like sea anemone, velvety mucosa. Turn Mira inside out, smear his hands inside.

Lust and urgency made him bold. He nuzzled Mira's ear, the only part he could get inside.

"Don't you want to kiss me?" he murmured.

Mira's eyes widened in her solemn face. "You can't imagine the things I want to do."

Ben read that as he wanted. The shed was too cramped for the real deal, but there was plenty they could manage. He needed to convince Mira that it was okay, to make his case. He reached for Mira's mittened hand and tugged it bare, then thrust it inside his jacket, through the gaps in his shirt against his thudding heart.

"Feel it," Ben said, remembering Mira's words. "Don't you know what's in my soul yet?"

"It's not what's in your soul. It's what's in mine." Mira pulled him down to the dirt floor, heart racing, and they kissed in every way. He, baby kisses across the whole of her mouth. She, tugging his upper lip with her teeth. He, tracing her lips with his fingertips. She, grabbing the back of his head hard with her hand and pulling him in, then planting a kiss that left him breathless. He, kissing her fast then pulling away, in a game of keep-away.

The last one was too much for both of them. Mira rose up and wrapped her legs around Ben's waist. She leaned in close to his ear. Ben groaned: this was it.

"I have to get back before Francesca sees I'm gone," she rasped.

And with that she left, sawdust rising where she had kneeled. The shed door swung shut. Ben stayed unmoving for fear of shattering the memory, or for shock. At some point, his eyes fell shut, and when he awoke in the frigid morning light, an ache hung in his chest, worse than his frozen feet. His father's shirt was tented over him.

Ben felt for his father's shirt now and shrugged it on. The stiff flannel lined with down smelled of gasoline and moth-balls. Ben tucked his fingers in the chest pocket. The hard edge of Mira's note met his fingertips.

He opened it under a crack of light along the wall.

Francesca's lips are so dry. Daddy says he will force
her to eat and drink from a tube in her stomach if she
doesn't stop her protest.

For the first time, Ben found himself sorry for Francesca. She had done everything in her power to fight what her father was doing to her, including wasting away. He remembered how gaunt Francesca had looked toward the end, especially after Connie had died, but even before. Here he was, thinking this was a simple crush. He felt anger stir deep, the kind he felt for Mr. Cillo, the kind that might turn into a new hate for Mr. Falso, and for his own father, for trying to drug him to keep him impotent. He wondered if he was always going to hate old men.

Ben stepped out of the shed and looked up at the night sky. It wasn't black; night skies were never black in Bismuth. The all-night artificial lights from the gas stations and the strip malls and the high-rises washed out the starlight. So much light flooded the sky that the electrical was constantly going out, superfluorescence jamming the power grid. In that moment, he knew Mira was not there, not in a heaven where she could look down and judge him for action or inaction. She was fire and heat, too volatile and angry to be exiled in some peaceful cloudy otherworld. Mira was beside him, in his ears and mouth and inhalations and exhalations, down his shirt collar and under his skin. Urging him to do something. Those notes were written to make him hold Mr. Cillo accountable. He breathed deeply, smelling a sweet thread of woodsmoke, and for him it was the smell of Mira, and he let it fill him. He closed his eyes and searched for something brave inside.

When Ben opened his eyes, he was staring into the dark holes of the Cillos' windows, and he knew where he needed to go.

FEBRUARY 2016

If Mr. Falso had leaked Francesca's news to Father Ernesto, he didn't let on.

The near-deaf priest was happy to visit the girls, Francesca especially. The oldest daughter of Frank Cillo was his favorite: smart, levelheaded, and actually interested in Christian doctrine. She had so many questions he hardly knew where to begin. A good place seemed to be the pan of lasagna she set down in front of him.

The elderly priest tucked a napkin into his shirt. "Why don't you slice into that delicious-looking dish and I'll do my best to answer your questions."

"Ragù, béchamel, and Parmigiano-Reggiano," Francesca said, elbow sawing as she sliced the lasagna into a grid. "You won't find any ricotta in here." She set a plate down in front of him.

He raised a jelly glass of port wine. "To your mother, then."

Francesca's pride bristled. She played with her food, biting back the urge to tell him she'd taught herself to make authentic bolognese lasagna. There would have been no reason to invite the old priest over if Donata hadn't died. The old napkin-folder hadn't shown up at the food pantry for three days before her downstairs neighbor smelled her. Francesca had an actual healing right in the palm of her hand, to show Mr. Falso, and to make him love her. Now she was stuck pumping an old priest for strategy.

She raised a glass of water. "To my mother. Who taught us to cook at an early age. The right way."

"She had priorities. The right ones." Father Ernesto lowered his head and shoveled the lasagna into his mouth. "I've said it for years, and I'll say it again. You girls are a testament to your mother and your father." Smacking noises were followed by grunts. "When did you say your father was coming home?"

Francesca stole a look at Mira, who placed a carafe of sweet wine in front of the priest and sat. There was no answer to his question, since Thursday was the night Daddy stopped at Big Steven's Gentlemen's Club. The latest routine involved him checking in by phone every hour. He'd say he was working late in his office, but his office didn't have men shouting and cheesy pop music in the background. The girls knew for sure after Francesca followed him one night. For Francesca, it was a puzzle that she needed to put together: how could her father, who never left them alone, suddenly leave them alone? After Francesca reported back to her sister, they never discussed it again. Sometimes, his hourly calls were handled in rotation, with one sister lying about the whereabouts of the other. Other times, it gave them reason to behave even more piously, superior and secure in the knowledge that they were the ones being good.

What Francesca did not know was that Mira shadowed their father. The compulsion was no different from her other unacceptable urges—to pinch the nose of a newborn baby, scream the C-word in silent study hall, flash her breasts at the priest across the table. Watching her beloved father degrade himself by paying for a lap dance was just another impulse that grew in the crowded corners of Mira's brain. More and more,

Mira gave in. More and more, she heard her mother's voice telling her to silence them.

Francesca raised her voice, and Mira jumped.

"Don't you remember, Father Ernesto?" Francesca over-enunciated. "I said our father won't be home tonight at all."

"In the fall?"

"Not in the fall. At all. Daddy's working late."

The priest dragged a napkin over his lips. At eighty-five, with his health declining, he seemed to fear every meal might be his last. He smiled mildly at the girls, having given up on the question, or having lost the thought entirely. Sometimes, he called them by each other's names.

The phone trilled. The girls stared out over their plates. Mira snapped to first, smiling sweetly as she pushed her chair from the table. In the kitchen, she forced a cheery voice, loud enough to drown out Father Ernesto's voice, whose volume increased in proportion to his difficulty hearing. On the phone, their father was quick, ending his verbal bed check before the girls heard too much background noise and deduced Thursday nights at the office involved Manhattans and using a lint roller in the car to remove stripper dust from his suit jacket.

Father Ernesto pointed a shaky fork at the ruffled ridge of Francesca's lasagna. "Remarkable! I wish you'd eat something."

Francesca cleared her throat. "About the saints, Father. The path to sainthood?"

"Hmm?"

"The path to proving someone is a Catholic saint."

"Oh yes." He pointed the fork at her. "Canonization."

Francesca considered the word. It sounded regal, like *coronation*.

He jammed a forkful of lasagna into his mouth and felt around his lap. Francesca handed him her napkin.

"Canonization?"

"Oh yes. A lengthy process. Can take decades, sometimes centuries to complete. Doesn't happen overnight."

Mira returned to the dining room and slipped into her seat. "What did I miss?"

Father Ernesto dabbed pearls of perspiration from his forehead with the napkin. "You girls are very slender. And you've hardly touched your plates! Are you trying to tell me your father's going to eat that leftover lasagna by himself? How is your father?"

Francesca set her glass down hard. The priest's head bobbed, startled. His eyes glittered, wet and wary, as he looked sideways at Francesca, who said, "You were about to tell us about the process of canonization."

Mira's voice pitched high. "Daddy's great. He's such a workaholic; he was so sorry he had to work late tonight and miss you. But really, this dinner was our idea. You have so many fascinating stories, Father. About the saints, for example."

"Oh, yes! The saint stories. I'm surprised you girls are interested in the lives of saints. Their stories can be shocking."

He took a long draft from his glass. When he set it down, Mira refilled it. "It's hard to understand how they could do such terrible things to their bodies in the name of God."

"Terrible things to their bodies?" said Mira.

"Purification rituals, starvation. Exposing themselves to leprosy," he said.

"I thought those were stories," said Mira.

"And then, the things that were done to them! Relentless persecution, by the Diocletians, then the Romans. Saint Tatiana, thrown into the lion cage at the zoo. Saint Agatha— oh. Never mind."

"Tell us how to prove that someone is a saint, Father," said Francesca.

The priest settled back into his seat. "I understand. You don't want to talk about the gory deeds. I don't blame you. But I believe that's a mistake. You have to accept saints for what they are, even when the stories of their lives repel you. Separate the horror from the faith system that drove the desperate acts—"

"The pope!"

Father Ernesto drew himself up and looked stiffly over his shoulder. "I'm sorry?"

"The pope. What does the pope say about the path to sainthood?"

"Oh, that's an easy one. Papal ruling says the path to

sainthood involves either of two steps: successful completion of a miracle, or martyrdom."

Mira's hand flew to her chest. "Martyrdom?"

"Oh sure!" He leaned back over his plate and resumed eating. "Sacrificing your life for your faith in God. Very big in the thirteenth and fourteenth centuries. You don't see it so much anymore, I suppose. Miracles, though. Those are another thing entirely."

"How do you know if a miracle really is a miracle? Say a person was . . . lame, for example. And the saint put his or her hands on them, by accident, even. And the lame person could suddenly walk again?" Francesca asked.

"Miracles having to do with healing are hard to prove. The wheels of canonization grind slowly. To examine claims, the Church looks at hundreds, sometimes thousands of pieces of evidence. There's no rubber stamp that says 'Saint.' The evidence must be incontrovertible. The situation or illness doesn't have to be terminal or even dramatic. The cure simply has to be rapid, complete, and utterly inexplicable by ordinary means."

"What do they do, exactly?" Mira said.

"First the original doctors who treated the sick person are interviewed by the Church. Then outside medical experts are hired to independently examine the records. Nothing is left to chance. Mother Teresa herself had to wait nineteen years after she died for them to prove she cured a woman of stomach cancer. And you'd think she would have been a shoo-in," he said, winking.

Francesca ignored his wink. "You're saying healings are considered suspect until proven otherwise?"

"That's it. You see, the problem is, you've got these charlatans we call 'faith healers' mucking things up. Now there's a win-win! They heal someone, they get credit. They don't heal someone, they get to say that person didn't believe hard enough in God."

"It sounds hopeless," Mira said. Francesca looked at her sharply.

"Unless . . . ," said the priest.

Francesca's head snapped. "Unless?"

"We stop trying so hard to prove miracles, and accept them as the wondrous things that they are," he said, gazing mildly at the ceiling.

Francesca's head dropped. Father Ernesto shook his jowls. "Wait; that's not what I was going to say at all." He laughed softly. "I fade sometimes. The train of thought derails. What I was going to say was, it's much easier to prove a resurrection."

"A resurrection? From the dead?" Francesca nearly shouted.

"More than four hundred instances of saints resurrecting people from the dead have been recorded and verified. Saint John Capistrano, Saint Ignatius of Loyola, Saint Paul of the Cross. Saint Philip Neri, Saint Francis of Paola, Saint Peter of Alcantara. Saint Dominic! Saint John Bosco. Saint Joseph of

Cupertino. Saint Bernardine of Siena, Saint Agnes of Montepulciano. Blessed James Salomoni . . ."

Francesca pawed at the table blindly, as though reaching for a pen.

"Saint Rose of Lima. Blessed Constantius of Fabriano *and* Blessed Mark of Modena . . ."

Mira tried to catch Francesca's eyes, but they were ping-ponging around the room.

"Saint Padre Pio, Saint Charbel Makhlouf, Saint Francis Xavier, Saint Francis Jerome, Saint James of Tarentaise, Saint Cyril of Constantinople, Saint Felix of Cantalice, Saint Bernard of Abbeville, Saint Gerard Majella, Saint Francis Solanus, Saint Hyacinth, Blessed Sebastian of Aparicio, Saint Martin de Porres, Saint Peregrine, Saint John Francis Regis, Saint Philip Benizi, Saint Pacific of San Severino, Saint Stanislaus of Cracow, Mariana de Jesus of Quito, Saint Louis Bertrand, Saint Margaret of Cortona, Saint Andrew Bobola, Saint Rose of Viterbo, and of course, Saint Patrick, the Apostle of Ireland. To name a few." He chuckled. "I guess my memory is better in some areas than others."

Francesca whistled.

"And Saint Vincent Ferrer! How could I forget Saint Vincent Ferrer? Did you know he marched right into a synagogue and converted ten thousand Jews to Christianity? And that was before he raised a dead man."

"I did not know that," Mira said.

Francesca stood. "The lasagna is dry."

Father Ernesto held both sides of his plate, like a child about to have his food taken away. "It's perfect, dear."

"Coffee, then. You need coffee. I'll get it. Is instant okay? That's what Daddy likes, so it's what we've got. Mira, can you help me in the kitchen?"

Mira smiled apologetically at Father Ernesto. "Do you mind sitting here by yourself?"

"I don't mind, but I'm not quite ready for coffee, I'm afraid. I'm still working on my lasagna." His head dropped sadly over his plate. "Though I think it's gone cold."

"Let me heat it for you!" Mira gently tugged the plate from the old man's hands. "Don't worry. I'll be back in a sec."

Mira backed into the kitchen and swung around.

Francesca was pacing back and forth. "Think," she said, spinning on one foot. "Help me think."

"About what?"

"About what else to do. We'll never be able to prove to Mr. Falso that what happened in the soup kitchen was a miracle now that Donata is dead. Besides, she's already been cremated. I made calls."

Mira braced herself. Slowly, she set the plate in the microwave and reached for the instant coffee and a mug from the pantry shelf. "Then what are you thinking?" She moved to the gas stove.

"You heard Father Ernesto. My other choice is martyrdom. To die, Mira. For my beliefs. Or else I have to be able to perform a second, confirmable miracle."

Mira tucked her lip. In times like this it was best to stay quiet and listen to everything Francesca had to say. She turned the gas to medium.

Tick tick tick tick tick.

"Dramatic. Incontrovertible. Undisprovable," Francesca said, pacing.

The burner wouldn't light. Mira removed the teakettle to a different burner and lifted the metal grate, then the burner cap.

Francesca stopped short. "I have to raise someone from the dead."

Mira looked up, holding the cap aloft, back still turned. "How would you find someone who's died?" she asked slowly.

"I missed my chance with Donata. It would have to be a recent death." Francesca started pacing again. "A hospital, maybe. God, that would be impossible." She stopped and whispered a prayer into her hands for taking the Lord's name in vain. The pacing started again. "The VA hospital in Jamaica Plain is supposed to be kind of sketchy. Or the nursing home on Union Street! I bet that's easy to break into."

Mira set the cap down onto the burner port and turned the knob. *Tick tick tick tick tick.* The gas smell bloomed.

Francesca covered her ears with her hands and stomped.

"Oh, dear Lord. Think, think! I have the power, I know I have the power. I just have to show *him*. But how do I find someone who died?"

Tick tick tick tick tick. Mira willed the blue flame to appear.

"Who do we know that's close to dying? Nana Pignataro? She's at least ninety-eight. Maybe I could start going over there to help with chores. Keep tabs on her. But what if she wanted to die? I mean, how much fun can it be to keep living when you're ninety-eight and your friends and kids are dead and you've got a hump in your back? No. This has to be a miracle worth doing. A tragedy that someone has died. And a spectacular miracle that they've been brought back to life. Like a kid—"

"Don't dry out that macaroni now! That would be a crime!" Father Ernesto called from the dining room.

"—but I don't know any kids. Or kids about to die. I don't even know any kids who take unusual risks. Unless you count Kamil Kulik and his heroin habit, and no one would want him back from the dead if he OD'd. It's hopeless!"

Gas fumed thick. "Nothing's hopeless," Mira said brightly. "There has to be a way to make this a win-win for you and for some . . . deserving . . . person. Someone you can save who needs saving. It might be a matter of waiting for the right moment, but when it comes, you'll know it and be able to act. Then everyone will know. And he'll know."

"Girls?"

"I wait until someone has an accident and hope that I happen to be there?" Francesca said. "That's insane."

"Not really. Think about it. The potential for accidental death is all around us." Mira glided to the drawer and removed a matchbox. "The quarry is incredibly dangerous. Someone dies diving there every summer. I hear Steven Pignataro is into huffing these days; maybe he'll go too far, and he's right across the street. Then there's a whole host of kids in school who have EpiPens because they're deathly allergic to peanuts. A guy eats a peanut butter sandwich and kisses a girl in the cafeteria: it could be deadly. And you could be right there." Mira lit a match and touched it to the holes in the center of the burner. The burner lit in a neat ring. Mira turned and smiled. "Your gift would be proven in front of hundreds of witnesses."

Francesca grunted. She froze at the kitchen window and crossed her arms, hooking her index finger around her chapped top lip.

"The weak and vulnerable are everywhere. You just have to find them." Mira licked her finger and drew it through the flame. It tingled, but it didn't hurt.

Francesca parted the checked curtain and gazed out over the Pignataros' cape to the shingled wedge of the Villelas' rooftop. "Or I can create my own miracles," she said.

Mira turned the knob until the flames reached high: blue,

red, orange, white. If their house exploded, and they were consumed in an airless blaze and returned to ashes, it would be terrible, but it would also be quiet. The urges that tugged and bit at Mira would be evaporated.

Silence could be a wondrous thing too, Mira thought. Her mother would agree.

PART 6

Throat

Ben dropped his bike to the grass and shoved his hand in his front pocket, feeling for the mushroom-shaped bottle as he walked toward the brick buildings and grounds office. The pills were supposed to take the edge off. Ben shook the bottle as he walked. He liked how it reminded him of the wormy Mexican jumping beans he used to play with as a little kid. It was easier to tell himself the bottles were toys than the truth: that the pills were his insurance, in case he couldn't handle being there.

Nobody understood why Kyle wanted to work in a cemetery, especially *that* cemetery. Never mind that it was the kind of job described as "semi-skilled," where your coworkers might be prison inmates. Kyle was smarter than most people knew. He'd managed to complete the EMT course nights and weekends in the required eighteen months, though he lasted at the job less than one whole summer. Kyle said his new job was easy. All you needed were a strong back, a little knowledge of hand tools (read: shovels), and the ability to compartmentalize, with grief crowding you every day.

Also, it gave him lots of unsupervised time outdoors to smoke weed.

Ben peered into the window of an office hut. Seeing it empty, he turned to look for a sign of Kyle. As far as cemeteries went, this one was a nice place to land. It was the size of two football fields and framed by the Blue Hills, which meant some graves had views (though Ben couldn't figure why this mattered to someone six feet under). It was considered fancy by most folks in Bismuth in the same way the boat club was considered fancy, but wasn't. Ben had overheard his friends' parents talking about it at the Villelas' house after Connie's wake. Mr. Cillo had pulled strings to get Connie in there, and to get the girls in four months later. You had to be a decorated vet or a Kennedy or Frank Cillo to get that kind of real estate, they joked.

An engine roared. Ben shaded his eyes toward Kyle driving a banged-up golf cart straight for him, then jamming on the brake just short of Ben's toes. Kyle swung himself out of the cart and peeled off canvas gloves, tucking them in the back pocket of his shorts. Dirt crusted over his bare knees. He slipped a cigarette pack from his front pocket and tapped one out, flicking a retro, chunky metal Zippo and lighting the stick under his cupped hand, protecting it from an imaginary draft.

Ben eyed the lighter glinting in the morning sun. "They let you smoke on the job?"

Kyle blew a shot of smoke. "Anything that keeps the nerves tamped down is acceptable. Long as you're not near sobbing guests."

"Guests?"

"Family members of the recently departed."

"You got the lingo down."

Kyle eyed Ben's fist. "Whatcha got there?"

"Oh, this?" Ben held the bottle out. "Something some doctor wants me to take."

"Most prescriptions are. What is it?"

Ben held the bottle at a distance and read as if for the first time. "Ser-tra-line."

"You mean Zoloft."

"I do?"

Kyle took a long, slow drag and blew the smoke out even slower. "Yep."

"Right." Ben stuffed it in his pants, where it made a bulge. "So, you like your new job?"

Kyle looked over his shoulder toward the office. "If you rode your bike from Powder Neck for small talk, we can hang here. But if you're here for a medicinal consult"—he pointed to the bulge—"we ought to move on."

Ben tipped his chin at the golf cart. "In that thing?"

"Hell, yeah." Kyle mashed the cigarette on the cement with his boot, then peeled it off the ground and tucked it in his back pocket. He smiled. "Some poor sucker's gotta keep this place clean, you know."

Ben swung himself onto the cracked cart seat. "I think I know the guy. Real loser."

Kyle laughed as he slipped in next to Ben and turned the key. The ancient cart lurched into drive and they putted over the hill. Ben was grateful the motor was too loud to talk over. He surveyed the neat lines of graves on his left, realizing he had no idea where exactly the Cillo plot was, since the interment of their ashes had been private. Ben turned that off in his mind. Now even Mr. Cillo's quiet burial of his daughters seemed suspect.

"How do you tell your way around this place?" Ben blurted, wishing his brain would stop chattering. "It all looks the same."

Kyle squinted, one hand on the wheel, his hair catching wind. "You figure it out pretty quick. See that white thingy that looks like a Greek temple? That's a whole family in there, the Neros. That's the west side. It's called a mausoleum, by the way."

"Good to know."

Kyle pointed off to the right. "Those granite tablets flat on the ground? You know what those are?"

"Graves of people whose relatives were too cheap to buy regular headstones?"

"Cremorials. Memorials for people who were cremated. Cremation, memorials. Get it?"

"I get it." *People or sisters,* Ben thought.

"Most of the cremorials are on the east side, with the Blue Hills in the background, see?" Kyle said, rubbernecking. "Those plots get the best views."

"Dead people prefer nice views?"

"Their loved ones do."

"Loved ones. Nice."

"The main gate is south. North is the only other way. If you get lost, you look for the hills."

"You really seem to be fitting in here. Where are the other people?"

Kyle wrenched down the high brake pedal next to a granite bench. "We're surrounded by people, dude."

Ben stung. To think that Kyle had become indoctrinated into this ultrasensitive new cemetery world, where Corpses Are People Too.

"Where are the guys you work with? I mean, I assume they're guys, right?"

"It's a big place. Not much natural interaction. No water cooler to stand around and chitchat." Kyle hopped from the cart and took an expansive breath, as if the air was cleaner here.

Ben sat down hard on the granite bench. "Is it lonely?"

Kyle smiled. "Not so much."

The bottle dug into the crease of Ben's leg. "Good. That's good. I'm glad."

"So. Last time I saw you, you had some anger issues. Those worked out?"

Ben dug his toe into the ground, remembering how good Piggy's cheek had felt under his knuckles. "My parents don't think so. Thus . . ." Ben gestured loosely at his hip.

"Zoloft's serious stuff. You taking it?"

"Nah, not yet. I mean, I'm not sure I will. I don't want to be relaxed, if that makes any sense."

Kyle threw his gloves on the cart and collapsed onto the grass, hands behind his head. With his rangy legs sprawled and his work boots flopping to the sides, he looked peaceful. It was a pretty spot, Ben realized. Nicest grass he'd ever seen, even late in the season, the lush blades tight, like a cushion. He imagined Kyle came here a lot, to smoke and to think. It seemed nice. For a moment, Ben let himself forget about what Mira was trying to tell him, what she wanted him to do. He swung his feet onto the bench and lay back, knees folded upward, the granite cold through the back of his too-thin jacket, taking in the wide blue expanse. He was surprised at how chill a cemetery could be.

Ben eased into the silence. "See, Kyle. I got a job to do. And it's hard to get work done when you're . . . unfocused."

"And a little high."

"Exactly."

"Except I don't imagine it takes much concentration to operate the hot dog rotisserie at the boat club snack bar." Kyle sat up on one elbow. "What kind of work are we really talking about, Benny?"

Ben stared hard at the sky. "I know why the girls jumped. Mira left me notes. The papers you saw at the quarry: that was them. She told me that her father caused their suicides. And I've got to make it right."

Kyle dipped his head so his hair fell over one eye. The effect was cynical, and Ben felt a stirring defensiveness. "She left you notes that said 'my father touched my private parts'?" Kyle asked.

"Not exactly. Well, basically. He was touching both of them, all the time. She said that."

"I don't mean to be insensitive, man, but did you ever consider that you're thinking this because of what happened with Coach Freck? I mean, what didn't happen, but almost could have happened. Like maybe you're prone to thinking this way?"

"What the hell, Kyle? She *told me*."

"She wrote to you." Kyle softened his voice. "And now you can't exactly ask for clarification. You get me?"

"I do not get you."

Both boys fell to their backs, silent. Ben steamed for a minute, then two. Finally, Ben spoke to the sky. "I'm gonna do something about it. Mira wanted me to."

He wondered if Kyle didn't hear him, on account of his bad ear. "Aren't you going to ask me what I'm gonna do?"

"Nope."

"Nope?"

"Doesn't matter."

"It doesn't matter?" Ben turned his head. "You're not going to ask me any questions?"

"A real man knows what he believes in. Once you know what you believe in, you don't have to check in with your friends or your parents or your priest before you go ahead and do something. You know what's right, and you do it."

Ben sat upright on the bench, his sense of peace vanishing. He was becoming annoyed. Here he was pouring his heart out to Kyle because he'd assumed Kyle wouldn't give him a hard time. Kyle had stood up for Ben, and backed Ben more times than he could remember. Been like a big brother to Ben, trying to make up for what a turd his own brother was to him, maybe, or because he felt bad when Ben's name turned up on Coach Freck's list. The reasons didn't matter to Ben. Yet here Kyle was, talking about old shit that didn't matter anymore, playing games with him. Something was off. Ben craned his neck to check Kyle's eyes. Maybe he was on something and Ben hadn't noticed.

Ben's stomach hardened as a thought occurred to him. "Are you saying you don't want to hear any of this?"

"Are you a man, Benny?"

"What does that mean?"

"What it sounds like. A man sticks to his course. Doesn't change it when things get rough, or when people try to throw stuff at him that's gonna get in his way."

Ben heard Mr. Falso's voice in his head, talking about pulleys and clamps and footholds, and retreating when you've gone too far. His anger stirred.

"If they know you're fighting it, they're gonna watch to see if you take it. Even if they're not the suspicious types, the doctor's gonna tell them they have to." Kyle's voice dropped an octave. "This is what you're gonna do. Use your tongue and push it down so that it's between your bottom lip and your teeth. When you leave for school, you can pick it out and toss it, preferably somewhere outside, in the grass or a bush. Some of it will have melted against your gums. Make sure you got a water bottle with you and swish some water around in your mouth, then spit it out. Even a little can have an effect: you gotta get the residue out."

"Okay."

"Have you spoken with anyone else about this?"

"The Zoloft?"

"Mr. Cillo's grabby hands."

Ben thought of his parents, with their logic and their worry and their tent-hugs. And their barely hidden distrust of Frank Cillo. "Not to anyone who will repeat it."

"Good. Stop talking about it. You need to catch the old man completely off guard. When you confront him, you'll know by his pure reaction whether or not he's telling the truth."

"What if he tries to, you know? What if he slugs me or something?"

"Is that what you're afraid of? Or are you afraid of what you might do?"

Ben winced. How had Kyle known how much rage he felt toward Mr. Cillo? That he wasn't afraid of the man's hammy fists or his Popeye arms, or the fact that he used to box, knuckles scarred and the nose to prove it. That this skinny kid, the son of a disgraced accountant, had become so convinced that Mr. Cillo had driven his daughters to suicide that he fantasized about pummeling him? Did Kyle know that his hate for Mr. Cillo had started before, for cloistering his perfect daughter, the girl next door, who should have been so easy to reach, but might as well have lived on the moon?

This was a town better off with no old men.

"Afraid of what I might do," Ben replied.

"Then you can't take the pills," Kyle said firmly. "You need every ounce of smarts and strength you can get."

Kyle was far from stoned. Ben let his rage ebb away, let the calm rationality of Kyle's voice settle him. With his hot cheek cool against the granite, Ben studied Kyle, whose hair fell away, leaving his misshapen ear exposed. It was funny. Usually when Ben talked to Kyle, he had to make eye contact, let Kyle watch his lips while he overenunciated everything.

"You hear me, Ben? Don't do it."

"I won't take the pills," Ben said, his voice husky.

"Glad I was able to help. And I won't even charge you for

the session." Kyle popped a piece of grass in his mouth, chewing up at the sky, his jaw working happily.

Ben knew what was different: Kyle was hearing him fine. He rose too quickly, about to say as much, and everything went awash in white. Ben gripped the sides of the bench as his eyes cleared, and his fingers slipped into ridges of etching. The letters felt sharp and new. He brushed his fingers over them, the curve of a C, the long, tall l's, the unmistakable o. Ben leaned over the side and snapped up. The grass between him and Kyle was lush and brighter than the rest, with seams traveling south in neat rows.

Fresh sod covered the urns that contained the ashes of two sisters.

Ben choked out the words. "Why didn't you say anything?"

Kyle plucked the blade from his lips and tossed it to the side. He gathered up his legs crisscross like a gangly Buddha. He smiled. "Chill, bro."

Ben scrambled off the bench as though it was burning hot. He paced. "Why. Are. We. Here?"

"You need to relax."

"I will not relax!" Ben threw up his hands. "You—led me here. You didn't even say anything. I shouldn't have been lying on that bench; it's disrespectful!"

Kyle waggled his hair at the ground like a dog. "You couldn't be more wrong. See, the girls touched people in different ways.

When Mira touched you through those scraps of paper she left behind, she gave you what you needed. A kind of spark that made you restless, gave you purpose. Something to believe in. Me, I got healing." Kyle's lips curled up and his nose dipped down. "And it keeps getting better and better, the more I stay close to them."

"Mira touched you?" sputtered Ben.

"Not Mira," said Kyle. "Francesca."

If something went wrong, Ben would press nine to speed-dial Kyle's number.

He hooked his thumbs under his backpack straps. In the front pocket was the original envelope containing the notes that Mira had left him, along with a nunchaku, which Ben didn't know how to use, but a baseball bat wouldn't fit in the pack, and the nunchaku fit nicely, and he had nothing else. Since his old phone was prone to dying fast, he'd bought an old-school tape recorder with a prominent button he could feel deep in his bag, and little tapes behind a plastic window that would whir quietly, recording Mr. Cillo's confession.

Ben had written and memorized a script meant to catch Mr. Cillo off guard, like Kyle advised. Enough questions to make it clear to Mr. Cillo that Ben knew his dirty little secret, without saying it outright. Ben would know by the look on the man's face. He would pretend to be selling lacrosse calendars.

Only costs a dollar, sir! Gets you coupons to the carwash, dry cleaners, you name it! Support the team! The final touch was a money bag stuffed under his arm.

Ben waited until after six thirty on Thursday night. He was sure his parents would never leave for their respective meetings, first his father, running out the door gripping a chicken sausage wrapped in oily paper towels in his hand, then his mother, forgetting her coat, then keys. He even let her drop him off at the indoor turf field, making excuses about feeling sick before Coach Taylor could stop him, and jogged home. As he rounded the bend, he saw his dark house, then the Cillos', lit from the inside like a pumpkin, with the old white Chevy Lumina parked in the driveway. He yanked the prepacked backpack from its hiding place in the rhododendron bush at the front of his own house. Dumped his lax stick, gloves, and helmet inside the front door but kept his chest pads and shirt on, figuring it gave him cred with a guy like Mr. Cillo. *Lacrosse in November? Why, yes, Mr. Cillo, the best players play year-round! What, they didn't have lacrosse when you were a boy? Not my dad either, not that he's that much younger than you, 'course he wasn't the high school athlete that you were, Mr. Cillo. I've heard the stories . . .*

Ben stopped the chattering in his brain. He cleared his throat and rang the doorbell with a jab, checking his shadowy reflection in the glass. It was a good call to wear his uniform. It made him seem more innocent, a reminder that he was still a boy, no matter what foul accusations came from his lips.

Besides, his chest pads might serve as some kind of protection, if things got rough. But really, Ben knew that his uniform bulked him up, and he wanted that bulk when he faced his enemy. He studied the Lumina, as though it had been an earlier trick of light. He pressed the doorbell, longer this time, and shifted from foot to foot. It got dark early now, and he was cold in shorts. He tried to remember how long his parents' meetings were. Was it his father who'd be home by nine, or his mother? He had no time for things to go wrong.

Ben glanced over his shoulder at Piggy's house. The Winnebago sat in the driveway like an aluminum-sided whale. Piggy would still be at lacrosse for another forty-five minutes, and his mother would be sacked out with the rest of his overweight family in front of the TV, except Mr. Pignataro, who rarely left his Gentlemen's Club, not even to sleep sometimes, according to his son.

Ben noted how easily thoughts of others crowded his head when the one person he should be focused on was Mira. He bit his lip and knocked on the door, a fast rap that meant business. The door gave a little. Ben spread his hand flat against it and pushed. It creaked open.

"Hello?" Ben called into the same living room his own front door opened into. Every light was on: the flush overhead oval, the lamp above the Barcalounger, the matching table lamps bookending the couch and trimmed in velvet brocade. Even the tiny stained-glass lights behind the windows painted on the velvet picture on the wall. Mr. Cillo had been taking his meals on a chair in front of the flat-screen TV, given the crumpled napkins, empty glasses, and crumbs on the table beside.

Ben fingered the straps of his backpack as he took careful footsteps around the living room. "Mr. Cillo? It's Ben Lattanzi, next door! The door was open! Anybody home?" He cringed at *anybody* since nobody besides Mr. Cillo lived there anymore. Then he checked himself, remembering this was no time to get soft. His eyes caught a set of two brass frames on the mantel, eight-by-ten school photos taken the year before. Francesca had tipped her chin down—had probably been told to by the photographer, Ben thought—and the result was pure mockery. Her eyes nearly twinkled, a you've-got-to-be-kidding-me stare down her nose that made Ben's belly twist. He blinked hard and looked to Mira next. The photographer had done that thing only school photographers and morgue beauticians were capable of: he'd made her look like someone else entirely. Her face was frozen in a fake smile, her eyes fixed on some unseen object. These were not the hot Cillo sisters anyone thought of, and he was struck by the fact that they seemed to have ruined their pictures deliberately.

Ben stepped backward and landed on a rubber cat toy. It squeaked, and he jumped, stumbling over a pair of worn wing tips, the source of a tangy funk that repelled Ben in its intimacy.

Ben shoved a bent finger under his nose. "Mr. Cillo?!" His

voice reverberated through the house. He waited, still and listening, for a bathroom flush, a footfall, a snore. The silence was heavy and complete. Ben relaxed his shoulders. Mr. Cillo was somewhere without his car—with a drinking buddy, probably.

The longing came on hard, to see and touch everything from the girls' final days. The weird stuff they wore during the last days anyone saw them: Francesca's shapeless hand-me-down dresses, Mira's ratty knit hat. He could walk right up into their bedrooms and look in their drawers. Mira had brought him here sure as if she had dragged him through the front door by his wrist. The notes had done that; Ben had the proof right in his backpack, should he get caught. Ben gazed out the window. With every light on, Piggy didn't need his Winnebago perch to see Ben. Anyone driving down the street, walking a dog, even a teenage boy looking out his bedroom window could see him standing in the middle of the Cillos' living room. Ben moved away from the window to the edge of the couch he knew well. A thrill ran through him in a detached way, like a history buff seeing the blood-stained pillow from Abraham Lincoln's death bed for the first time. Ben ran his hand over the back of the couch, imagining he might find a strand of blond hair. He looked through the window again, up to his own bedroom, dark but for the faint blue glow of his computer.

Ben shivered. Living in this house was like living in a fishbowl. He and Mira could have gotten caught so easily.

It'd been December, and they'd planned it for weeks, when Francesca would be working late at the rectory on an Advent food drive, and Mr. Cillo would be at his club. Ben had lied to his parents about hanging at Eddie's (a walkable distance being critical) then ducked into the Cillos' backyard, where Mira had let him in the back door. They'd kept the lights off, in case Ben's parents looked out their side living room window. Ben, in a low voice pretending to be his father: "Carla, tell Benvenuto to get off Mira Cillo!" which Mira met with silence. Her single-minded seriousness that night only drove Ben more mad. They'd dropped to their knees on the floor, right where he stood, in front of the couch. Mira undid Ben's fly with surprising deftness and pushed him backward. Mira's sharp knee on Ben's thigh, holding him down. In the half-dark, her eyes carried depths that Ben had never seen, and he wanted to touch every part of her at once. Mira's mouth slammed his, her muscled tongue pressing hard, stealing his breath, then breathing her own life force down his throat and into his lungs. Ben's lips bruised, and she moved lower, biting his throat. Her eyes met his, and she rose above him again, shapeshifting into something urgent and furious. Ben's blood swelled to meet hers, but he was aware that it was deficient. She had been cooking in her own want for so long, a want that Ben understood, but could never match.

Tonight there would be no fade to black. Here again, in front of that same couch, Ben would remember every part—mouth neck arms stomach waist back hips thighs inside—every part remembered.

After, they lay stuck together, their parts fitted perfectly, Mira gazing up, making sure Ben was real. Once, she made a small, upset noise, raising on an elbow and blowing softly on his throat where she'd left a mark.

He owed Mira her truth. No one could stop him.

It came without warning, the sudden whine of bald tires turning hard. The driver had spotted Mr. Cillo's driveway late. Ben's bowels dropped to the floor. Car door slams were followed by men calling to each other, the words indistinct and loud: drunk. Ben could be spotted plainly if Mr. Cillo looked through his own living room window. Ben turned to take the stairs, knocking the backpack off his shoulder. He stooped to pick it up. As he raised his eyes, he saw the note, pinned to the underside of the couch near where they'd made love. White-winged and folded, waiting to be set free.

Ben raced up the stairs, note in fist. Like downstairs, the girls' bedroom was inexplicably lit. He wished the room was dark—how could he hide in a lit room? He opened a closet stuffed with trendy clothes and shoes the girls had stopped wearing. Downstairs, the front door slammed. Ben couldn't risk Mr. Cillo hearing his footsteps. He jammed himself in and sank to the floor, backpack behind, propping him upright. A boot heel dug into his thigh. Francesca's, he thought, as he eased the closet door open a crack, like he'd found it. Though Ben felt sure Mr. Cillo never came in this room, the scene of his crime.

Except for the closet, the room was unnaturally orderly for any girl, even ones acting unnatural. It reminded Ben of a furniture store display, decorated with potpourri and generic art. He tried to distract himself by attaching objects to each of the girls, then considering how they might have used them. On the dresser, the plastic paddle brush he decided was Francesca's was picked clean. He imagined her plucking at the tangle, dropping dark tumbleweeds of hair into the trash can. It seemed curious to Ben that a soon-to-be-dead girl would clean her brush for the next person when there was no next person. Under one twin bed, Ben spotted a paperback of *Their Eyes Were Watching God*, the same edition he'd been assigned in tenth grade: Mira's. He imagined Mira slipping it under the bed the night they died, as Francesca shrugged on a sweater and told her to hurry. Pink Post-it notes fringed the top and sides. Ben wondered what passages Mira had marked important.

Clatter-crash! rang out from the kitchen below. Mr. Cillo was preparing canned something on the stovetop, and having a hard time. What would become of Ben if Mr. Cillo set the kitchen on fire and he couldn't escape? Would the charred body in the closet become one more mystery surrounding this family where anyone young kills themselves before they grow old, and the old ones go on and on?

Mr. Cillo stumbled, followed by a squeak and a bang—the cat toy thrown against a wall. Ben wondered if he'd committed a crime, breaking and entering. After a while, the noises settled into a television drone that worried Ben more than swears and crashes. It could be hours before Mr. Cillo fell asleep, and then deeply enough that Ben could tiptoe past and out the front door, or the back, through the kitchen. He told himself it was a waiting game he could win as long as he didn't panic. He nestled among the clothes in an effort to get warm, and realized he was leaning against the collection of shapeless dresses that Francesca had taken to wearing. He wished there was something more of Mira in this room, objects that would remind him why he had pulled this stunt to begin with.

Eventually, he opened the note.

Francesca says it's as though
he has a knife to her throat.
She is out of options.
End at the end.

And so he was coming to the end. He already knew the option that she—they—chose. And Mira wouldn't have chosen it unless she was out of options, too.

Ben had trouble breathing. He leaned through the closet
doorway for air. That's when he saw the hat. It hung over the
back of a chair, barely more than a slub of yarn, a knit thing that
had sat sideways on Mira's head starting around April, after the
girls came back to school following Connie's wake. Mira wore
it no matter the temperature, no matter that winter was over
and she hadn't even worn it in the winter. When most of the
girls who had something to show off (and even the ones who
didn't) began to expose knees and arms and backs, Mira covered up more. During those last weeks, in Semantics, Ben
watched as she wound her bright hair around the widest part
of her hand and stashed the bunched knot underneath the
terrible thing. He had come to hate the hat, not only for hiding what most guys noticed first about Mira, but for mark-
ing her as sullen and weird, which it did better than if she'd
dyed her hair black and tattooed a tear on her cheek. Ben remembered the day their Health teacher asked her to remove
the hat—girls, snarky and jealous, said it was for fear of lice—
and when class ended, she left it on the metal rails under her
chair. Ben had waited until she was nearly out the door before
he stood and walked over to it, poised to snatch it and stuff it
in the boys' room trash can, deep under piles of mealy paper
towels. But Mira remembered and rushed back in, creating a
standoff where for a moment, Ben thought she would speak
to him. Instead, she turned red and her eyes widened, a look

that he could neither tolerate nor place. Clutching the hat to her chest, she ran from the room.

A choking noise escaped Ben's throat. He wondered how many missed chances there had been, when Mira would have spoken to him, but didn't. Had he done other things, too, that made Mira distrust him enough not to tell him what her father was doing until after he could do nothing about it?

He gazed at Mira's bed through watery eyes. He wondered if Mr. Cillo had touched Mira in that bed, which was so close to the other bed. It was hard to imagine things could happen to one sister without the other knowing. His brain flashed to the girls protecting each other from the monster by sacrificing themselves. It was so easy to envision the sick beast moving from one girl to the other. Starting with Francesca, then—

Ben paused his thoughts and stared at Mira's bed. He banished the thought of Mr. Cillo's sweaty visage looming over Mira. Ben felt certain that was how it had gone down, why Francesca had taken such pains (and he felt sure Francesca had led the charge) to cleanse the room of their personal selves, which they took with them to the quarry. Their bodies, finally, their own.

Ben wished he could get out of his own head.

He felt for his phone in his back pocket and found it black. He pressed hard on the power button, but nothing came. He swore, then cursed himself for cursing. Downstairs, upbeat music from the television floated to meet him.

Ben felt the sense of ice tongs squeezing the sides of his brain. His vision narrowed.

As his panic grew, he ticked off the things the dead phone meant he could not do. He couldn't text his parents a lie that he'd gone somewhere after practice. He couldn't send a panicked message to Kyle for help.

Kyle. He needed Kyle.

The ice tongs squeezed harder. The closet got darker. Ben squeezed his fingers into the spaces behind his temples.

Worst of all, and he wasn't sure why this was the worst, but he couldn't tell the time. This was how a blindfolded hostage felt. He guessed an hour, maybe more, had passed. If the best way to torture someone was to force them to lose sense of time, Mr. Cillo was torturing him.

Keep talking to yourself, Ben. Keep talking.

Ben reached down blindly and felt the outline of the pills in his lacrosse shorts. Wasn't this what the stupid pills were for? Taking the edge off? Because this might be a good moment for that. Ben heard Kyle's voice in his head: *You hear me, Ben? Don't do it.*

Ben yanked the bottle from his pocket. He squinted at the bottle: *Take two tablets with a full glass of water.* If two was good, three was better. He wrenched off the cap, popping three dry pills and swallowing hard, the bitter taste burning his tongue.

He leaned into the clothes and sighed. The clothes embraced him. He listened for signs that Mr. Cillo had discovered some overturned item, some misplaced shoe that revealed someone had broken into his house, and at some point he stopped listening at all. Thick golden warmth flooded him. Ben eased the closet door wider and was surprised when it made no noise. He tested his footstep for creaks. Finding none, he stepped out of the closet and stood in the middle of the girls' room. The warmth stayed with Ben, and seemed to transfer to an affection for the bed, the bureaus, the tiny violets on the old-fashioned wallpaper. Every object called to him to be touched, lifted, gazed at. Held. Even Mira's bed was inviting, and he knew it shouldn't be. He ought to be thinking of her there, helpless, seeing things happening to Francesca, or shutting herself off to things happening to her.

No, he had to get his head right. Stay on his toes. Because despite the danger that lay below, he was, in fact, getting sleepy.

Ben rubbed his eyes. What time was it? Mr. Cillo had been out drinking hard, probably at Piggy's father's club, and no one came home from Big Steven's early. The sounds from downstairs were the news, and not the six-o'clock news, since he'd rung the doorbell well after six, and the earliest the news came on was ten. And those same sounds had been going for a while. Was it past ten? It was the kind of time-suck that happened at the quarry, only he was in a different place illegally, and he was going to get caught.

Unless the beast was asleep.

He inched his way across the room, walking in slow motion, heel, pad, toe, his arms akimbo, as if balancing on a wire. He made it as far as the square patch of landing before the stairs when he realized he'd left his backpack in the closet. He turned to repeat his heel, pad, toe pattern back to Francesca and Mira's bedroom when the telephone rang loud. The ring came from every direction: the living room, kitchen, and from Mr. Cillo's bedroom, next to where Ben froze. Nerves rose from Ben's bare arms like static electricity. As it rang a second time, Ben heard the alien, female voice echo through the house, flat, with inhuman beats and pauses.

"Call from"

"Paul"

"Lattanzi"

APRIL 2016

"We'll use the EpiPen," Connie told Mira. "It's a foolproof plan."

Mira turned to Francesca. "Do we know how to use it?"

"Don't question." Francesca collapsed on the edge of the bed. Her shirt gaped as she leaned over her knees to tie her sneakers. Mira stared at the sharp ridge of her clavicle and the hollows above. She knew Francesca's body as well as she knew her own. Her sleeping and eating noises, shapes and shadows. Mira could close her eyes and see Francesca turn away in her strappy tanks, her rounded scapula like wings rising as she breathed. Her pale wrists flexing at the breakfast table as she twisted sleep from her bones. Francesca had always been strong, and proud of it, using her muscles, taking over jobs a boy might do, if a boy lived in the house. Lately, though, she was all sharp angles. Her shoulders ended in points, with recently emerged knobs and hollows. Francesca's body was changing, as though something was carving away her soft parts.

Francesca blew hair from her eyes and rose. "Stay or go, your choice."

Mira's mouth grew dry. "Of course I'm going."

Francesca slipped inside the moth-eaten A-line coat she'd taken to wearing and stared at Mira's feet. "You'll need sneakers, not boots." Francesca searched her face for a moment, then touched two fingers to Mira's brow, smoothing the cleft between her eyes. "Have courage, sister. We're all blood here. No one's hurting anyone."

Connie wavered in the doorway. "Can we go? It's getting dark soon."

Francesca moved to Connie and draped her hands over her shoulders. "Concetta Marie. Are you sure you want to do this?"

Connie smiled gamely and looked only at Francesca. "I'm sure. *Mio sangue.*"

Mira's eye fixed on the slip of green sequined T-shirt that dragged past the hem of Connie's short purple parka. She'd worked her hair into a beachy, wavy style that Mira knew took hours of coaxing with salt spray and a clip-less curling iron. Her glossy lips were the color of cotton candy. On her feet were trendy boots with chunky heels not made for running. Francesca had let the mouse in her experiment wear whatever she'd wanted, because she knew something about this nightmare experiment fed into Connie's desire to be the center of a drama in which she was the main character, or as close to it as she'd ever get. Even if Connie died, she knew she'd look good doing it.

"*Mio sangue.*" Francesca gazed over her shoulder at Mira. "You've got the phone to record?"

Mira nodded.

"Let's roll."

Francesca flew down the stairs. Mira grabbed Connie by the elbow.

"Are you sure you want to do this?" Mira whispered harshly, over Francesca's footsteps echoing heavy on the stairs.

"It's what I want." Connie's eyes darted over Mira's face. "You heard me."

"What if Francesca's miracle doesn't work right away?"

"Then she'll use the pen." Connie winced. "Why are you questioning me?"

"I want to make sure you understand what we're doing."

"I know the plan."

Mira knew she was talking about the official story that they had rehearsed, one that involved overexertion, a faulty EpiPen, and a divine miracle. "I meant the risk."

Connie's eyes went dark. "Who are you to talk about risk? You, who makes Francesca hide the antifreeze in the cellar so you won't drink it? Who can't take her temperature with a glass thermometer because she'll bite it? Who stays back from the edge of the altar so she doesn't hurl herself into the quarry?"

Mira swallowed hard. Connie had never spoken so harshly to her. Yet everything she said was true: she was a hypocrite.

"It could go wrong," Mira said.

"You don't get it," Connie said. "I live a padded life. I can't play sports. I don't do gym. I can't swim at the quarry. I'm not even supposed to have strenuous sex!"

"Connie . . . ," Mira murmured.

Connie touched Mira's forehead with one polish-chipped fingernail. "Have courage, sister."

Have courage, sister! Mira blew out a breath that shook her lips. Connie was prone to repeating anything. They'd made a cruel game of it when they were younger, one sister dropping a preposterous fact to see how long it would take Connie to repeat it to the other sister. Did you hear Louis Gentry's mother was a former underwear model? That gypsy moth caterpillars were a plague from God that meant the world was ending?

That Coach Freck was falsely accused? Who knew? Connie did! But this wasn't simply Connie parroting Francesca. She had bought into her plan utterly. Mira had been (conveniently, now that she thought about it) doing odd jobs at Daddy's office when Francesca had convinced Connie to allow her to test her powers by risking her life. She wondered how that conversation had gone down, and almost laughed thinking about it, it was so preposterous. She knew Francesca only had to say she needed it, and that they were blood, and that was enough.

"I want everything to turn out right," Mira said weakly.

Connie grabbed her hand. She smelled fruity from what she'd washed her hair with, slicked on her lips, or chewed. She squeezed Mira's hand.

"Mio sangue," Connie said, pulling away.

Mira listened to Connie's feet hammer, the slam of the back door followed by complete stillness, and Mira suddenly couldn't remember if she had ever been alone in that room. She closed her eyes and inhaled Connie's lingering scent, which now smelled of decay.

Mira snatched her coat off the bed and flew down the stairs.

It was the first week in April and the ground was hard under Mira's bald bicycle tires. Connie, who wasn't allowed to own a bike, clung hard to Francesca's back, knees squeezing her waist. Though in her mind, Mira was there to protect Connie, it was Francesca she stayed close to, riding to the left of her shadow, forcing cars to pull around her first. She jumped as a pickup truck barreled past and honked. Mira had started noticing the looks when they rode their bikes, and they weren't the looks she was used to. Only girls under the age of ten rode bikes, never mind to actually get somewhere. Mira saw them through the eyes of the drivers who passed: Francesca in her bag-lady jacket, with Connie on her back. Mira on the rickety, oldest, hand-me-down bike, the gearshift forever stuck on one. She suspected that the rules their father set—not riding in hardly anybody's car, for one—were starting to peg the Cillo sisters as plain weird. Now with Francesca determined to prove herself a modern-day saint, Mira wondered if it wasn't true.

Francesca braked at the blinking light where the two-lane highway spun into a rotary that contained the exit to Johnny's Foodmaster. It was nearly rush hour, and a badly timed merge could take out all three at once. The wind was punishing, and the day's warmth sank fast as the sun fell. They waited. Mira squeezed her arms close to her sides to keep warm as she rested her foot on the ground. Francesca tore out in a flash, and Mira hitched back up on her bike and flew into the rotary, pedaling fast to catch up. They coasted off the exit and rode around to the back lot of Johnny's Foodmaster, chaining their bikes to the metal stand. A boy in stained white pants nodded to them as he hauled a bag to the nearby Dumpster, bringing a waft of ocean and rot. When Mira had trouble keeping her bike upright in the slats, Francesca didn't seem to notice, staring out toward the quarry, wind whipping her hair. After she was done, Mira stepped into Francesca's view, but found that her eyes were closed, and she was murmuring a prayer.

Francesca's eyes flashed open. "I'm ready."

Connie rose and fell on her toes, hands jammed into her parka. Mira looked toward the boy, and considered calling to him as the supermarket door slammed shut.

Francesca held out her palm. "The pen, please."

Connie's eyes flashed fear, though she made a sloppy half smile.

"We won't need it. *Mio sangue*," Connie said, swallowing hard. She dug into the small bag strapped across her body and handed the plastic bullet-shaped case filled with adrenaline to Francesca.

Francesca threw her arms around Connie's neck. "Blood."

Francesca let her arms fall. She pointed the EpiPen in the air, then at Mira. It glowed orange against the slate sky like a flare.

Mira frowned at the pen. "You want me to hold it?"

"You should be in charge of it, since you're the only one who thinks we'll need it."

Mira turned away, her face flushed dark red, as she shoved the EpiPen into the back pocket of her jeans. She had never felt so separate from Francesca, and it hurt her, somewhere vague in her chest, an ache that she realized had been there for weeks. When she turned, they were already small, running up the steep hill that led to the scabby woods encircling the quarry. Francesca led, then Connie, her dark head bobbing as she tried to keep pace with Francesca, her scarf flapping behind like a misaligned rudder.

PART 7

Heart

Below Ben, a mechanical lounger wheezed, followed by drunken fumbling noises.

"Hello?" Mr. Cillo growled, his voice thick with mucus and sleep. He cleared his throat with a hack.

From the hall, Ben couldn't hear the voice on the other end, but he could measure out the beats of his father's greeting, laced with apologies for having woken Mr. Cillo, and Ben cringed, for he imagined they sounded wimpy. Ben's mind flashed on every reason for his father to call his hated former boss, and none of them made any sense . . . unless. Unless they had somehow discovered his intention to lie about lacrosse practice and enter their neighbor's home.

Why would his father—or mother—call Mr. Cillo?

"Well, this is a surprise." Mr. Cillo's voice was smoother now, alert.

Ben's gut flinched.

"Slow down, Paul. I'll see what I can do. No, it's fine to ask a favor, and anyway, this is an emergency. That business: it's not relevant. Let me call my guy at the station and I'll see what

I can do. But it's only been four hours, you say?" Ben heard Mr. Cillo scratching around, for a notepad, perhaps. "Five feet, eleven inches? One hundred fifty pounds? He's not seventeen yet, right? Sixteen you say? That's good. Last seen walking alone from the indoor turf field complex place toward the Neck, around 6:35 p.m. Any idea why he might've left practice? Sick, okay. Listen, Paul. I've got to ask you this, because they're gonna ask me. Is there any chance your boy may have run away? Because if there's any chance, you've got to tell me now. Number one, this is sooner—way sooner—than they usually do these kinds of things. Number two, if they find out the kid is a runaway, and they posted an alert, there'll be hell to pay. Not tonight or tomorrow, but later, if you ever have any problem at all: crickets. You got me? It becomes a boy-crying-wolf kind of thing . . ."

Ben's knees went weak. His parents thought he'd been abducted? Suddenly it wasn't sappy respect he imagined in his father's voice, but terror. His chest caved in shame. He'd been so single-minded in his mission to extract the truth from Mr. Cillo that he hadn't considered the full-on terror his parents lived in: that he was losing his marbles. They thought he'd run away, and the only way, the most efficient way they thought they would get him back was by using this man they hated.

Ben smiled.

Downstairs, thunderous steps moved across the living room into the room off the den. Exposed in the hall, Ben felt sure

Mr. Cillo could hear his ragged breaths. If he ran across the living room, past the den and out the front door, Mr. Cillo would see him, plain as day. But there was no other way. He couldn't be certain the back door off the kitchen wasn't locked, and a struggle with a locked door wasn't something he had time for. Ben's heart sped as Mr. Cillo read aloud from the scrap of paper, the Facts of Ben: his height, his weight, the circumstances of his disappearance. "Color of his hair? Heck, I'm not sure. Light, blondish, like my Mira."

(Chokes here. *Faker,* Ben thought)

"Parents said brown eyes. Skinny build"—

(*When was the last time he even looked at me?* Ben thought)

—"kind of kid a pedophile might like."

(*Takes one to know one,* Ben nearly spat)

"Computer-savvy, supposedly. Could have been led by some guy online. He was one of those list kids—forget it, I'm muddling matters. Listen, the boy's my next-door neighbor, and I know the parents. St. Theresa's people. Good people. I know it's early and doesn't follow protocol, but do it, okay? As a favor for me."

Ben's face burned. "Good people." That was rich. What a phony. Suddenly, Ben's reason for being there came to him, clear and true. He would surprise the monster, confront him with his accusation, make him sweat. Because now that he was missing, he was like a ghost himself. Mr. Cillo would have no time to adopt his big-man persona, his nice-guy posing. Ben would get clear, unadulterated shock and guilt: that flicker of recognition he'd been imagining and savoring for weeks. Ben let the drug do its job, and his muscles relaxed. He walked down the stairs, slowly, staring into the den. Mr. Cillo was turned to the wall, a sweat stain pressed into his back, a bald spiral mashed into the back of his hair by the chair. He was silent, on hold while his crony on the other end did his bureaucratic missing-child thing to get the AMBER Alert started. Ben opened his mouth to speak—the phrase *I know what you did* on the edge of his tongue—yet Mr. Cillo remained unmoving, his back to Ben, face inches from the wall. It was an unnatural pose, and Ben cocked his head, wondering, briefly, if he'd had some sort of standing stroke, if those kinds of things existed. Then he saw the barely perceptible shake of his shoulders glued to his inelegant hump of back, made of old manly injuries. The phone stood upright in its charger. Ben placed his hand on the cold doorknob, easing it to the right with a soft click. As he stepped into the night, the note held aloft between two fingers, he was followed by a wracking sob.

Ben watched the action in his house from the Cillos' rhododendron. Downstairs, window lights flickered as his parents paced past. He imagined the scene when he walked through the front door. He would have to face their panic, and lie that he had tried to run away. It had consequences, but it was the only excuse that was credible. There would be lecturing and berating. His mother would cry. It would be hours before he felt his pillow beneath his head.

The night air smelled crisp and cold, and he drank it in as an antidote to whatever the Zoloft was doing in his system. He thought he might like to stay outside all night, and he knew it was wrong and possibly evil that he should be happy at this moment. He ought to be feeling dread, for the punishment that awaited him, and disappointment, for his failure to confront Mr. Cillo. But the air was invigorating, and Ben was heading for a relic that he alone could interpret, contextualize, catalog.

It would be days before his parents would let him out of their sight, if they allowed it at all. His future in Bismuth was tantamount to a prison conviction. He would need a plan, but not now. Ben slid the note into his shorts and jogged through his side yard to the corner of the cement patio. He was relieved to see the long vertical blinds to the kitchen slider drawn tight. Flashes of red and blue light backlit the house; the cops had arrived, and parked at the front curb. He wondered if the cops were the same ones that had arrived seven years before, after dinner, on another crisp November night when the police came to personally deliver the news that Ben was on Coach Freck's special list, and to prepare his parents with their own list, names of experts trained to talk to children who had been victimized. Ben's breathing went trippy. He slipped from his backpack and flattened himself against the house, the vinyl siding cold against his back, and tried to steady his breath. He listened to the robotic bleats of walkie-talkies, and the doorbell chime, then sprinted across the backyard to the play set, taking its stairs in one step and tucking his long body into the lookout. He collapsed to the floor and studied the blinds for movement. Certain they were still, he pulled the note from his pants pocket.

End at the end. Only one place left to go.

Ben ran his eyes over the note once, then twice. He squinted and read it a third time. From the front door came the grateful voices of his mom, then his dad, followed by the formal voices of policemen. Ben folded the note in half, stashed it low in his pocket, and set his jaw. He swung his legs over the stairs and eased down, slipping through the backyard and into the shed. He felt for his father's heavy plaid work shirt hanging on a long nail until his hand brushed its satisfying heft. He needed warmth for where he was going.

Ben slipped from the shed in the shirt and crusty work gloves, a flashlight under his arm and a trowel weighing down the left pocket of his lacrosse shorts. He lifted his bike from its side and mounted it, tires swishing on the night-damp tar. As he coasted down his driveway, something made Ben look right. In the window of the living room that was also his living room, Ben saw a sliver of the den where Mr. Cillo stood, facing the wall, in the same spot Ben had left him.

Ben rode like a demon, bare calves and thighs numbing fast in the wind. They might notice his bike was gone, not a detail the police would check, but a detail his parents would check, were they sure he had stopped home before running away. They might have found the pills he didn't swallow in the bushes, another fact they'd leave out when sharing their grief with the officers, who'd seen so much from this neighborhood, being as it was nearly three months since the Cillo girls' drowning. Do you call it a drowning when you put rocks in your pockets? Ben let these thoughts race through his head, because they distracted him from the maddening fact that it was *taking so long to get there.* Mira wanted him to go to the quarry, like she had, on a warm night when the wind from his bedroom window blew soft across his belly, a tickle or a kiss. Not like this night, when the wind punished him in proportion to the speed with which he rode, drove him backward, made every rotation of his pedals feel like a Sisyphean feat. Camped beside the front door of his enemy, the night had lured him, and now it fought him.

Or maybe it was the drug.

He couldn't get to the ledge where she stepped, in bare feet, and fell, weightless, her energy spent by her own race to get to the quarry and the labored hike through, drenched with sweat. It would probably be easier to exhaust yourself than to let adrenaline kick in and begin flailing, trying to save yourself as you dropped one hundred feet into the water. His monkey mind tossed this away—it was too visceral—and he focused on his feet, unfeeling now, two clods at the bottom of his legs that needed to press. He stood, forcing his weight into his feet, and cars slowed as they passed him, surprised to see a bicycle on the highway at this hour, cursing him for being young and reckless.

He reached the rotary in twenty-six minutes. He knew that, despite what his parents had decided to tell the police, they still had to have the quarry in the backs of their minds. And there was the fact that the quarry was a dumping ground for everything, from refrigerators to old paint to bodies. The police would come to the quarry. They might even come to their ledge, his ledge, the place where Mira was sending him. And for that reason, he needed to be inhumanly fast.

Ben coasted into Johnny's Foodmaster. In the lot sat the usual few abandoned cars in the glow of the store's after-hours low light. Ben rode wide around the cars, behind the store, past the bike cage and to the end of the asphalt until he reached the woods. His pedals resisted, then his wheels caught traction. He rode as far as the underbrush and the incline allowed, about a quarter of a mile, until mud mired his tires and he could go no farther. He slid off his bike and wrapped his chain twice around a young tree and locked it. The moon was large. He pitched the flashlight deep into the scrub, and covered the bright metallic bits of the bike with branches. Up the hill, the trapezoidal shadow that was the top of the quarry loomed, and he ran his hands through his hair until it stuck up in the front. He rubbed his palms together, but they felt disconnected, so he stopped and began to climb. After a while, the aquatic roar of the expressway grew fainter, and he thought he heard laughter. Shivering, he focused on the crunch of his feet on gravel, walking harder. He patted the note in his pocket, reminding himself that this quest was not something he'd constructed, a distraction from reality. Twice, he stopped to place his hand on his belly and breathe. Alone on the hill, his breath sounds were magnified, and he hated the Darth Vader sound, which he was sure made him seem weak to Mira looking down from heaven. Fixing his breath was something he hadn't had to do since the year after Coach Freck. He was no longer scared that his parents were spiraling with worry, or that he'd broken into a man's home. He wasn't even terrified of what he might find.

It was that some element would be off, and he would not experience it the way she had.

When he reached the clearing, his legs buckled and he staggered to the altar, sinking down. Mica stuck to his knees. The exhaustion was sweet, and he let it wash over him.

"This is how she felt," he said in his most convincing voice.

His vision was hazy, and again, sleepiness crept in. He rubbed his eyes with the heels of his hands, speckled with mica, and he felt the tiny shards against his eyelids, working their way in, but he was too tired to care. He sat for a moment, rubbing, until he heard a noise. He froze, listening for far-off sirens and the voices of grown men brandishing flashlights and barking dogs.

"Why did you have to touch her?"

Ben palmed the rock and twisted his upper torso. At the edge of the clearing stood a girl in a ragged, loose-weave sweater.

"I'm hallucinating," he said in his surest tone, meant to ward away mirages and ghosts.

The image shimmered.

"That's good," he whispered. "You are a figment of my imagination. Go away."

The image shimmered again. Ben made fists and dug at his eyes. He stopped and opened them slowly. The image remained.

"Go away!" he yelled, trying to stand but falling, his legs like water.

"Why did you have to touch us?" the girl said as she came closer, not walking exactly, her feet never grazing the ground. Ben fell and scrambled back to his feet, backed up and fell again, his legs sprawled. As he neared the tip of the altar, rocks came loose underneath and tumbled over the lip.

Ben blinked hard, but the image remained a few feet in front of him. Francesca slid her jaw side to side with tiny clicks. Ben realized she was waiting for an answer. A stock image from every cheesy movie he'd ever seen played before his mind, of a man talking to a ghost, then the camera pans back, and he's talking with no one. That was what this was, he decided. Not real. He had three pills in his body that he'd never taken before and no food. He'd ridden to Johnny's in twenty-six minutes. He'd spent half the night jammed into a dead girl's closet. He was a little high, and possibly asleep, and Francesca had invaded his dreams.

Why not Mira? he wondered. Never Mira.

"Listen, I figured out Mira's notes. I know what your father did to both of you. And I can make it right," Ben pleaded. "I'm gonna send a letter to the newspaper, and everybody in Bismuth's gonna know what kind of a guy he really is."

The mirage laughed, and it was the sound of splintering glass. Ben shielded his face as though shards flew at him through the air.

"*You* broke us!" it shrieked. "*Every single one of you* broke us! Look at me!"

Ben dropped his hands. Its face—her face—was perfect and intact and hard, beautiful in the way people had said Francesca Cillo was beautiful. She loomed larger, and Ben forced himself to still. "My *father* had nothing to do with this. My *father* had the right idea, keeping us away from all of you. The minute we let you in you destroyed us."

Ben struggled to sit up. "You're right. I was as bad as the rest of them. Please, just let me wake up." Ben closed his eyes and reopened them. She was still there, an angry shimmer. The air carried a new, sonic buzz, loud and getting louder. It was like the sound of june bugs; impossible in November. Francesca pointed her chin at the frigid water. "Go on. She wants you to find it. She wants you to see the truth."

The image fragmented into glints, and then there were only the trees that lined the clearing. Ben felt the charge in the air dissipate, and a chill followed. Beyond, a siren rang in the distance. Then the dogs. It would take them exactly twenty-eight minutes to reach the clearing, if they didn't stop to see the bike, and if they weren't hauling dredging equipment and diving gear.

Ben stood at the ledge's tip and looked down into the freezing, molasses-colored water. He was going to have to jump.

Logistics flooded Ben's mind. According to Kyle, when the girls went missing, the ambulances had come in on the other side of the quarry, the only way passable by emergency vehicles, and the divers, rather than jumping, made their way down to the lowest ledge on the opposite side and basically waded in from the shallows.

He would be jumping right into his rescuers' arms. Unless he was quick.

His head pounded, blood or panic overloading his brain. The dark quarry water terrified him. But once the police found him—and they would find him—he might never get here again. And not reading Mira's words was more terrifying than any poison.

Ben emptied his sagging pockets: phone, pills, trowel. He

exhaled hard and long, then filled his chest with night air. Flexed and rose up on his toes, and lifted his arms to the sky. Pushed away from the rock. And dove.

Flying through the air, Ben shut his eyes against the g-force rush around him, streaming wet granite veined with glitter. And then he hit the surface like a blade, and his ears fuzzed over in an underwater vacuum-hush. His outstretched hands touched something hard—quarry trash, plant matter, a skeleton—and he pulled away, panicked, arms and legs flailing, pushing his way to the top, where the moon rippled like a beacon. He swam for it.

In an explosion, Ben broke water. The air seared his lungs. For a while, he only bobbed and gulped oxygen. In the distance, he heard a demented ambulance siren, warped by the quarry acoustics or some tweaking of his own inner ear. He swam for the wall, kicking hard, still gasping, his arms pulling him along to the scooped base rock where he had begun his ascent that summer day past Connie to Mira, shame turning into exhilaration with the touch of her falling hair. He boosted himself out of the water and shivered uncontrollably in the hard moonlight. The siren whine again. Ben moved like an animal, on all fours, his nose close to the ground examining every spot of the low landing ledge, for this was the only place left. One rock seemed deliberately placed. He rolled it aside and felt the depression in which it had sat. His fingers grazed something man-made, plastic and paper, and he held the object up to the moonlight. He knew the orange EpiPen was Connie's before he read the typed prescription that said *Connie Villela* on the wrap-around label. Covering the prescription was a note secured by a purple ribbon. He sat upright and placed the pen in the middle of his folded legs. He tugged off the ribbon and unfurled the note.

Francesca thought she was touched by God.
But we couldn't prove it. And because of that, Connie died.

We didn't plan for Connie's heart to stop forever. We didn't plan for our hearts to be broken.

Here's what we learned: when you touch things, they can break.

MARCH 2016

The sludge of mud and pine needles gave way to baked earth as they entered the clearing where the slope flattened before dropping off. Everyone called it the field, but it looked more like a scorched battleground. Oak saplings stretched a few feet toward the sun, shedding brown leaves in the slight breeze. Patches of shaggy pines grew low, dwarfed by species or conditions or both. The girls paused to rest, smoke blooming from their mouths. Mira smelled moisture locked in rock, and it smelled clean, not like the other smell that sometimes rose from the quarry lake, like rotten eggs, a hot smell that would be yellow, were it visible. Mira wondered if it smelled better because it was nearly spring, and she had never been to the quarry any time but summer, and never alone.

Francesca's hair had escaped her ponytail and it fell wild across her shoulders. She raised her arms to the sky.

"Do you feel as amazing as I feel?" she called.

Mira opened her mouth to speak, but it was Connie's voice that came.

"I feel free!" Connie said, twirling, her face turned to the darkening sky. Connie giggled, leaning backward and spinning in circles. Mira turned, realizing Francesca had stepped behind her. She had ditched her coat, and her clavicle rose and fell above the collar of her blouse. "We've never come here alone before," Francesca breathed. "It feels good. Don't you think so, Mira?"

Mira said nothing.

Francesca stepped closer, the side of her white hand brushing Mira's cheek. Mira stiffened.

"Keep your faith in me, sister," she said.

Mira stepped back. A rush of wind tumbled toward them from the city below, and Connie crushed against Mira and giggled while Francesca stood tall, her hair blowing about, framing her face like a dark halo. *Francesca feels everything too much,* Mira thought, and pulled her own jacket tight around her.

The afternoon grew purple.

"It's getting late," Mira whispered. Her voice was hoarse and hot in her throat. No one seemed to hear her, and Mira wondered if she'd said it aloud.

Francesca clapped. "Time to play! Hide-and-go-seek tag. I'm it!"

Mira touched her throat. Her memories of hide-and-go-seek tag involved the neighborhood boys, sweaty and flushed, trying to corner and kiss them. Eventually she and Francesca had refused to play, though Connie was always up for a game. The only boy who hadn't tried was Ben. He'd found Mira hiding behind the fence door with the black metal latch that, propped open by thick grass, formed a perfect pie wedge in which to hide. Ben had bounded up, thrown the door shut with a click, and crouched, staring at her, panting. He was supposed to yell "It!" Instead, he turned and ran away, toward Piggy wedged beneath the carriage of his Winnebago.

Francesca covered her eyes. "One, two, three, four, five . . ."

The girls shrieked and ran.

"Mira!" Connie stabbed a finger toward a thatch of pines. "Hide!"

Francesca flicked open one eye. "Nineteen, twenty!"

Mira thought: *run.* She darted for the scrub and crouched

behind its thickest parts, still visible to Francesca. Connie lay on her side behind an oak log.

"Ready or not, here I come!" Francesca beelined for Connie. She scrambled from the log but was overtaken by her cousin, who slapped her on the back. Connie howled.

"You're it!" Francesca said.

Connie turned and ran toward Mira. Mira blinked, for the Connie gunning for her looked younger, hair streaming, cheeks pink. And it was that gangly Connie run, the opposite of self-conscious, the way she'd moved in the years before she noticed boys. Frozen, Mira smiled despite herself.

Connie was upon her.

"You're it," Connie cried, dancing a victory jig. "Now you have to play! The party pooper has to play!"

Mira thought she saw Francesca rolled in a ball, making herself even smaller behind her scraggly pine. As Mira ran toward the tree, Francesca stepped in her path. Mira bounced off her chest and fell backward. Connie laughed, and her laughter seem to come at Mira from every direction.

"You took me out!" Mira sputtered.

"Now I'm it!" Francesca slit her eyes and scanned the field. Mira turned cross: Francesca had slammed her hard, and the ground was cold. She rose slowly, rubbing her behind. Connie called, "Me next! Me next!" from her scrubby hiding place. Francesca's shoulders pitched forward, and she ran toward her, elbows pumping fiercely. Connie screeched in delight. She took off, heading east in a wide arc around the quarry mouth. Francesca followed, but Connie had at least a yard lead, and she was strong, stronger than she ever seemed, Mira thought as she joined the chase. Again and again, Francesca lunged, but Connie dodged her grasp. The girls shrieked in pleasure with each near miss; even Mira began to shout, rooting for Connie to get away. Connie squealed, reveling in moving. As her lead grew she became brave, stopping and switching direction, taunting Francesca from behind spindly oaks, her pursuer struggling, shreds of leaves like torn butcher paper in her hair. She tracked Connie closer to the crest, to the drop-off into the quarry proper, with its ledges and water. Ahead, the Boston skyline blinked, festive. Mira knew Powder Neck glowed, too, behind and below them, a steady blue-white.

Mira stopped. Francesca was forcing Connie to the edge.

Mira cupped her hands around her mouth to scream "Stop!" and Connie did, turning to face them, her head loose on its stem, bobbing slightly. Francesca stopped short a few feet from Connie. Mira approached, slowly, squinting. As she came closer, she saw Connie's eyes were unfocused, her hand waving around her throat.

"Connie?" Mira said.

Connie fumbled with her jacket zipper. Mira stepped forward and yanked it. When it caught, Mira yanked harder, rocking Connie like a rag doll. Finally the zipper split and Mira threw the coat open. Pink welts traveled down Connie's throat and joined, forming larger ones that disappeared into her low-cut shirt.

"What are those?" Mira cried.

Connie splayed her hand against the lacy pattern, as if someone had said something surprising. Francesca pushed Mira aside for a better view. She peered at Connie's chest.

"Hives."

Connie's breath got loud and ragged. Her fingers closed around her throat. Miles away, on Powder Neck, an ambulance siren wailed, jolting Mira.

"We need help," she said. "This is bad. We need to call someone right now."

Connie staggered and swayed, dropped to her knees and retched. The sound carried. Mira crouched beside her and wiped Connie's mouth with her sleeve. She rubbed Connie's back, murmuring, "You're okay, you're okay."

Francesca's eyes flitted over Connie.

Mira looked up at Francesca. "I'm using the pen."

Connie looked up weakly. "Don't," she whispered.

Francesca's eyes flashed at Mira. "You heard her."

Mira felt Connie stiffen under her arm. Mira stood and looked around wildly. She reached around to her back pocket and felt for the bulge of the pen. As she did, Francesca walked swiftly toward Mira and knocked her to the ground. Mira stumbled a few feet away. She blinked hard at the dusk and scrambled to her feet. Francesca had rolled Connie onto her back and now kneeled beside her, her hands on top of one another upon Connie's chest, about to perform CPR.

Mira felt relief sweep over her. Francesca was going to do the right thing, like she always did, big sister sweeping in and taking control. How could she have doubted?

Francesca closed her eyes and tipped her chin to the sky, murmuring, "Jesus, you commanded your apostles to heal the sick, raise the dead, cleanse the lepers, cast out devils: freely I have received, freely I give."

Mira gasped.

Connie's body twitched from its core.

"Quickly!" said Mira.

"Give me your grace, oh God, to perform a miracle, to give breath to this girl where there is none . . ."

Mira cried. "Is it happening? It needs to happen, there's no time!"

Francesca threw her head back. "Oh Lord, you put saints on Earth after the apostles to follow Jesus's command to heal the sick and raise the dead. Let me be your vehicle, dear God . . ."

Mira drew the pen from her back pocket and held it in front of her nose. "I can't see. What do I do with it?" The pen slipped from Mira's spastic hands, flying into the air and landing soundlessly in the dark. "I lost it!"

Francesca's head snapped up. "Pray! Pray now with me!"

Mira crawled on her hands and knees, fumbling blindly on

the ground. Loose rock and mica shards sliced the soft under-sides of her hands. "I can't find it!" Tears streamed into her mouth and nose. "I can't find it!"

Francesca dropped her head. The ledge was filled with chanting, verses of the Lord's Prayer, broken with sobs.

"Mira!" Francesca's voice was shrill. "Pray with me!"

Mira crawled onto the altar rock. It seemed impossible that the EpiPen could have bounced that far, and as she thought this, another thought, her father's words, intruded: *No good comes from running around alone and unchaperoned.* She pushed it from her mind and ran her hand in front of her in a semi-circle. Her fingertips grazed plastic. She snatched up the cigar-shaped shadow and held it up to the lights of Boston. She spotted a soft indent below the cap and twisted the top. The cap fell to the ground with a soft tick. Clambering to her feet, she turned, and froze.

In the half-light, Mira thought she might be gazing at a me-dieval religious painting. Francesca, serene and lovely, now kneeled at Connie's head, her hands long underneath, pale slices cupping Connie's darkened cheeks.

Alone on the ledge, Mira shivered deeply. On the ground, Connie's twitches had stilled, and she appeared to be sleep-ing. Francesca's voice floated past Mira, past the tip of the altar rock, out and over the chasm. Mira knew the quarry did queer things with sound, warped and threw it. But never this. Her voice magnified and multiplied, and soon it sounded like a hundred girls praying from every ledge. Mira felt the voices bounce back and fill her, and the reverberation entered her body and warmed it. If the prayers were a color, they'd be white, Mira thought, a pearly white light. Mira imagined the light pouring into Connie, and that seemed good.

"Our Father, who art in heaven, hallowed be thy name."

And then she heard her mother's stern voice. *Pray, Mira.*

Mira walked as if through water and kneeled next to Connie. Francesca swayed now, her eyes upturned. Mira's eyes widened as she marveled at her own voice soaring back to her tenfold.

Mira's fingers flexed around the pen.

Francesca prayed louder. "Thy kingdom come, thy will be done. On Earth as it is in heaven."

Mira straightened her back and prayed louder too. Francesca reached across Connie's waist to grab Mira's wrist, chanting, her eyes smiling at the corners. She shook her wrist, still chanting, and suddenly Mira realized her sister needed her, needed her voice to join the chorus or Connie would die.

Mira closed her eyes and prayed.

"Give us this day our daily bread, and forgive us our trespasses."

Mira listened to her own voice multiply and divide. A thousand Miras surrounded her, and their voices were beautiful.

She swayed.

"As we forgive those who trespass against us, and lead us not into temptation."

She chanted louder.

"But deliver us from evil."

As if obeying an unspoken command, the girls fell silent, but their voices carried for another minute across the chasm. Mira opened her eyes. Francesca looked down. She dipped her head over Connie, and her hair spilled, draping her in darkness. Her ear pressed against Connie's mouth. Mira froze, staring at the black crown of Francesca's head for a full minute.

"Oh no," Francesca whispered, convulsing over Connie.

Mira blinked hard, shaking herself awake. Her hand that clasped the pen had gone numb. She switched the pen to her left hand and raised it to the sky. With a primal scream, she jammed it down hard. The needle pierced Connie's jeans and punctured her thigh. The pen stood upright as her hand moved away, her fingers aloft and quivering in the air, her scream echoing across the chasm.

She didn't respond, and Mira knew that was not good.

PART 8

Ash

DECEMBER 2016

On the same day Ben walked out of Piggy's basement for the last time he ever would, he waited for his parents to fall asleep before slipping into his moonlit backyard clutching Mira's notes against his chest.

Stealth was required. His parents had been watching him closely since the incident. His mother had collapsed at his feet; his father had wept. Drenched, cocooned in a Mylar emergency blanket, the cops pushed Ben over his own doorstep. Now, his father's wing tip toe nudged the side of his sneaker under the kitchen table, his mother's fingers brushed the tops of his shoulders. Constantly, they touched him. Ben couldn't blame them, since it seemed like the teenagers of Bismuth were disappearing into the ether. Ben had even agreed to weekly dinners with Mr. Falso, which had to be easier than seeing a real therapist. Like his parents, Mr. Falso had accepted his excuse: that he'd gone to the ledge that night to get peace. His swim was deemed a sad reenactment of what his lost girlfriend had done months before, but resulting in hypothermia instead of rigor mortis. What they didn't know was that he'd brought something back with him from that night. Something he couldn't shake.

In the yard, a wet *click click* in his ear.

Softly, he placed the notes inside the patio chiminea and lit the match, each time snuffed by the wind, until the third time when it caught. The smoke blew away from his house, the smell of ink and char rising out of the neighborhood and over the Neck, out across the water and toward the city, where it would mingle with the smells of salt and city and new beginnings.

He no longer needed the notes. He could tell their story now using his own words. Mira's and Francesca's and Connie's.

Do something to one of us, you do it to all.

But first, there was business.

He stepped lightly across the frozen grass to his front yard, flush against the house so as not to set off the sensor lights his father had installed to discourage further escapes. From the bush in his front yard, Ben could see Mr. Cillo in his office, hunched over his desk, head resting on forearms. He had watched Mr. Cillo every night since he'd hidden in the man's dead daughters' closet. Graying gelled hair on a massive head. Meaty hands with scarred knuckles cupping elbows. Epaulettes of an ancient Members Only jacket worn indoors. Always the same.

Ben checked his watch: 11:19—arguably too late. But he was still a kid. Harmless if he showed up on a doorstep. He knew vaguely that the old Ben would have realized it was inappropriate to ring his neighbor's doorbell after eleven o'clock at night. But somewhere on the altar ledge, the new Ben had lost the compass that told him what normal kids did not do. For sure, his new lack of a filter had contributed to his near-friendless state. Since that night, Ben had felt Francesca's disapproving presence.

The sense of Francesca hit a crescendo in Piggy's basement, when Piggy began comparing the Miller girls to the Cillo sisters and everyone started weighing in, sizing them up. Ben's indignance had risen with every jaw-click in his ear. He'd yelled at Piggy, then each of them, and when they laughed at him, he threw his Xbox controller at Louis's lap, nailing his balls and starting a fight. Kyle tried to call them off, even said it was Ben's meds making him a nutbag, though to his knowledge, Ben was still faking his daily dose.

The sense of being watched was growing stronger.

And then, without remembering he had walked across his own driveway and the small patch of lawn that separated them, he was ringing Mr. Cillo's doorbell.

The door creaked open slowly. Framed by the indoor gloom, Mr. Cillo's form was rumpled and aged. A belly had developed that winter. Streetlight glare caught in a pair of never-before-seen glasses. Behind Ben, the wind whipped up. Something about the house seemed cozy, and for the first time in ages, he wanted to be inside.

"I know it's late, sir. But I have something to say to you."

"I'd say it's late, boy. It's almost midnight. Do your parents know you're out here?"

Ben looked down at the stoop, his cheeks hot. Mr. Cillo was referring to Ben's runaway escapade, one that he had been drawn into, a favor that he knew was unwise, hadn't wanted to give. The sureness of purpose Ben had had moments before evaporated.

"No, sir. But I couldn't sleep. I know you can't either. I see you awake every night."

Mr. Cillo wrinkled his brow, and Ben noticed his eyebrow hairs were long and tangled. He crossed his arms over his gut. "You peeping in my windows, son?"

"I can't help but see. We're so close, our houses . . ." Ben was fumbling. In his ear, the impatient *click click* of bone in socket.

"I wanted to say I'm sorry," Ben blurted. A leak had given way, and something hot and heavy poured out of him.

"Yeah, well. We've had our differences, your dad and me. But you got a good family. Show me how sorry you are by sticking close to your mom and dad and not scaring them anymore."

"Yes, sir." Ben told himself that it didn't matter what Mr.

Cillo thought he meant, only that he said it. He had been mistaken in his belief about Mira's father, and now he had atoned.

"And stay away from the quarry. Nothing good comes out of that place." He raised his arm to close the door, ready to sulk back into the dim.

Ben wondered if he understood the irony of what he'd said—the quarry had given him a living, and it had taken away his daughters. The filter was gone. Before he could stop himself, he said, "It's like the Bible says. First it gives, then it takes away."

Mr. Cillo let his arm fall. He opened and closed his fists. Ben cringed, ready for him to come after him, deliver him a smack for his insolence. But the wrinkles around his eyes grew soft, and his fists loosened at his waist.

"I feel sorry for you, kid," he said, shaking his head. "That coach really messed you up, didn't he?"

Ben felt the emotion rising in his throat. There was a time when he would have done physical violence to Mr. Cillo for his words. But Ben was beginning to master his own white-hot rage. Turn it into something else.

He straightened his shoulders and turned away from the Cillos' home. There was nothing here that he wanted.

* * *

APRIL 2016

Pale thimbles floated in a congealed Crock-Pot of pasta e fagioli. Spatulas under squares of lasagnas in colored Pyrex invited takers, but every slice remained. Children had filched all of the Jordan almonds from the pizzelle trays, and the cookies lay unadorned.

Everything had gone switchback, sideways, wrong. Francesca couldn't take it any longer. Mr. Falso had spent the entire night counseling her aunt, though she was barely responsive from the Xanax, and could easily be attended to by any one of the priests who had come to the house directly from the cemetery. Even her father—no fan of Mr. Falso, not really—had squeezed his shoulder at one point and offered him a cigar and an escape, but Mr. Falso had refused. Francesca was beginning to see Mr. Falso's behavior as one big attempt to avoid her, and she would not have that. Not now, when she needed him most, for comfort, of course—Connie had been her cousin, her blood—but her spiritual resolve was in jeopardy, never more so than now, since her dream had confirmed what she had begun to suspect.

She would catch him when he couldn't say no.

Francesca broke away from Mira. It was stifling, anyway, the way she clung to her, gave her no room to breathe, depending on her to get through her own terrible guilt. How could Mira feel guilty when the guilt was Francesca's to bear? It seemed almost selfish to Francesca, the way Mira sucked up responsibility for what had surely been Francesca's fault. But that was their way: one body, shared blood. *Mio sangue.*

Mira tugged at her sleeve. "Will you ask Daddy if we can go home?"

Francesca caught her reflection in a mirror. She was a ghost of herself, in her favorite black dress, the same one she'd worn to the wake, shapeless skin and bones under a cheap spandex blend, with hollows under her eyes. She looked like crap, really. But that was to be expected when your little cousin dies.

But not Mira.

Somehow Mira looked okay, in her flowy dress, her eyes sad but beautiful. Surely she had been tortured as much as Francesca by what happened to Connie. It had been a dumb trick, a stunt too soon to try, since she'd had so little time to explore her latest power. Mr. Falso's waning interest had set her on an accelerated time line. Francesca's eyes narrowed on Mira. Her cheeks had color; Mira hadn't lost weight like she had. Her small belly was soft and slightly rounded under her dress, her arms still full. Perhaps Mira felt less guilty, because she'd tried to use the pen to save Connie? What ever happened to that pen?

"Why are you looking at me like that?" Mira said.

"It's nothing." Francesca smiled gently. "I'll ask Daddy if

we can go in a minute. I promise. Stay here and don't talk to anyone." She waited half-hidden behind the corner of the Villelas' hutch until Mr. Falso broke away to get her aunt a paper cup of punch. The other women seemed relieved as they swarmed Mrs. Villela's chair; they couldn't leave without sharing regrets and a proper goodbye, and Mr. Falso's monopolizing had stalled them for a good hour.

Francesca waited until he set the crystal ladle back in its bowl with a soft clink.

"I need to speak with you privately," she said curtly.

Mr. Falso spun and punch splashed onto his curled hand. With his eyebrows raised, the creases in his forehead and around his eyes and mouth seemed deeper than before, making him look old and clownish. Francesca set the thought aside.

"Now."

"Of course!" Mr. Falso looked over Francesca's head toward Mrs. Villela, surrounded by mavens, not in need of punch anytime soon. He set it down on the table and forced his expression into something more sober. "How are you doing, Francesca?"

"Privately."

"Yes, right." They walked past clumps of neighbors and Connie's classmates to the back of the house. Each time he turned for approval, Francesca shook her head. Finally, they came to the back stairs.

"Up here," Francesca said, mounting the stairs.

Ash

"Francesca, I don't think—"

"I don't care what anybody thinks is appropriate or inappropriate. Half the guests are only here to look good for my father and my uncle anyway. They don't care about Connie. She's *my* dead cousin. I'm the one in pain. You're supposed to counsel me, do you understand?" She shook with the force of her words, angry at him, but more angry at the tears forming at the corners of her eyes that meant she was losing control. Silently, he passed her, and she followed him up the stairs. He paused in the hall until she grabbed his wrist and pulled him past Eddie's closed bedroom door and into Connie's bedroom.

Someone had drawn the nubby purple tab curtains that covered the room's only window. Francesca dropped Mr. Falso's wrist and strode to the window. She yanked the halves apart and light streamed in. He shaded his eyes. Flowers, brown and desiccated, hung from a noose of ribbon. The walls were covered with posters of pretty boys with puffy lips. In a corner, a rigged strip of lightbulbs above a sheet of mirror, under which a slab of plywood jutted from the wall, fashioning a makeshift vanity. The plywood was laden with small bottles of flesh-colored liquid, sticks, and tubes. Above, the mirror was coated with a film of hairspray from cans lined up on the floor below. A stool with a round seat topped by a frilly pink circular pillow came to half the height of the makeshift counter.

Mr. Falso sat on the edge of a padded chair and moved his folded hands in front of his groin, crossing his legs in a feminine pose, as if to hide all the parts of him that made him male. Francesca paced the pink braided rug, swearing every time the heel of her shoe got caught on the weave.

She stopped and stared at him. "That's right, Nick. I actually say *curse words*. Just another reason for you to make the case that I am not, in fact, saint material."

Hours before, Francesca had envisioned this very scenario, the two of them alone. Herself crying on Mr. Falso's shoulder, and there's where it would get difficult for them both, her frail loveliness pressing against him, tears smearing her mascara. He would allow her to soak the breast of his button-down shirt, wear it downstairs like a badge. Tip her jaw with thumb and forefinger and look deeply into her eyes, and say, "Your cousin is safe with God," and then, "And you are safe with me."

She hadn't gone to her father for help when the rest of the town turned only to Frank Cillo to solve their problems. She hadn't gone to a priest, or one of the myriad uncles, genetic and in name, that their father positioned around the town like grizzled watchdogs to monitor his daughters. She came to him, Nick Falso, Friend of Teens. She trusted him. He could be trusted.

"I'm not making a case one way or another. You're in pain, Francesca. You've lost someone you loved deeply. This is a confusing time. Don't begin to think that I don't care."

Francesca's eyes jittered. She grabbed her elbows and rubbed them. "I haven't been in this room since I was twelve. Connie practically lived at our house." She stalked over to a knick-knack shelf and raised a photograph in a cheap brass frame that said *Sisters* in curlicue letters: Connie, across the laps of the two Cillo girls, their feet stretched toward the camera, animal slipper heads cocked in different directions. They wore ponytails and pajamas, and their faces were coated with green pasty masks like Day-Glo mimes.

Mr. Falso smiled. "She was like a sister to you, wasn't she?"

"But she wasn't our sister. She wasn't actually our sister."

"I'm sure you treated her like a sister."

Francesca twisted the side of her mouth into a crooked smile. "I treated her like blood. You do anything for blood. Connie understood that."

"Connie was an extraordinary girl. She never allowed her physical limitations to keep her from leading a good life, filled with love."

Francesca laughed then, a gruff noise, and placed the frame back on the shelf. "Connie loved to be loved."

"And now she lives with God."

"It must be nice to know where you stand with Him."

Mr. Falso coughed. "We should be getting back downstairs. Your aunt will wonder where I am."

"You need to hear me." Francesca rushed to the chair and fell to her knees on the braided rug. Mr. Falso's head snapped

toward the door; there were only the same distant murmur-
ings of middle-aged parents, tired and thick-waisted, searching
for the space between mourning and sociability. His gaze fell
to Francesca's hollowed cheeks and perfectly carved jaw, and
he seized Francesca's hands and tried to raise her, but she pulled
him down and he was drawn forward, closer to her face, on his
knees.

"You don't understand," Francesca pleaded, her eyes bright
and wet. "Satan came to me in my dreams. Last night, and
the night before that! It was awful: he looked like he does in
pictures, only he was little, a little demon, with an awful mouth
and sharp teeth, and his mouth was filled with light, but not
good light, a hot, rank light, like fire, a fire caused by something awful burning, like . . . skin. He speaks, and his voice
is terrible; I'm saying 'he' but the voice could have been a man
or a woman. He taunts me, tells me I should give up wanting
to be a saint, because I'm not good enough!"

"Francesca . . ."

"But here's the thing: I was protected. There was a light
around me, a different sort of light than the one coming from
his mouth. And I had the sense"—Francesca's eyes ran over
Mr. Falso's face—"I had the sense the light was protecting me
from him."

"That's good. That's very, very good, Francesca. That's your
faith protecting you." Mr. Falso shifted, his wrists still caught

by her slender, strong hands. "Protecting you from a bad dream."

Francesca's mouth fell open as she dropped his wrists. "A bad dream?"

Mr. Falso rubbed his wrists, settling back in the chair. "Yes. And if I were going to interpret it, I would say that Connie's death tested your faith. This is common: when bad things happen to good people, we ask, Why, God, why her? Why me? That's what the whole book of Job is about: God testing people with terrible trials. You're like Job, Francesca. You won't stop believing in God because your beautiful, vibrant young cousin died! Your faith will win out."

Mr. Falso sat back in his chair, satisfied. As if he could have had a cigarette.

Francesca set her jaw hard.

"If you know so much about Job, how about Saint Teresa of Avila? She had visions of the devil—*visions*, not dreams—on a regular basis. On a regular basis, Satan taunted and tempted her, tried to get her to give up being a saint. She describes them exactly as what I saw!" Francesca stabbed the rug with her finger. "Exactly! The light pouring out of his mouth, the light around her! It's exactly the same, you can google it . . ."

Mr. Falso leaned forward, his voice soft. "And did you?"

"Did I what?"

"Google it?"

"Well, yeah! But that was *after* I had the first dream! What are you saying?"

"Francesca." Mr. Falso reached out and stroked her hair with the back of his hand. "I'm saying nothing, except that you are exhausted. You've experienced things that are confusing to you, and then had a terrible tragedy. You're looking for answers."

"I'm looking for someone who believes me." Francesca grabbed his hand in midstroke and pressed it to her cheek. "You have to believe me, Nick."

His name hung there in the room as the sun dropped behind a cloud, or below the horizon. Francesca had lost track of time. In her mind's eye, she knew she had made herself ugly to him, her cheeks like onionskin, thin, with veins showing underneath, her dark eyebrows drawn in crayon strokes.

Gently, he slipped his hand from underneath hers and rested it in his lap. "You are not a saint."

Francesca blinked heavily, then gazed down sharply to her right as though struck.

"I have to go downstairs. Why don't you take a few minutes here alone? I'll let your family know you're lying down. Your sister will bring you a glass of punch, okay?"

Francesca was silent.

"Okaaay, maybe not." Mr. Falso edged from the room, looking around as though the objects might save him, something interesting and upbeat to note, some capper that might make light of their circumstances. At the window, a dried bud fell to the floor.

Kneeling, head torqued as though she'd been slapped, Francesca remained still.

"You rest, then." He slid from the room, leaving the door open a crack.

Minutes passed, then an hour. The room ebbed from blue to purple to black. Francesca's legs went dead, and her neck ached. Still, she did not move. She had slipped into a sweet numbness. She wondered if this was where Connie had existed before she died, when her body was overtaken by histamines and her mind stopped flashing, in this pale, cottony place of no feeling. It wasn't so bad, she thought. She was resting.

Mira crept into the dark room. She felt for the lacquered dresser and placed a cup of punch on it, and fumbled with a lamp topped with a ceramic canary finial. The canary fell to the floor and splintered. When the light switched on, she saw it was split in two.

"Oh!" Mira said.

Francesca fell onto one hip, legs useless, propped on one arm like a tent pole. Mira snatched the paper cup from the dresser top and handed it to her. Francesca took a sip.

Mira thrust her neck forward. "Did Mr. Falso do something to you?"

Francesca laughed huskily, bright red punch dribbling down her chin. The depth of her voice was at odds with how weak and dejected she looked, on the floor. It frightened Mira.

"No, of course he didn't," Mira said quickly. "Mr. Falso would never *do* anything to you. I thought, since you were on the floor . . . never mind." She scrambled up and pulled a dusty tissue from a box on the dresser. Kneeling beside Francesca, she dabbed at her sister's chin tentatively, the way one approached a wounded animal.

Behind the tissue, Francesca smiled bitterly. "You're right. He would never do anything to me."

Mira crumpled the tissue and made a big deal out of tucking it into her little bag, giving herself time to consider how to yank Francesca back from her dark place. "It's probably wrong to say, but he looks handsome tonight."

Francesca laughed again, her pitch ticking up. Mira knew it was not right. Her laugh sounded sharp and rangy, like it was looking for something to puncture. Mira tucked her lip to keep herself from speaking any more. Minutes passed, and the silence between them thickened. Through Connie's window, Mira saw the outline of a tree against the grape-colored night sky. The leaves trembled, and she buried her chin. The tree alarmed Mira, like a lot of things (the ropy underside of a dog's neck, a dead mosquito fat with blood). Inexplicable threats that made her press the insides of her elbows into her forehead until her thoughts stopped racing. It was those times when Mira would remind herself that Ben Lattanzi was right next door, and she could go to him, and his presence would force her into normalcy. Connie could have used a Ben. She'd never had a real boyfriend, or real friendships, really, beyond her cousins. Everywhere hung reminders of the smallness of Connie's world, flimsy, curly-edged things made of paper: ribbons, movie posters, photos with cheeks pressed together.

"I told him about my visions."

Mira startled. "About the devil from your dreams? What did he say?"

The sockets in Francesca's cheeks hardened.

"Visions. Not dreams. Of course," Mira corrected herself. "What was his face like when you told him?"

Francesca struggled to raise herself on bloodless legs.

"I imagine he wanted to comfort you." Mira lifted her slowly by the arm. "Protect you, I imagine."

Francesca pulled away and steadied herself. "You can imagine."

"He must have known you were terrified."

Francesca shuffled toward the door. "The word he used was 'exhausted.' But the word he meant was 'delusional.'"

Mira fixed on the point at Francesca's waist where her leotard bagged, where a man might lift her, were she a real ballerina. She envisioned a man's hands around Francesca's waist, fingers overlapping. Why couldn't this man, this "spiritual director," lift her?

"He needs time."

"He thinks I googled Saint Teresa of Avila, and that I'm acting out the things she wrote."

Mira knew Francesca's confessions to Mr. Falso were dangerous. He didn't know how close to the edge Francesca's mind twirled, that disappointment could cause her to spiral. Or maybe he did know. In that moment, she hated him, and the hate felt like something Francesca could see. She crossed back to the window to hide her face, tugging the curtains together against voices drifting up from the yard below.

Mira threw back her shoulders. "We'll just have to try something new."

Francesca sagged against the doorframe. "After what happened to Connie? You want to try again?"

"Not in the same way. Not with someone we know."

"We murdered her."

"Girls! Time to go!" Their father's voice boomed from downstairs, a yell meant to smoke them out without having to stumble across something private and embarrassing.

Mira spun and stepped lightly across the room toward Francesca and closed the door softly behind them. "Truth be told, it was probably going to happen sooner or later. Connie wasn't going to live like a teacup for the rest of her life. Eventually,

she was going to test her limits. In some ways, it was a beautiful thing, that we were there as witnesses."

"I should have been able to save her."

"You're not saying that you don't believe in your own gifts
anymore?"

"Girls!" their father called again.

From the bottom of the stairs rose the clucks of women
rushing to aid Frank Cillo.

"You can't discount Donata's hands. Did you tell Mr. Falso
about Donata's hands?"

Francesca gazed at her sister, smiling, her eyes lit softly,
like the faint glow from a long-dead star only now reaching
Earth.

Mira swallowed hard. "Did you tell him?"

"It wouldn't have done any good. He wouldn't have
believed me."

Mira's protests faltered as Francesca took her hands in her
own, scars grazing their tops. She drew Mira's hands to her
mouth and kissed them.

"It's always been that way for saints, since the beginning of
time." She dropped Mira's hands and turned the doorknob.
"He doesn't want me while I'm living. But he'll have me when
I'm dead."

Mira hung ten paces behind Francesca, watching as her
sister's shadow lengthened between them. At the bottom of the
stairs, Francesca turned right toward their father's voice in the

parlor. Mira needed a moment; she needed to find Ben, to whisper directions to meet her somewhere. It wouldn't be easy: they'd have visitors coming and going at their own house now, at all hours and for days, dropping by to touch their shoulders. She and Francesca would be expected to greet them and accept their Saran-wrapped packages of concern. Mira would have to nod at the injustice of Connie's leave-taking, as though she had boarded a flight for spring break, and as though Mira herself had no relation to the event.

Mira searched the dining room, still stuffed with bodies. No Ben. She looked for him among the parlor bustle, and was relieved to see her father and Francesca waylaid by a circle of biddies from St. Theresa's. She ducked out fast before they could spot her, cutting through the den and onto the back porch, past her father's Rotary Club pals smoking cigars and watching the Red Sox on TV. She leaned over each of the grizzled men, accepting cheek kisses while shoving each one off a little. When she finally stepped down the porch into the yard, she exhaled and looked up at the sky. On the other side of the fence, the old rottweiler, Lupo, panted hard, his wet teeth visible through the slats. Lupo was bad to the core; Mira's uncle blamed Lupo for the cat's bad eye, had sworn many times to take a shotgun to the beast himself.

Mira heard her mother's voice in her head.

Touch it, Mira.

Mira stepped toward the fence and stretched her finger through the slat.

"I wouldn't pat that thing."

Mira whirled around, dress floating around her legs, Lupo howling. Louis Gentry was perched on the highest rung of staging set up in the Villelas' backyard. Her uncle had planned to paint his house that coming summer; Ben was going to help. More money for something special he was saving up for, he'd told Mira.

Mira set her chin low. "I wasn't going to pet it."

"Sure looked like it. And I'm not sure this family could handle another freak accident." Louis cocked his head toward the house. "Looking to get air?"

"I was leaving. Have you seen Ben?"

"I did. Hey, do you hate these things as much as I do?"

"I hate them when they're waking my flesh and blood, if that's what you mean," Mira said sharply, rubbing her arms. She smelled the ocean and a worse smell, dog mess from next door, probably.

"I didn't mean to be crude. You know I cared about Connie."

"Um, none of you guys cared about Connie. You cared about what you got off Connie—that would be more accurate."

Louis gave her a look of hard disappointment. "Now that

isn't fair. You know, this whole thing gets me thinking about how fragile life is." Louis leaped off the staging like a cat and walked toward her. "Say it was you instead of Connie who got hurt up there."

Mira had known Louis nearly half her life, but something in his eyes now looked manic and empty at once. "It wasn't."

He came closer, staring right into Mira's face. She could feel his breath. "I never could have gotten over it."

Mira stepped backward. "You said you saw Ben. Where is he?"

Louis laughed to the side, his hand on the back of his neck.

"What are you laughing at?" Mira demanded.

"Yeah, I saw Ben. I saw him leaving. With Gina Tramondozzi."

"You're lying."

Louis shook his head. "It's nothing new. He hooks up with Gina T. every time he gets lonely. They go way back. She's, like, your body double or something. A bad one, but you take what you can get. Not me, of course. I'm discriminating in my tastes."

He said it so surely, so effortlessly. Mira's eyes went dark.

"See, you can't tease a guy, hooking up every once in a while, when you feel like it. Growing guy like Ben Lattanzi's got needs," Louis said.

Mira felt her sureness disassemble and fall away. "You don't know Ben's needs." She faltered.

"I know Ben's human. And Gina's a warm body. It's hard to resist when it's right there in front of you, just asking to be taken," he said, the corner of his lip flicking up.

"He would never," she said, her voice tightening to a squeak.

"The thing about urges is, eventually you gotta give in, or they'll keep coming back." Louis stood over her, lifting a hank of hair from her eyes. "And back. And back."

Mira spun away from Louis and staggered to the front of the house, filmy-eyed, her gaze gone dead, her mother's voice in her head.

It's quiet here, Mira.

By mid-May, the cherry tree on the Cillos' front lawn began to bud, then bloom. By the end of the same week, its petals blanketed the fallow lawn. Mira sat under the tree sometimes, cradling a new kitten gifted by one of Mr. Cillo's associates, and initially, Louis used the cat as an occasion to stop and talk. Mira whispered one-word answers and refused to lift her eyes from her lap, where the kitten lay curled in a tight C. He brought the cat a toy purchased from Claws and Paws, a wand with blue and purple feathers on the end that looked like a ravaged feather duster, which Mira accepted without protest or thanks.

When the grocery delivery van pulled up one day, Francesca poked her head inside the passenger side window, her foot kicking up playfully behind her. She laughed and dug cash out of her purse, which she shoved through the window, jamming it back into her bag when it was refused. Francesca moved to the back and slid boxes out through the doors, stacking them on the curb. Mira didn't budge from her spot under the bare tree, as if watching her sister stockpiling for an apocalypse was unremarkable.

Francesca moved the boxes into the house. Mira took mental inventory. Twelve canisters of Maxwell House instant coffee. Overgrown cylinders of sugar, salt, and pepper. Canned tuna, salmon, chicken, and turkey. Mega-packages of Charmin, Kleenex, Bounty, and napkins, in multiples. Barber pole–striped shaving cream cans in a beer box. A mountain of hamburger trapped under an arc of plastic wrap. Powdered milk. Black licorice nips in a plastic barrel. Racks of short ribs laminated in plastic. Envelopes of Red Cap pipe tobacco packed upright in a slant-cut box.

Mira tickled the kitten with the feather duster. It batted the tuft. It was cute, not more than a gray ball of fluff, its bones loose and light, a barely there creature you could hardly feel in one hand. Mira cupped the kitten's tail end with one hand and pinched its nose with her two forefingers with the other. The kitten became a writhing ball of fluff, then settled as Mira released her fingers. She repeated the squeeze again, each time tweaking a little longer. When the kitten stilled, she carried it into the house and left it in its box underneath a blanket, and went looking for something else pleasing to touch.

Mira didn't remember when the fishbowl had come into the Cillo house. They had never had a fish, nor any pets before Mira's kitten. Francesca said it wasn't a real fishbowl, but an enormous cocktail glass that their parents had won as a prize at some boozy Lions Club fund-raiser many years before. Mira loved touching the smooth glass, and the thick lip that folded over itself at the top. There was something perfectly round and lovely about it, and even though it left the tiny notes she had started writing Ben over the last few months exposed, Francesca didn't seem to notice or care, which always made Mira wonder, since as sisters, and in particular sisters who lived on top of one another, anything seemingly private—diaries, magazines with cute boy bands, diet logs—was fair game. Why the notes were left alone mattered little now. Francesca was so caught up in their preparations, she wouldn't notice that the notes were gone.

Daddy would be left with everything he needed. Stocking so the supplies wouldn't be found was another matter, and it meant hiding things in the basement. Mira was supposed to be inputting Daddy's profile into online dating sites, because it wouldn't be long before the supplies ran out—six months for perishables, eight months for paper goods, twelve months for canned goods. After trying and failing to interest him in

Louis Gentry's mother, who had been single since Louis's dad died in the Iraq War, the girls knew they needed to get a wife for their father some other way, and if they hit enough sites, the law of averages said they'd make a connection. Francesca ran the outside errands, the ones that required begging for rides and interactions with the outside world. She convinced Kyle's delinquent older brother Kamil to bring his bus by on a Wednesday afternoon before Mr. Cillo got home from work and load the bikes up so Francesca could take them to the bike shop for a tune-up. Mira suspected Francesca's outside errands included visits to the parish center, where she no longer worked. Her services were not needed, would be too much strain after Connie died, was Mr. Falso's strong feeling.

Mira did not like looking too closely at Francesca. She was no longer sleeping, afraid of the nightly dreams where the devil tempted her into abandoning her "path." Dusky circles under her sister's eyes extended along the line of her thin nose, and she squinted. The corners of her mouth drooped, and she seemed to have trouble finding words for things.

"Stack the—cans, cans of, fish, whatever—away from the hot water heater. They might spoil; we don't know!" she'd shout.

"The tuna or the salmon?" Mira would ask.

"The salmon. Tuna! Oh whatever, the cans!" she'd stumble to say.

The fishbowl contained exactly five notes. Mira scooped out

the notes one by one. Francesca would be home soon from her visit with Kamil, trying to get cyclobenzaprine, which was supposed to make you fall asleep. Francesca had hoped that Kamil did what she asked and got it beforehand, and would not make her sit in his car waiting to meet his "associate." But since they'd been gone three hours now, Mira assumed things had not gone as planned.

Mira folded the notes she planned to leave for Ben to find, and placed them on top of one another until they made a precarious tower. In a way, she hated the notes. Most of them were cryptic and stupid. They contained an accounting of ugly things. Each one had been shed, a flake sloughed from her heel as she ran. It was tempting to edit them, clean them up. But she knew that was dangerous. Her intention, for Ben to tell their story, was vulnerable. So simple to touch their father's lighter to the top note and make a pile of ash. No. She would give Ben the notes, and then he would see her. All her parts. For a time, that was what he had wanted the most.

What was missing were instructions.

By the time you get this, I'll be gone, she wrote, recounting what she knew people would call them, and how some of it was true. Her eyes filled with tears, and the paper went blurry. It felt impossible to keep going.

In her mind's ear, she heard her mother, gentler than she'd ever been in life. *Tell him to tell your story, Mira.*

She could do that. So she did.

Six notes. They had been together a total of seven times in seven places. A seventh note ought to be a kind of summary, she thought. A guarantee Ben would get the story right. She slipped her hand into the desk drawer and felt for the EpiPen she'd hidden there last March. On a new sheet of paper, she wrote:

Francesca tried to raise Connie from the dead
to win Mr. Falso's love. And because of that,
Connie died.

She wrapped the note around the pen and tied it with a purple ribbon from her wrist. She tried to stack the rest of the notes into a neat pile, then gave up and settled for a messy polyhedron. She set one note, the sixth, aside and stuffed the rest of the wad into a manila envelope. It would take a few days for her to get around town and hide most of the notes where they needed to be. They'd been planning for this moment for two months. Now, she had only a few days.

A few days was good. Merciful. If she waited any longer, she might change her mind.

Mira slipped the instructions into an envelope and addressed it, wondering how long a slightly misaddressed letter would take to find its way. She knew from her aunt's long career at the post office that a misaddressed letter without a return address ran the risk of ending up in the dead letter office, which was somewhere in Boston. It could be opened, even. But one with a nonexistent street name that sounded a lot like an existing street name would end up with the "lost ladies," a cadre of blue-haired postal employees whose only job was to decipher cryptic addresses, trace mangled mail, and return stolen wallets dropped in mailboxes to their rightful owners. Her letter would be in good hands; it would just take awhile for it to get there. Mira counted on this.

Headlights illuminated the living room window. She snapped her head, then dropped it as the dark crowded back in. Not Francesca, not yet. She was probably fending off Kamil, who always expected something in return for a favor. It was hardly fair that Mira sat at their father's desk while Francesca was out doing the dirty work, but Francesca had wanted it that way. Mira pinned note six to the torn liner underneath the couch, steeling herself against memories of the last time she was with Ben. She tried to complete her father's profile, which she thought with some pride reflected the right mix of rugged manliness and lovability. But her eyes kept wandering to the window. The street was dark. Her stomach gripped; a thought niggled at the edge of her brain. It was a good plan, it was fair and just. And yet. In confessing, she condemned Francesca. Even if Ben never told anyone, he would always know that Francesca had killed Connie. He would judge her.

And Francesca's wasn't the only heart broken.

She grabbed a lighter from the desk drawer, removed the note attached to the EpiPen, and set it on fire. As she watched the paper flicker, slowly, it seemed, she remembered the time she, Francesca, and Connie had smoked for the first time on the back deck of Connie's house, in the middle of January, Connie freaking out that the wind would blow the smoke back in through the screen into her kitchen. She thought of how easily Francesca had convinced Connie to steal her mother's Parliaments. How Connie had exhaled a thin strip of smoke with her eyes closed, and how silly she had looked. Francesca told Connie she looked older smoking, and that was what it took for Connie to get hooked. When Mira and Francesca got in trouble after their father smelled smoke in their hair, Connie took the blame, earning herself a full week without her phone. She'd been happy to take the punishment, Mira thought, because it made her more like them, her cousins, the Cillo sisters she worshipped and emulated. Only Connie could romanticize their electronic-less existence, their strict rules. Only Connie could view it as exotic and enviable. Only Connie would give her life in an effed-up experiment to prove one of them was a saint.

Mira ran her finger through the flame a few times before she doused the flame. She collected the half-burned note and its ashes onto a sheet of legal paper and dumped it into the trash can underneath the desk. On a new piece of paper, she wrote:

Francesca thought she was touched by God.
But we couldn't prove it. And because of that, Connie died.

*We didn't plan for Connie's heart to stop forever. We didn't plan
for our hearts to be broken.*

Here's what we learned: when you touch things, they can break.

She attached the new note to the EpiPen with the ribbon
and stashed it in her bag on the floor.

Mira lifted her chair so it did not scrape as she rose, flicked
off the overhead lights, and sat on the couch enveloped in darkness. She crossed her arms over the back of the sofa and rested
her cheek on the fold of her elbow. The phone rang. *I'm asleep,*
she told her father, without moving. *Francesca's asleep too.* He
would realize quickly and hang up. Three rings, half a fourth,
then . . . silence. She smiled. With the lights off, Mira could
see straight through the Lattanzis' living room window, past
where Mrs. Lattanzi sat at her own small desk, pooled in a
computer screen's blue light, into their kitchen, where Mr.
Lattanzi passed by the doorframe with a dish of something
in stunted hands, which she realized were encased in oven
mitts. She knew by the smile on Mr. Lattanzi's face that
Ben was seated at the dining room table out of Mira's sightline,
waiting for his dinner. Mira knew Mrs. Lattanzi loved her
work, and there she was, working on her computer. She knew
Mr. Lattanzi had helped coach Ben's lacrosse team that night,
and that they were having a late dinner after practice, and that
his ears were still red because it had been cold on the field.

Mira marveled at the clarity with which she could see straight into the heart of Ben's house, where everything was as it should be, where everything was what it seemed. Where no one had been touched by gifts that became curses, and fathers knew what was going on in lives they allowed their children to live, and mothers didn't beg daughters to join them in the ether.

Mrs. Lattanzi yelled something over her shoulder and Ben loped into sight. Mira lifted her face from her arm and sat up on the couch cushions. Ben stood behind his mother as she showed him something on the screen, and he laughed. As he laughed, he turned to look out the window, and Mira froze. She wondered if the light from the basement was filtering in somehow, and he could see her, it had caught her hair, made her visible. Mira wanted to yell, to wave her arms. She knew at that moment that she wanted to be seen by Ben. He may have failed her, screwed her, and run from her crazy, but she still loved him, for his beauty, and his wounds.

She remained still.

Ben squinted, his eyes searching in the dark, until he looked away, collapsing on the couch and chatting with his mother, reassured that he had seen nothing.

JULY 2017

Ben gazed out the Kuliks' screened porch. His vision was loopy, caught on the tiny wire squares, and he squinted to see beyond them to the abandoned ball field where kids had stuffed red Solo cups to spell out the class year. Beyond the field, he saw the redeveloped Superfund park, with joggers and middle-aged walkers and baby strollers bouncing above loamed and seeded poison. Beyond the park, he saw the red blear of headlights on Route 3, and the perfectly gray Atlantic behind.

Now everything was crystal clear. His letter would tell the truth about what happened to Connie: a big fat mistake that would drive anyone with a conscience to a desperate act. It was all anyone needed to know, that the girls weren't crazy, just good. Too good for this world. How good would be Ben and Kyle's secret, because after the shameless parade of graveside selfies, the webcam someone installed claiming to see the girls' ghosts, and the endless articles and littered beer cans and the rumored TV movie chronicling the sisters' last days, Ben and Kyle both knew that calling out Francesca's specialness would only make the lurid interest in the girls worse.

The light was falling fast.

"You almost done, Tolstoy?" Kyle stretched his legs on the cot he slept on in his sunporch and mined his teeth with a safety pin. That summer, Ben had noticed it looked a lot like Kyle was living out here, having moved in a cube fridge, printer, TV, and a laundry basket full of clothes. The Kuliks might not have such a hard time of it when Kyle left.

Ben wiggled his cramped fingers over the keyboard. Waves of pain shot through his butt. The wrought-iron filigreed chair

and matching table Kyle had brought in for the task were per-
ilously dainty beneath him. The story that had taken him five
months to start, and another six months to rewrite, was finished. Tonight, as he came to the last page, his hands were
connected in a direct line to his brain, his typing feverish, and
the only sound he heard was his own breathing. Now it was
go time. He unfolded his long body and hit Print, shoving the
hot documents into three envelopes addressed to the Cillos; the
Villelas; and the *Bismuth Evening Gazette.*

Kyle arched an eyebrow. "You sure about that last one?"

"I'm sure."

"We'll be long gone by the time it blows up, anyway." Kyle
rolled off the cot and shoved his pillow into his trunk suitcase,
bouncing on it until it clicked shut. "Your bags in the truck?"

"On top of the tools." Ben sealed the last envelope and
tugged at the front of his shirt. It was a dry, cool summer night,
the kind that didn't happen much near the ocean, but Ben was
sweating buckets. "Help me lift?" Ben grabbed the handle on
one end of the trunk and Kyle grabbed the other, and Kyle
whistled as they hoisted his worldly possessions into the flatbed of his truck. Ben slid in on the passenger side.

The truck rumbled to a start. No one in the house came
out; no one asked where they were going, and Kyle didn't
bother to look back.

"Post office?" Kyle said.

"Yep," Ben replied.

They cruised by the darkened Powder Neck branch of the post office and dropped the three envelopes in the nighttime slot. With the wheeze and slam of the handle, Mira's words were out there. No turning back.

Ben didn't anticipate how dark the cemetery would be, but Kyle's vision was freakishly sharp, a cosmic balancing for years of near-deafness. They came to the Cillo plot and decamped, carrying the shovels and file from the back of the truck swiftly, like men for whom grave digging was an everyday thing. Ben rubbed his hands together to dry the sweat (so much sweat) and they set to work, each to his own task.

Bats pinwheeled low above their heads. After a while, the mosquitos found them, and Ben's bites had bites. The moon was a lucky break: it shone with a clear ferocity so that when the shovel slipped from Ben's raw and clumsy hands, he spotted the long white outline of its handle and lost no time. Three hours later, sweat soaked their shirts, and every part of their bodies burned, including, inexplicably, Ben's crotch. But there was no stopping until they hit bottom, because once the letters telling Mira and Francesca's story had been dropped, everything else had to follow.

"I hit something!" yelled Ben. He went into overdrive, dropping to his knees and digging around the small box with a hand spade. Kyle dropped his file and kneeled beside Ben, using his hands to dig. When they cleared enough dirt to lift it out of the ground, they stood, swaying like drunks, taking in the unearthed treasure. Ben would have liked to stand like that for a while, honoring whichever sister it was. But Kyle brought him back.

"Time, dude," Kyle said softly.

Ben rubbed his chin, squinting at the urn.

"Dude?" Kyle said, louder. "They deserve to rest in peace. This is not peace."

Ben held his mouth, unsure.

"Ben: it's time."

Ben kicked the ground like a horse. "Yeah. I know. They deserve to rest in peace," Ben relented, repeating the words he and Kyle had told each other over and over that summer.

They worked together, digging up the second plot, and soon the box revealed itself. When they set them both in the flatbed and slipped into the safe carriage of the truck, reality set in, and Ben was relieved to get away from the girls. Kyle seemed spooked, too, gunning it so fast out of the long cemetery road that Ben was mashed up against the door. Ben tried not to think about the urns knocking around inside the boxes: it was unconscionable for the urns to be left loose inside these things not unlike plaster beer coolers, with nothing to protect them.

The boys fell quiet. Ben's wet shirt stiffened, and the dirt on his arms and legs dried to a floury paste. They hadn't made a plan for getting clean, but Ben couldn't think that far ahead when they still had so far to go. He blinked and rubbed grit from his eyes until the headlights of oncoming cars bled together. Cars roared past and the truck rattled, but the noise did nothing to mask the *klunk!* in the flatbed.

Ben shivered uncontrollably.

Kyle looked over at him. "You all right?"

A sedan with pink LED lighting on its undercarriage cut Kyle off. He slammed the brakes.

Klunk! and a rattle.

"I've got a confession to make," Ben yelled. "I used to hate driving with you."

Kyle grinned, teeth gleaming in his grimy face. "Oh really?"

"You were the worst driver. I deliberately wouldn't talk the whole time so you wouldn't take your eyes off the road to watch my lips, or give me your good ear, or whatever it was you used to do. But somehow, I think you've actually gotten worse."

Kyle laughed. "And here I thought you were always quiet because my driving made you carsick."

"Still does."

Ben noticed Kyle's right hand resting on the seat next to him. The hand looked wrong, bent at a strange angle and twitching, like its nerves were frayed and accepting the wrong signals.

"Your hand any better?"

For three hours, while Ben had dug, Kyle had worked the file like a demon, sparking as he grated the rough edge against the granite. By the time they'd finished, they had both used up every part of their bodies, and they were starting to become unglued. Ben's shoulders screamed, lactic acid already seeping inside the tears in his muscles. But Kyle had it worse, performing the same motion on the bench for hours, filing the girls into anonymity.

Kyle regarded his hand and whistled through his teeth. "When am I ever whole?"

Ben laughed. "You're right about that." *Maybe she can fix it,* Ben wanted to say.

Ben knew their plan involved an element of hypocrisy. Using Francesca's gift could be considered an exploitation along the same lines as that of the freak-seekers who made pilgrimages to the Cillo gravesite. The activity had gotten heavier in the last few months, and Ben had started to think of their plan less as righting a wrong and more like a rescue mission. Vandals were getting braver, most recently spray-painting other graves with arrows pointing to the Cillos' bench, which Ben and Kyle realized early on was too heavy to move.

Off the exit, Kyle took the corner around Johnny's Foodmaster too fast, and the truck lifted on two wheels. Ben leaned toward Kyle, sure they would tip. The truck righted with a bounce—*Klunk!*—and flew past the rusted rack where the kids left their bikes before they entered the quarry. Ben hadn't considered that his and Kyle's escape out of Bismuth might be accelerated by dying. Though that would be right in line with

Bismuth's new rap. Consider *People*'s article on what was being called the "Deadly Quarry Mystery." The article was less about the girls and more about Bismuth as a place where young people disappear ("Famed 'Town of No Old Men' Now Losing Its Youth," December 2016). Ben had memorized the first line: *Some call it a karmic correction, others see it as the inevitable result of the town's youth's unrestricted access to the dangerous Bismuth quarry. Regardless, a spike in suicides and accidental deaths among the town's young people is a reversal for this rough "town of no old men" nine miles outside of Boston, where for decades, silicosis meant death for many by middle age.* A trio of reporters had done some creative demographic addition that showed the number of deaths of citizens ages eighteen to thirty was triple the number of most towns in the Commonwealth. Ben noted that eighteen to thirty didn't include the ages of the Cillo girls, or Connie, for that matter. A special insert box explained the nature of the poisonous quarry, that had "given so much and taken so much away." Ben, who had taken to collecting clippings about the Deadly Quarry Mystery, would have known about the story anyway, since "local epidemiologist" Carla Lattanzi was a primary source.

Kyle looked over at Ben.

"You ready?" he asked.

Ben locked his fingers underneath his seat. "Now or never."

Kyle jammed the accelerator, and the truck's wheels spun dirt as they climbed the steep incline. He weaved in and out of saplings and drove right over the smallest ones. Ben could barely see ahead of them, and he bounced on the seat next to Kyle, who screamed and hollered, "Yee-haw!" Ben answered with a lame whoop. Ben checked over his shoulder for their precious cargo, strapped tight but probably bouncing around inside, though Kyle would remind him that human ash is indestructible and he needed to chill. Besides, it was too late to tell Kyle to stop. If he did stop, they could tip or get stuck in the mud. A couple of times he was sure they would die. The hill to the quarry seemed much steeper than it did when he hiked it, and he came to thinking about Mira, and Francesca and Connie, and the day they took Connie's last hike. It wasn't hard for Ben to understand how Connie had overexerted herself; perhaps she'd even run. He knew no one ran without being chased, or without a goal to reach at the top, and he wondered which of these it had been. Or did they have to convince her? He saw Connie that day on the ledge, looking like a rejected puppy, gazing at Ben with those wide-spaced eyes—"I thought, I mean, if you did like me, too, we might . . ."—so unconvincing on her own.

Who had held the EpiPen while she struggled to breathe?

Kyle hit a rock and Ben slammed his head against the roof. For a second, he saw black, and an electronic hum dulled the crashing noises of the truck tearing up the hill.

Teenagewasteland blogger Grim Reaper, a.k.a. thirteen-year-old Tyler Peavey of Jenkintown, Pennsylvania, blogging from his parents' house to more than one million subscribers, had instituted a Countdown Clock on his home page wherein he ticked off the deaths of teenagers and children in Bismuth, Massachusetts. Ben wondered if he would be another statistic to the Grim Reaper, or if he'd make his connection to the sisters at all. It would depend, he imagined, on whether or not Kyle got out alive and completed their mission. Surely it would be a big story if they were discovered here, splayed on the ground next to the toppled truck, with their stolen goods locked in the stowaway trunk. They'd say he and Kyle were fetishists, necrophiliacs, whacked on drugs. Who would tell their story?

Kyle shook Ben's sore shoulder.

"Ouch," Ben murmured, pulling his arm away.

"You smacked your head again. You gonna make it?"

Ben blinked and rubbed the top of his skull. "Yeah, I'm good."

"Then get out of the truck. We're here."

Ben had slunk far down in the seat, and he shimmied upward, dazed, until he could see over the windshield hinge. Kyle had parked in the tiny clearing before the ledge. Ben knew if he looked backward, he might crap his pants, because going down meant jamming it into reverse, at least until they had enough room to clear a three-point turn. Kyle jumped down and strode to the back, shaking out his dead hand. Ben's legs felt heavy, like the magnitude of the act had lodged in them.

He wasn't ready to say goodbye. He began looking for excuses. "They said last night on the news they might drain it."

Kyle came back around to the front of the truck. "Your mother said it's too expensive and it'll never happen."

"What if they find out what we did, and then this place becomes a theme park, the way the cemetery is now?" Ben asked.

"We'll cover our tracks by hand," Kyle replied.

"What if it backfires on us? What if, since there's nothing for them to look at in the cemetery, they start coming here because it's the scene of the crime?"

"The papers said the electrical fence project starts next week."

"Fine. But that's three days from now."

"Dude . . ."

"The gawkers might still come to the cemetery to see Connie."

"It's different for Connie. She wanted the attention. You know that. In a way—"

"Don't even go there."

"Right. I won't. Because we don't have time." Kyle checked the skyline. A squiggly red line glowed at the horizon. "It's almost daylight. We do it or we don't do it. Unless you want to take these babies home and hide them in your bedroom closet, we need to execute."

Ben looked over the swirling quarry water to the Boston

skyline. Black night brightened into gunmetal as the sun stirred somewhere below. He slid over the seat and circled the truck on spent legs, back to the flatbed. Kyle followed and stood on the opposite side.

Kyle smiled. "How do you want to do this?"

"You take one, I take one," Ben replied.

The urns were pearlized white and identical, except for names and dates, and pristine, having been inside their individual protective vaults. The boys stood, paralyzed and awkward, as though they were at a school dance and faced with deciding which of the girls to dance with. Kyle cleared his throat and took charge, like he would at a school dance, being oldest and knowing both probably wanted to dance with him. He lifted the first urn and squinted. Earlier, they'd weighed a ton, but now they seemed lighter. Ben was unfazed by the discrepancy. He'd expected the quarry's sense-warping magic to be at work on this night. The screw top was silver, with imprinted flowerwork and the words *Loving Daughter, Mira M. Cillo*.

Kyle looked to Ben, who nodded and accepted the urn in his arms, then rested it at his feet. The second one Kyle pulled up read: *Loving Daughter, Francesca M. Cillo*.

"You ready?" Ben murmured. He had been thinking about blond waves and thighs, bone shards and dust. His eyes stayed dry, but he could feel the familiar sag that had come to his face this last year, a frown weighting his cheeks.

Kyle set Francesca's urn aside and took a deep breath. He looked into Ben's eyes, unflinching, the way no one had in a long time. "We're doing the right thing, Ben."

"What if we're not?"

Kyle hefted Francesca's urn to his chest, his arms wrapped around it. "She wanted someone to believe in her gift. We're those people." He turned the urn over and shined his flashlight on the bottom and a round, threaded plug. "And there she is."

Ben handed him the screwdriver and looked away. "I'm not sure I can watch. What if it breaks?"

"It's not"—Kyle grunted—"gonna"—he grunted again—"break." The seal popped off with a suction noise.

Ben reached around his neck and pulled from his shirt a small leather bag on a cord. At the same time, Kyle stuck his hand inside the urn and lifted out a plastic bag of ash. Ben held the leather pouch away from his chest and Kyle poured some of Francesca's ashes inside. Ben closed it quickly and tucked the bag into his shirt. The pouch hung next to his heart. Ben supposed he had imagined it, but he felt the bag pulse.

"What about you?" Ben asked, looking down, chin to chest.

"I'm not greedy. She helped me already: I can't ask for more," Kyle said. "I hope she helps you get over what that bastard did. You deserve it, man." Kyle replaced the bag and fitted the plug into the urn. "The sun's coming up, and we gotta hit the road. We wanna be on the highway by five thirty if we're gonna get to New York by noon. It's time to say goodbye."

"They deserve to rest in peace," Ben said stiffly, fighting tears.

Kyle sniffed hard. "It's what they would have wanted." He carried Francesca to the fingertip of the ledge. When Ben didn't move, Kyle lifted Mira. When Ben finally raised his eyes, he saw the urns standing side by side on the edge, glowing amphorae from another age.

"Are you ready?" Kyle said.

Ben looked at Kyle's hand, dangling at his side. "This might be your last chance at fixing your hand."

Kyle considered his crooked hand in the moonlight. "Nah. I told you, dude. This isn't about me."

Ben nodded. In that moment, he knew that even if he was like the others, Kyle was not.

Kyle moved forward and lifted Francesca's urn. He crouched, brushing his lips lightly over the silver tracings, and murmured thanks. He stood and held her aloft for a moment before letting go.

Ben waited for the splash. He lifted Mira's urn and held it high, and did not trace the words with his fingertips, or press it to his cheek, or kiss its smooth face. He did none of these things: he only let it go. A whoosh of air, and the urn became small until it was enveloped by the platinum mist that hung above the water, then a fast, neat plop.

Kyle stepped back and rested his hands on his hips. "Now there's nothing to look at."

The sun broke over the horizon. Kyle gazed toward the city, and farther, then up at the sky, his throat bare to the heavens, where two glittering emerald birds circled, one following the other, swirling up and out of the quarry.

Ben checked the still water below. Not a ripple, no evidence of a break. The quarry had absorbed the girls, delivering them to a place where they would remain untouched by hands, and unbroken by hearts.

ACKNOWLEDGMENTS

My novels begin with my own moments of sudden discovery. *Beautiful Broken Girls* is inspired by the work of Virginia Woolf, who gave my teenage self the words, finally, to describe the male gaze.

Speaking of the teenage self, thanks are owed to Gary, for everything, but especially for his younger years, which I mined shamelessly for this novel. Also, I used the boys I have known who are now men, and will never recognize themselves here. Thanks also to the members of The Circle of Silence, in particular, Chrissy Byrnes Conley, who would say, "*This* is going in your novel someday." It all did.

Thanks to Sal Caraviello, Saint Mary's spiritual director and all-round marvelous person, on whom Nick Falso is *not* based.

I am grateful to my agent, Sara Crowe, for her early guidance. You can, in fact, have too many sisters. This is largely a novel about a town, and it is better for the excellent eye and sharp mind of Larisa Dodge, who owns the strongest sense of place of any writer I know.

Thanks to my personal saints at Macmillan, Morgan Dubin

and Kallam McKay, who champion my work early and often. And to Candace Gatti, who wields her PR wizardry and local connections on my behalf, unasked, every single time.

Thanks to Elizabeth H. Clark for her breathtaking cover design. I didn't think you could top *After the Woods*. I was wrong.

Thanks to Janine O'Malley. You are, as Eddie would say, "one of the good ones." Your editing of this unusual novel was so respectful and smart. I would not have entrusted it to anyone else's hands.

Finally, Dad, thank you for a lifetime of changing my casino chips into cash. I am rich for being your daughter.